Borrowed Crime

Center Point
Large Print

Also by Laurie Cass and available from
Center Point Large Print:

The Bookmobile Cat Mysteries
  Tailing a Tabby
  Lending a Paw

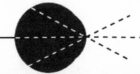

**This Large Print Book carries the
Seal of Approval of N.A.V.H.**

Borrowed Crime

A Bookmobile Cat Mystery

Laurie Cass

CENTER POINT LARGE PRINT
THORNDIKE, MAINE

This Center Point Large Print edition
is published in the year 2015 by arrangement with
New American Library,
an imprint of Penguin Publishing Group,
a division of Penguin Random House LLC.

The text of this Large Print edition is unabridged.
In other aspects, this book may vary
from the original edition.
Printed in the United States of America on permanent paper.
Set in 16-point Times New Roman type.

ISBN: 978-1-62899-616-6

Library of Congress Cataloging-in-Publication Data

Cass, Laurie.
  Borrowed crime : a bookmobile cat mystery / Laurie Cass. — Center
Point Large Print edition.
    pages cm
  Summary: "When a volunteer dies on the bookmobile's route, a
growing stack of clues points towards murder"—Provided by publisher.
  ISBN 978-1-62899-616-6 (library binding : alk. paper)
  1. Women librarians—Fiction. 2. Murder—Investigation—Fiction.
    3. Large type books. I. Title.
PS3603.A86784B67 2015
813′.6—dc23
                                                              2015012330

To all who have known
the love of a good cat.

"Mrr."

Borrowed Crime

Chapter 1

Some people are practically born knowing what they want to do with their lives. People like my older brother, who had his life plan scrawled out on a piece of paper by age seven, are the kind of folks who move from one goal to another, ticking things off their lists and achieving Big Things.

Other people wander through their early years without a clear path in mind, but still end up where they should have been all along. These would be people like my best friend, Kristen, who enjoyed high school chemistry so much that when the college-major decision came up, biochemistry seemed the obvious choice, and she ended up with a PhD. As it turned out, however, she did not enjoy working for a large pharmaceutical company, so she quit, came home to northern Michigan, kicked around ideas about what to do with the rest of her life, and opened up Three Seasons, which quickly became one of the finest restaurants in the region.

Then there's me.

From age ten I knew I wanted to be a librarian, but beyond that I had no course charted out for my life. When I found a posting for assistant director at the district library in Chilson, Michigan, not long after I was handed my master's degree in library and information science, though, I felt a ping of fate.

Chilson is a small tourist town in the northwest part of Michigan's lower peninsula. It was where I'd spent childhood summers with my aunt Frances. It was where I'd met Kristen. It is a land of lakes and hills and has a laid-back atmosphere where "business casual" means "clean jeans and a shirt without too many wrinkles." It was my favorite place in the entire world, and getting my dream job in a dream location was something I could not possibly have planned.

Of course, there were drawbacks, and that wasn't even counting the facts that at thirty-three I was never going to grow past the five-foot mark, that my curly black hair was never going to straighten, and that I didn't know how my beloved new bookmobile would handle the upcoming winter.

"He's doing it again, Minnie," Aunt Frances said.

We were sitting in her kitchen, because although the dining room that overlooked the tree-filled backyard was a lovely place to eat during the warm months, when the weather grew cooler, chill drafts curled around our ankles and the two of us beat a happy retreat to the warmth of the kitchen.

In summer, though, the kitchen wasn't nearly big enough, because in June through August my aunt took in boarders. Six, to be exact: three female and three male, each of whom was single and unattached.

My aunt had an extensive interview process for her summer folks. Though she told the prospective boarders that she wanted to determine compatibility for the unusual living arrangements (the boarders cooked Saturday breakfast), she was actually starting her process of secret match-making. No one ever knew that they were being set up, and, in her years of taking in boarders, she'd failed only once, and even that wasn't a complete failure.

But that had been last summer, back in the days of warmth and sunshine and a town busy with tourists. Now, in early November, the summer residents were long gone, the tourists wouldn't be back until late May, and my aunt and I were rattling around in a house far too big for two, even with most of the upstairs rooms closed off.

Of course, sometimes it wasn't nearly big enough for three, considering the nature of the third.

"Do you hear him?" Aunt Frances asked.

I did. I started to stand, but she waved me down. "Finish your breakfast. I'll clean up his mess after the two of you leave. It's not—"

"Mrr."

Eddie, my black-and-white tabby cat, padded into the room and jumped onto my lap. His head

11

poked up over the tabletop and he reached forward.

"Not a chance, pal." I moved the bowl of oatmeal out of his reach. "You know the rules."

Aunt Frances laughed. "He may know the rules, but I don't think he has any intention of following them."

Gently, I pushed at his head, trying to make him lie down, but he pushed it back up.

Down I pushed.

Up he came.

Down.

Up.

Down.

"You know he's going to win," Aunt Frances said.

"Shhh, don't let him know."

"From the noises we just heard, I'd say he already won the battle with the toilet paper."

In summer, I lived at a marina on a small houseboat, but Eddie and I moved to the boardinghouse after my aunt's guests were gone and the weather started to turn. Since then, Eddie had discovered that his new favorite toy was the roll of toilet paper in the kitchen's half bath. And to Eddie, a toy couldn't be a favorite unless he did his best to destroy it. Happily, toilet paper wasn't expensive. At least in small quantities.

"You know," I told the top of his head, "even

things that aren't expensive can get that way if you have to buy them new every day."

Eddie had gone through bouts of destructiveness with paper products all summer long, and it looked as if the trend was going to continue. What he'd be like in the winter, I didn't know, because I'd only had Eddie since late April.

I'd gone for a walk on an unseasonably warm day and found myself wandering through the local cemetery, enjoying the view of Janay Lake. My calm reverie had been broken by the appearance of a cat, who had materialized next to the gravesite of Alonzo Tillotson, born 1847, died 1926.

Though I'd assumed the cat had a home and had tried to shoo him away, he'd followed me back into town and charmed the socks off me by purring and rubbing up against my ankles.

I'd taken him to the vet, where I'd been told that my new friend was about two years old and needed ear drops. I'd run a Found notice in the newspaper, but even though I'd dutifully paid for a normal-sized advertisement instead of the tiny one I would have preferred, no one had called. Eddie was mine.

Or I was his. One of those.

"I'll stop and stock up on my way home." I got up and took our dishes to the white porcelain sink, which was so old it was trendy again. I'd seen similar ones in antiques stores selling for bizarrely large sums of money and realized that my aunt could make a fortune by taking the boardinghouse apart and selling it bit by bit. Of course, then she wouldn't have anywhere to live. Besides, she loved the place, despite its drafty windows and problematic plumbing. And so did I.

"Do we need anything else from the store?" There was no answer. I looked over my shoulder and saw Aunt Frances still sitting, her elbows planted on the old oak table, her chin in her hands and her gaze on Eddie.

My cat was sitting in the middle of the spot I'd vacated. He was looking back at Aunt Frances with an intense, yellow-eyed stare. I knew that stare well, and it often meant trouble.

"You know," my aunt said in a faraway voice, "I think it would be nice to get Eddie his own chair."

Trouble, my friends, right here in the boarding-house kitchen.

I went back to the table and gave my feline friend a gentle push, sending him to the floor. Aunt Frances started to protest, but I shook my head. "He got you again," I said. "Beware of the power of the cat. He was trying to convince you to cater to his every whim, and he would have sucked you in if I hadn't interfered."

Aunt Frances laughed and got up from the table. I could tell she didn't quite believe me. Well, I didn't quite believe me, either, but what other explanation was there for lying awake in the middle of the night, desperately wanting to straighten your legs but not doing so because straightening them would disturb a cat's sleep? I also didn't believe that Eddie's brain grasped more than a handful of human words, but there were times when it seemed as if he understood life better than I did.

My aunt, being eight inches taller than I, was a much better candidate for putting away the dishes, so I washed while she dried.

"Did you get a card from Kristen yesterday?" Aunt Frances asked.

I grinned. Indeed, I had. My best friend worked hard in her restaurant from spring through fall, then hightailed it south. The restaurant's closing date had more to do with the weather forecast than anything else, and she studied the early-snowfall predictions of the *Farmer's Almanac* all summer.

One mid-October morning, she'd tromped into the library and flung herself into my office's guest chair. "I'm out of here," she'd announced.

I'd glanced up from my computer. "A little early, isn't it?" She didn't usually close the restaurant until the first week of November. Then she drove to Key West, where she tended bar on the weekends and did absolutely nothing during the week. Come spring, after I e-mailed her pictures of melted snow and ice-free lakes, she would return, refreshed and ready for another summer of hard work. It wasn't a life I would have wanted, but it suited her perfectly. "What's the rush?" I asked.

She slouched in the chair, sticking her long legs out into the middle of the room. At six foot, with straight blond hair, Kristen was my physical opposite. We were opposites in other ways, too, come to think of it, the most obvious of which was that I wasn't interested in cooking anything more complicated than canned soup, while about the only food Kristen didn't try to improve was an apple. And even then she'd often slice it up, add a touch of lemon juice, and serve it with chunks of a cheese variety I couldn't pronounce.

"Supposed to snow week after next," she said. "I've talked it over with the staff, and they're okay with closing down early. It was a good summer, but 'good' means 'a lot of work.' They're tired, and I don't want to push them."

It wasn't just her staff that was tired. I studied the droop of her broad shoulders and the fatigue scoring lines into her face.

"What about Scruffy?" I asked.

Last summer, I'd accidentally started a romance between Kristen and Scruffy Gronkowski, a very nice man who was anything but untidy. He was the only person I knew under the age of sixty who took the time to iron creases into his pants, and he was also the producer of a cooking show that was occasionally filmed in Chilson because the host, Trock Farrand, owned a house nearby.

She grinned. "He's at Trock's house, trying to figure out how to fit my restaurant into next year's schedule."

Jumping to my feet, I flung my arms out and ran to her, shrieking for joy all the way. She laughed and hugged me hard. "Mid-July, he thinks, so it could be a nutso-busy zoo the rest of the summer."

Kristen's restaurant was doing well, but having it appear on a national cooking show could zoom it past the marginally profitable zone and into a place where she could think about hiring a manager. Not that she would—she was too hands-on—but there's a big difference between not wanting to and not being able to.

"And how does Mr. Scruff feel about your Key West destination?" I asked.

She looked at me, all wide-eyed and innocent, a look she hadn't been able to pull off even when she had been innocent. "Oh, I didn't tell you? He's planning to come down for Christmas."

I whistled. Or tried to. Whistling wasn't one of my most developed skills. "That sounds serious."

"Now, don't go all wedding dress on me," Kristen said. "My mother's bad enough. Scruffy just hates the snow." And that was all she'd say, no matter how sneaky I was about trying to get more information out of her.

The night before she left, we sat in her restaurant's empty kitchen, eating the last crème

17

brûlée in the place and drinking a bottle of her best champagne.

"Postcards," she said suddenly.

Since we'd been guessing how long the new downtown gift shop would last—my estimate was less than a year—I blinked at her. "What?"

"Postcards. Key West is full of them." She topped off our glasses with more bubbly. "I'll send you a postcard every week." She smiled, showing her white teeth, and for a moment she bore a striking resemblance to a great white shark.

"A Scruffy report?" I asked. We'd be e-mailing or texting practically every day, but the thought of getting a postcard in my mailbox was appealing.

"Maybe. But only if I get Tucker updates."

The good-looking, blond, and tall (but not too tall) Dr. Tucker Kleinow and I had been dating since last summer. Though we'd hit a stumbling block when we discovered his allergic reaction to cats in general and Eddie in particular, our relationship was progressing nicely, thanks to Tucker's willingness to take an allergy medication when he was Eddie-bound. "Deal." I held up my glass, and we toasted our pact.

Now that I'd received two postcards, I was realizing what had lain beneath her sharklike smile. Postcard number one had been a picture of blue skies and sandy beaches. On the back she'd written *Key West, a steady eighty-one degrees. Chilson, forty-five and dropping. Sucker.*

Aunt Frances had stuck it up with a thumbtack on the doorframe to the living room, where, in a few weeks, it would be surrounded by Christmas cards. She was amused by the whole thing and had been wondering if Kristen would keep it up all winter.

Now I nodded toward my backpack, which was sitting on the end of the kitchen counter. "The new one's in the outside pocket. Go ahead and take it out."

Postcard number two had been a picture of blue skies and sandy beaches. On the back she'd written *Key West, eighty degrees and sunny. Chilson, snow coming soon. Eww.*

But Kristen knew that I didn't mind winter. I actually liked it. Soft and white, it transformed the world into something completely different, something fresh and clean and unexpected.

I stood there, my hands in the soapy water, daydreaming ahead to skiing and skating and snowshoeing. All sorts of activities that started with the letter *S* were done on a substance that also started with an *S*, namely snow, and—

"Mrr!"

I jumped. "Right," I said, nodding. "We need to get going, don't we?"

From his perch on my chair, Eddie looked straight at me. I didn't need a cat interpreter to know that he was saying, *Well, duh.*

Aunt Frances returned the last bowl to the glass-front cabinets. "Do you think Eddie would like a half wall? About so high"—she held her hand at waist level—"and about three feet long. I've been thinking about taking out this door between the dining room and the kitchen for some time. It'll open up the space nicely. Maybe this is the year to do it."

Smiling, I dried my hands on the blue-and-white hand towel. "You think?"

She eyed the area of interest. "It's not a load-bearing wall. A sledge and a flat bar will take it down in no time. Then a little framing, a little drywall work, and a little trim. Shouldn't take long."

I snorted. "Have you ever heard that story about the shoemaker's children—you know, the ones who didn't have any shoes?"

My loving aunt whirled her drying towel into a tight spiral and popped me lightly with the end of it. "Out, you horrible child," she said, laughing. "Out right now, or you'll be late for work."

"Mrr."

And since they were both right, I grabbed my backpack, which was full of appropriate provisions for cat and human, and headed out.

I paused at the front closet to pull on my coat, boots, and gloves, and went outside into the dark of the predawn morning. But as I stepped off the wide front porch, empty of the summer swing that had been stored away, I saw that the world wasn't completely dark.

The sky was gray and was forecast to stay that way for the foreseeable future, but the ground was covered with a light dusting of white.

My heart sang with pure pleasure. Maybe by February I'd be tired of the cold, and maybe come March I'd be tired of brushing snow off my car, but at this moment I was enchanted with the sprinkling of fairy dust.

Humming to myself, I started my car, set the defroster to high, and got the ice scraper from the floor of the backseat, where I'd put it at the end of September, because you just never knew.

The ice scraper had a long handle and a brush, and it had been a gift from my father when I'd bought my first car. He'd wrapped it himself, the bright yellow and red paper tight against the plastic, revealing the object's shape so obviously that a five-year-old could have guessed what it was, and had handed it to me with gravitas. "Don't ever take it out of your car," he'd said solemnly. "Keep it in your trunk during the summer, on the floor of the backseat all winter."

It wasn't a bad idea—as a matter of fact, it was a pretty good one—and it had only taken me five years and one early snowstorm to start taking my dad's advice.

As I brushed the snow off the car's hood, I heard the sound of a door shutting. Which was odd, because it wasn't even seven thirty, and the only year-round people in the neighborhood were retirees who tended to stay inside until the morning got as bright as it was going to get. The vast majority of homes in this part of Chilson belonged to summer people. They might come up at Thanksgiving, a week at Christmas, and perhaps Presidents' Day weekend, but mostly the houses sat quiet and dark, waiting for the warmth of May to bring them back to life.

I turned and saw something completely unexpected.

Across the street, a figure was standing on the front porch, zipping up his coat and pulling on gloves. It was Otto Bingham, the house's new owner. At least I assumed it was him; Aunt Frances had heard that a gentleman by that name had purchased the house a few weeks ago, but she'd never met him. Though she'd gone over to the white clapboard house two or three times to introduce herself, he'd never been home.

"Good morning!" I smiled and waved, thinking that I'd have to tell Aunt Frances that I'd had an Otto sighting. The light from the porch illuminated a man who looked, at this distance, like he was in his mid-sixties and on the bonus end of the Handsome bell curve.

"The snow's pretty, isn't it?" I asked.

He looked at me, squinting, then gave a curt nod

and went back inside his house, shutting the door firmly behind him.

I stared after him, then shrugged. Maybe the guy hated snow, which would be silly for someone who'd just moved to this part of Michigan, but you never knew what made people do things.

Then I put thoughts of my aunt's curmudgeonly neighbor out of my head, gave the car's windshield one last brush, and headed back up the porch stairs for the cat carrier.

Because it was a bookmobile day, and no bookmobile day could be complete without the bookmobile cat.

"What I don't understand," Denise Slade said, "is why you feel the need to keep Eddie such a secret."

I glanced over at my newest bookmobile volunteer, then went back to concentrating on my driving. When the road was wide and straight and dry, piloting the thirty-one-foot-long vehicle was a joy and a delight. However, most of the roads in Tonedagana County were narrow and curving, and today they were wet with slushy early snow. Then again, poor road conditions were part of life Up North, and I was mentally prepared to deal with whatever Mother Nature tossed my way. But I wasn't so sure I was prepared to deal with Denise.

Denise was one of those stocky, energetic women who volunteered for multiple worthy organizations. She'd helped out with area environmental groups, she'd spent time on the local PTA, she'd baked cookies for the Red Cross blood drives, and she was now president of the local Friends of the Library, a volunteer group that raised funds for library projects and donated innumerable hours to helping out at library events.

Though she'd ruffled more than a few feathers with her take-charge attitude and her voice, which I'd heard described as the kind that goes straight into your teeth, I'd always gotten along fine with Denise.

Then again, that could have been due to the simple fact that I hadn't spent much time with her.

"Eddie," I said, "was a stowaway on the bookmobile's maiden voyage. He followed me from the houseboat"—the marina where I moored the boat in summer was a ten-minute walk from the library—"and snuck on board when I was out doing the morning inspection."

"Well, I know all that." Denise looked at the cat carrier strapped down next to her feet. "And I know that you didn't take him out again until that poor little Brynn Wilbanks cried to see the bookmobile kitty." She paused and slid a glance over to me. "How is she these days?"

"Great," I said, smiling. "She's doing just great." My smile filled me to overflowing, because five-year-old Brynn was still in remission from leukemia. She was doing so well that her mother had enrolled her in kindergarten, and the bookmobile would soon be making a stop at Brynn's elementary school.

"Good to hear." Denise nodded. "So, I get why Eddie started coming on the bookmobile, what with Brynn and so many other people liking him. What I don't get is why you have to keep him a secret from your boss. Keeping secrets from Stephen is a bad idea, Minnie. Trust me on this one."

I stifled a sigh and yearned for what could not be. My summer volunteer, Thessie, had been a perfect match for the bookmobile, for Eddie, and for me. She was funny, intelligent, and tall enough to reach the bookmobile's top shelves without having to get on her tiptoes. She was also a senior in high school and aiming for a college major in library science. Bookmobile life would be perfect if Thessie would only drop out of school. If only she would bury her ambitions, to ride on the bookmobile for no pay and no benefits and absolutely no future.

"What's so funny?" Denise asked.

"Just trying to picture Stephen covered with Eddie hair."

She leaned forward and reached through the wire door to pet the feline under discussion. "You do have a lot of it, Mr. Edward."

"Mrr."

Hmm. Denise was a little pushy and a little too

sure of herself when the circumstances didn't warrant it, but she was a cat person, and Eddie seemed to like her. Maybe he knew something I didn't.

Denise sighed. "Well, I hope you know what you're doing with Stephen and all. I mean, I won't say anything to anyone, but I have to say it's no wonder you're having trouble getting people to volunteer. What are you going to do on the days I can't come out? Because I can't promise I'll be able to come with you every time."

My half smile faded. I stopped thinking about my stick-to-the-rules boss, a man who wore a tie to work every day even though there was no reason to do so, a man who seemed to delight in giving me unachievable goals, a man who wouldn't blink at firing me if he found I'd been giving bookmobile rides to a creature full of hair and dander. I stopped thinking about all of that and concentrated on keeping my voice calm when I really wanted to shout. Loudly.

"Denise," I said, "you told me you could help out until next spring. You said you had nothing else going on and that you'd be glad to help keep the bookmobile running."

"I did?"

She sounded puzzled, and I glanced over. She was pushing her short, smooth brown hair back behind her ears and frowning slightly, deepening the lines that were starting to form in her face.

"Yes, you did," I said. "Please tell me you haven't made any other commitments. I just finished the new schedule and I don't want to have to cancel any stops."

Making the winter bookmobile schedule had driven me to chocolate more than once. I'd made up the summer schedule with no problems whatsoever, and had blithely assumed that fall would be the same way. My blithe spirit was no longer. Despite my best intentions, the new schedule wasn't anywhere close to what it had been in summer. But at least I now knew to contact schools and day-care centers in May about their fall programming.

And I also knew that I really needed to find money to hire a part-time bookmobile clerk instead of relying on volunteers.

Back in the days when I'd put together the book-mobile funding and worked through operation issues, the library board had laid down one cast-in-stone rule: no driving alone. I'd agreed readily, and had been happy enough to comply with their policy. Well, I'd once had to count Eddie as my bookmobile companion, but that had been a onetime thing.

Denise laughed. "Don't be such a worrywart. I'm going to volunteer a few hours a week at the nursing home, is all. Most of the time I'll be able to work around the bookmobile schedule."

Most of the time? "And what happens if you

can't?" My voice was going all Librarian. "Denise, if there aren't two people on the bookmobile, we can't go out. I need to know in advance if you can't make a trip. A week, at least."

"Don't worry," she said. "It'll be fine."

I wasn't worrying; I was thinking.

It was easy to convince folks that the bookmobile was a worthwhile cause for volunteering; all I had to do was give them a quick tour of our three thousand books, CDs, DVDs, and magazines, and tell them about the happy smiles on every face that came aboard. Selling people on how important the bookmobile was to the hundreds of people in the county who couldn't get to Chilson, home to the only brick-and-mortar library in the county, was the easy part.

The problem was, since Thessie had gone back to school, I'd had a number of people excited about riding along. Unfortunately, almost all had canceled for various reasons, and I'd had to cleverly winnow out a few who I felt might not keep the Eddie secret. Denise was the sole survivor.

What I needed was to hire someone. Or, more accurately, what I needed was to find the funds to hire someone. Until then, I had to rely on volunteers. And if Denise wasn't going to be reliable, I'd have to find someone else. Only who?

Thinking hard, I tapped my fingers on the

steering wheel. Thought some more. Tapped. Thought.

Then the sun broke through the clouds, skidding bright light across the countryside, and I stopped thinking so hard. It was turning into a beautiful day. Why ruin it with thinking too much?

"Wow. Did you see that?" Denise stretched forward, looking up. "That was one huge woodpecker!"

"Pileated," I said confidently. It was a newly formed confidence, because I hadn't known diddly about birds until I started driving the bookmobile. But now that I was out and about so much, I was using the bookmobile's copy of *Birds of Michigan* on a regular basis. The two weeks when someone had checked it out had been two very long weeks.

"Really?" Denise twisted in her seat, tracking the bird. "That's neat. I bet you see a lot of nature stuff. Have you ever come close to hitting a deer?"

"No, and I hope I never do."

She laughed. "You mean 'not yet.' It's just the way things are. And deer season starts on Saturday. When those rifle hunters get out in the woods, the deer will start moving around."

I wasn't going to worry about that, either.

Denise was looking around, checking out the wooded roadside. "I wish I had my book with me, that one listing where all the town and county names of Michigan came from."

"Why's that?"

"We're in Peck Township, right? If I had my book with me, I could look it up and see if I have any notes on it."

"A note?" I asked.

"Well, yeah. I make notes in a lot of my books. Reminders, mostly."

"You write in your books?"

Denise snorted. "Don't go all Miss Librarian on me. What, I can't do what I want with my own property? It's not like I'm marking up a library book."

No, but it seemed . . . wrong, somehow.

"It helps me remember things," Denise was saying. "Especially the long historicals. Authors just load up on the characters in those. If I didn't make notes about who was who, I'd forever be flipping around to figure things out."

Knowing that she was marking up works of fiction was somehow even worse than knowing what she was doing to nonfiction. Yes, they were her own books and, yes, she had the right to do what she wanted to them, but it still made me squeamish. I mean, if a person could write in a book, what else might she be capable of doing?

A road sign flashed past. "Our first stop is coming up," I said. "Ready?"

"You bet!" Denise grinned.

Well, at least she was enthusiastic. I glanced over at Eddie. He'd shoved himself up against the side of the carrier that was the farthest possible distance from Denise and pointed his hind end in her direction.

No. I was not going to use a cat's sleeping position as any kind of omen, good or bad.

Eddie opened one eye, used it to look up toward Denise, then closed it again. His sides heaved as he sighed.

Cats, I told myself, *cannot foretell the future. This is going to be fine.*

"You know," Denise said, "what this book-mobile needs is a decent stereo system. It's almost Thanksgiving; we should be playing Christmas songs. I just can't get enough of 'Grandma Got Run Over by a Reindeer,' right?" She sang the chorus and tried to start the first verse, but got stuck on the words and went back to the chorus.

I gave Eddie a quick look, but he'd already turned himself around so that his hind end was facing me.

At the end of the day, I couldn't decide what I'd wanted to do more: hug Denise or put her out by the side of the road.

She'd been both amazingly helpful and incredibly annoying. Once she'd been both at the same time, a feat I hadn't known was possible.

"This was fun," she said.

"I'm glad you thought so." For a moment, I considered launching into the story of the bookmobile's origin, how Stephen, my boss and the director of the Chilson District Library, had closed the smaller satellite libraries around the county in the name of financial savings, because now that the library offered e-books, he'd said there was no need for the branches' existence.

I'd felt differently, and had floated the idea of a bookmobile to the library board. They'd smiled at me indulgently, said it was a fine idea, and if I could come up with the money, they'd be glad to approve the program.

A few months later, I had a hefty check in hand from an extremely generous donor, and the surprised board approved the program. Stephen wasn't so thrilled. And though it was clear he thought that the bookmobile was a waste of my time and the library's resources, he had little choice but to go along with the board's decision.

At the time I thought I'd won a great victory. Now reality was setting in. Stephen was continually giving me more to do at the library, a strategy I suspected was designed to take me away from the bookmobile. If I didn't have time to drive the bookmobile, no one would drive it anywhere, because we had no funds to hire a driver, and then Stephen could sell it and pocket the check in the library's bank account.

I sighed and decided to keep it all to myself. If Denise was excited about the bookmobile, let her keep that emotion. Maybe she'd spread it across the land, where it would seep into Chilson's community psyche, and money would fall from the sky. Stranger things had happened, hadn't they?

"Next left," Denise said. "We're the third house on the right. That's it."

The week before, I'd told her I could drop her off on the way back into Chilson, since the day's return route went right past her road. It was a neighborhood of two-story homes on lots that my friend Rafe would call too big to mow and too small to farm. Denise's husband had dropped her off at the library that morning, and it was easy enough to make a short side trip, especially since her road ended in a cul-de-sac that fit the bookmobile's turning radius.

"See you Saturday morning," I said.

"Bright and early." She unbuckled her seat belt and reached forward to give Eddie a scratch through the wire door. "See you later, Eddie-gator."

When she was gone, I looked over at my cat companion. "So, what do you think?"

His yellow eyes blinked in slow motion, but he didn't say anything.

"That's exactly how I feel." I tried blinking the way Eddie did, but blinking slowly was a lot harder than I thought it would be. After two tries I gave it up and dropped the bookmobile's transmission into drive.

"On the plus side," I said, "we don't have to think about her again for four days. So let's not, okay?"

Eddie's mouth opened and closed silently, which, since I wanted to think he was agreeing with me, I did.

"Then we're settled. Time for a new subject." We moved on down the road, and when we were on the two-lane county highway, I said, "How about what season is best in northern lower Michigan? Spring, summer, fall, or winter?"

I studied the countryside that lay before us. The morning's snow had long since turned to rain and melted away the half inch of white stuff. Trees that in summer had been covered with leaves were now skeletons, revealing things that were invisible in warmer months. Houses appeared where you hadn't realized they existed, long views of lakes and hills emerged, and a whole new layer of the world was coming into view.

"It's like the skin is peeled back," I said. "In a couple of weeks, the snow will come and cover everything up again, just like in summer the grass and trees cover things. But now, and in early spring before things turn green, the bones are showing."

I was proud of my insight. It was almost poetic, really. Eddie, however, was snoring.

Until Eddie, I'd never known that cats were capable of snoring. Now I knew better. At least once a week I'd wake from a deep sleep to hear the not-so-dulcet tones of *Felis eddicus*, the species I'd decided was unique to Eddie.

There was still a short drive to town, so I went back to thinking about the seasons. Silently this time.

Winter was fun because of skiing and the sheer beauty of snow. Spring was fun because of watching the world turn green. Summer was fun because of the breathtaking freedom of being outside in shorts and a T-shirt, plus all my marina friends were back and the boardinghouse was full of new people to meet. And then we were back to fall, which was easy to love for its stunning colors and crisp mornings.

"Hey," I said, waking Eddie. "You know what? I don't have to decide which season I like best. I don't have to choose. I can like them all!"

Eddie sneezed and licked his face. "Mrr," he said.

Chapter 2

The next morning I left Eddie at home, to his great disgruntlement. Even Aunt Frances noticed his grumpiness.

"What's with him?" she asked, nodding toward his back feet, which were thumping up the stairs. If past performance was any indication of the imminent future, in a few seconds he would jump on my bed, stand in the middle as he viewed the pillow selection, then flop down onto the one that offered the highest likelihood of Eddie comfort.

I showed Aunt Frances my hands, which were empty except for the mittens I'd just pulled on. "No cat carrier. He's cranky because he thinks every day should be a bookmobile day."

She looked up the stairs. "Would some cat treats make him feel better?"

"Sure," I said, "but then you'd have to give him treats every morning, and he'd follow you around, asking for more, and you'd give them to him just to shut him up and he'd get fat." I zipped up my coat. "Then we'd have to find a kitty treadmill, find a place to put it, teach him how to use it, and make sure he got at least thirty minutes of exercise every day."

Aunt Frances handed my backpack to me. "Much easier not to give him treats in the first place, then."

"I'm glad you understand. Now, if you could explain that to Eddie, we'll be all set." I headed out into the cold morning. Two steps away, I turned around and poked my head back inside. "You know," I said, "one or two treats would be okay."

She grinned and, from the pocket of her oversized fleece sweatshirt, pulled out a small canister of cat treats. "Three at the most."

I left my enabling aunt and my cranky cat to their mutual devices and started my morning commute across town. Bookmobile days, due to the Eddie element, necessitated that I take my car to work, but on library days when it wasn't pouring down rain or howling with snowy winds, I walked.

My route first took me through streets lined with trees and filled with late-nineteenth-century houses built as summer cottages. People from Chicago had steamed up Lake Michigan to spend the hot city months in the coolness provided by lake breezes. More than a few of the houses were still owned by descendants of the families who'd built them, the walls decorated with the same pictures that had been hung a hundred years earlier.

I walked west, facing the rising wind, and fought the urge to tiptoe as I passed the sleeping houses, shut up tight until spring. A few blocks later, I was out of the historical district and into the section of town where normal people lived.

This was a neighborhood of narrow two-story houses, an occasional ranch house, and large old houses divided up into apartments; these homes had lights on in the kitchens and cars in the driveways. No sleeping here; there was school to attend and jobs to drive to.

Out on a tiny front porch, a woman was bundled up in a long puffy coat and was drinking from a steaming travel mug.

"Morning, Pam," I said. "Can I have some of your coffee?"

Pam Fazio, a fiftyish woman with smooth, short black hair, top-notch fashion sense, and an infectious laugh, clutched her mug to her chest. "Mine, mine—every drop is mine," she growled.

I smiled. Pam, owner of a new downtown antiques store, had an uncanny ability to match product to customer. It could have made entering her shop dangerous to the wallet, but she also had an amazing knack for sensing budgets.

"Are you going to drink morning coffee on your porch all winter?" I asked. Pam had moved to town from Ohio that spring; her long-term tolerance for cold and snow was still a question mark to many.

She took a noisy sip. "Every morning that I went to work in a windowless cubicle at a large company that shall remain nameless, I vowed that I would spend an equal number of mornings on my front porch, drinking my first cup of coffee in the fresh air."

"No matter how cold?"

"Cold?" she scoffed. "I'm not afraid of the cold. Not when I have coffee." She put her face into the rising steam. "Ahhh."

I laughed, waved, and started walking again. From here, downtown was only two blocks away. A left turn and then a right, and I was there: downtown Chilson in all its haphazard glory, an oddly comfortable blend of old and new architecture that attracted tourists and small-town urban planners from all across the region. But now it was the off-season, which lasted roughly eight months of the year, and business was not exactly bustling.

The only cars on the street were in front of the Round Table, the local diner. All the other storefronts were dark; many had signs taped to their front doors. CLOSED FOR THE SEASON. SEE YOU IN THE SPRING. Some of the shuttered stores were run by managers for absentee owners; others were owned by people who worked hard all summer long for the pleasure of heading to warmer climes over the winter.

My boots echoed on the empty sidewalks, which weren't nearly wide enough in summer when all the tourists were in town. I breathed in the fresh air, drank in the view of Janay Lake, looked around at the odd mix of old and new downtown buildings that should not have complemented each other but somehow did, and thought, as I almost always did when walking to work, that I was the luckiest person alive.

I was still thinking that when I let myself into the library, kept thinking it as I logged in to my computer, had it in the back of my mind as I brewed coffee, and let it settle there to keep me company as I got to work.

Two hours later, I was forced to revise my

opinion. No way could I be considered lucky if my boss was standing in my office, clutching a sheet of paper and shaking his head.

"Minerva, did you really think I was going to ignore this?"

In a perfect world—the world in which I would continue to be the luckiest person alive—yes, I would have expected him to ignore everything I wanted him to. Sadly, this was not a perfect world, and I was going to have to work hard to convince Stephen that, even though the grant I'd been promised from an area nonprofit group had vaporized when a major donor had gone bankrupt, there were still other methods of funding next year's bookmobile operations.

"There are other possibilities," I said.

"Possibilities of what?" he asked. "Spending even more time and money on efforts to bring a handful of books to a handful of patrons? Tell me how that's a sensible use of the library's extremely limited resources. We must think of the greater good, Minnie."

At least he'd pulled back from calling me by my full name. I took that as a good omen and started marshaling my arguments. They were the same ones I'd written into the memo I'd e-mailed when I'd received the bad news about the grant, but maybe they'd be more believable if I used positive facial expressions, persuasive oratory, and hand gestures that communicated sincerity.

"Exactly," I said, smiling and nodding. "Just like our mission statement says, we serve as a learning center for all residents of the community." Life didn't get much better than when I could back up my ideas with the statement Stephen had written himself.

He fluttered the e-mail again. "I don't see the connection between that and the loss of the bookmobile funding. And your latest foray into serving homebound patrons is only going to add more cost to your operations."

My chin started to slide forward into what my mother would have called my stubborn stance. I almost put one hand to my face to push it back. Getting red-cheeked and angry would not help my case. Logic—that's what I needed.

"All residents," I reminded him. "We're supposed to be a learning center for everyone, yet some of our patrons can't come to the library, especially in the winter months." I glanced at the window behind me, where a light snowfall had started. *Thank you, serendipity.*

"That's well and good," Stephen said, "but we cannot operate without proper funding."

I knew that. Of course I knew that. How could I not, when it was up to me to provide services on an annual budget that was getting smaller and smaller? For a moment, I wished fiercely for the settlement of the late Stan Larabee's estate. Stan's will had included a generous bequest to the library, but his relatives were contesting the will, and it was a toss-up if we'd ever see any of Stan's intended gift.

Worse, Stephen was right. The library simply could not operate in the red. There was some money tucked away, but that was for emergencies, not regular operations. I leaned forward and put my elbows on the desk, interlocking my fingers loosely, doing my best to project confidence and wisdom.

Well, confidence, anyway.

"I'll find the money," I promised. "Give me a few more weeks. As you can see from my e-mail, there are a number of possibilities." Not good ones, but still. And there was always the option of collecting returnable soda cans for the ten-cent deposit. And holding bake sales. Lots of them.

Stephen sighed. "You're assuming a best-case scenario, and that's a dangerous expectation."

Once again, he was right. I took a calming breath, then started to expand on the funding possibilities. Somewhere out there, there had to be a foundation that would like nothing better than to support a bookmobile program. All I had to do was find it. "I have contacts in library systems across the country, and with—"

Stephen held out a hand. "I've stated my reservations. That said, the current budget amounts show approximately six months of funding for the bookmobile. I see no reason why operations can't continue for that length of time."

"You . . . don't?" I blinked. "Thanks, Stephen, I really think—"

"I will also notify the board of my concerns. You can be sure that I won't be the only one scrutinizing the monthly expenditures."

I clutched at that a little, but only for a moment. "Don't worry." I smiled, happy once again. "It'll all turn out okay."

He looked at me straight on. "I certainly hope so."

A small piece of my ancient lizard brain reared up, shrieking with fear, but I told it to hush and went on smiling. "Six months from now, I'm sure something will have turned up."

"I certainly hope so." Stephen folded up my e-mail into small squares and tucked it into his shirt pocket. "Because when the bookmobile budget runs out of gas, so does the bookmobile." Chuckling to himself, he left my office and went up the stairs, heading to his office aerie.

"Very funny," I said to the wake of his laughter. Stephen occasionally smiled, but he rarely laughed, and the fact that he had laughed worried me, because what it usually meant was that someone was about to get in trouble.

I leaned back in my chair to think, and, in doing so, I dislodged an Eddie hair that had been on my jacket sleeve. It wafted into the air, spun about a few times lazily—*lazy? How appropriate!*—and eventually dropped in the direction of the floor.

That's when the penny, in the form of displaced Eddie fur, finally dropped.

Stephen knew about Eddie. Someone had told, and he was chuckling to himself, enjoying the two weeks until the next board meeting, when he would, without a doubt, recommend that I be fired.

"Stop worrying," I said out loud. But I didn't quite persuade myself that things would be okay. Stronger measures were in order, and I knew just how to get them.

I pulled my computer keyboard close, typed a quick e-mail with the words *Stephen Strikes Again* in the subject line, added two names, and hit the SEND button. I grabbed my coffee mug and made a beeline for the break room.

My best library friends, Holly Terpening, a part-time clerk, and Josh Hadden, the IT department, were waiting for me. Josh was a little younger than I was and Holly a little older, but the three of us had been hired about the same time, and that fact alone had cemented our work relationship into solid friendship.

Soon after our hire dates, we'd developed a pact. We would always support each other after a one-on-one with Stephen. For years I'd shored up Holly and/or Josh, but these days it was different.

"Ever since the bookmobile, I'm his favorite target," I muttered, leaning back against the countertop.

"Works for me," Josh said cheerfully. "He hasn't complained about the network in months, so thanks, Minnie."

Holly skewered him with a Mom Look. Her two smallish children had given her the skills to perfect that expression, and she used it both wisely and well. "Josh, we're supposed to be helping, remember?" A strand of her brown hair had escaped her ponytail, and she pushed it back behind her ear.

"Ah, Minnie knows I'm joking." He pulled a can of soda out of his cargo pants and handed it to me.

Popping the top, I thanked him and said, "I do know you're joking. But it would help if we had a hand signal."

I'd developed a thick skin at a young age, thanks to my efficient stature and my name (though if I never heard another Mini Minnie joke again, I would be okay with that), and had never been hesitant about going to Stephen with issues other library employees would have quailed at. As a matter of fact, I'd become such a Stephen expert that everyone now begged me to take things to the boss.

But I was no longer the golden girl. I was turning into the nearest dog to kick. Or so to speak. Because not even Stephen would kick a dog, would he?

I frowned and considered the question.

Nah. Stephen could be a royal pain in the patootie, but he wasn't *that* bad.

"Here." Holly sat at the table and reached for a plastic container. "I made a bunch last night for Anna's kindergarten class and decided the kids didn't need all of them."

Holly's chocolate-chip cookies were the stuff of legend. I pulled out a chair to sit, took one, hesitated, then took another one. "Thanks. You guys are the best."

"Yeah, we know." Josh thumped into a chair and reached out for a cookie. "So, what was the deal today? Too many kids in the library again? He hates that."

Which wasn't true—not exactly. What Stephen hated were the crumbs and dirt small children seem to inevitably leave behind. Maybe in a few more years, when the recently renovated building got a little more wear and tear, he'd relax a little. Probably not, but maybe.

I told them about his comment about the greater good.

"Seriously?" Holly looked at me over the top of her coffee mug. "That's a horrible thing to say."

"Well." I shrugged. "He's right."

Josh snorted. "Quit being so nice, Minnie. The only thing he's right about is . . ." With a dramatic flourish, he put his hand to his forehead and fake concentrated. "Huh. Nothing that I can think of."

"A year ago, I did tell him I'd find operations money," I reminded my friends. "Only Stan Larabee died and that ended that." Now, I could see that it had been a mistake to put all my bookmobile funding eggs into a basket labeled STAN, and then a second basket labeled GRANT THAT WILL SOLVE YOUR FINANCIAL PROBLEMS FOR AT LEAST A YEAR, but there wasn't much I could do about it at this point other than to keep searching for new grant possibilities.

I averted my mind from my two lost sources of funding. "Anyway," I said, "we can't take money out of the library's regular budget to fund the bookmobile. That wouldn't be right."

"What's not right," Holly said, "is that Stephen isn't supporting the best thing that's happened to this library in years."

I grinned. "You mean besides the millage that paid for the renovation of this gorgeous building?"

Holly waved away the multimillion-dollar project. "That's different. That's typical Chilson show-off stuff. We have to have a library that's better than everybody else's. So of course that millage passed the first time around; we couldn't let Petoskey have a nicer library than we do."

I stopped chewing and stared at her. Never once in the three and a half years I'd lived full-time in

Chilson had I thought of our wonderful library that way.

"And anyway," Josh said, "no matter how cool this building is, the bookmobile is way cooler."

"It is?" I asked.

"Well, sure." Holly swallowed the last of her cookie. "You've shown us the figures. The number of books borrowed is a lot higher for bookmobile patrons than for the people who come here. That's got to be boosting the overall circulation numbers for the library, right?"

It was, but not as much as she might think.

"Plus," Josh added, "it's famous."

I shook my head to bring my thoughts out of the spreadsheet daze they'd fallen into. "What is?"

My friends exchanged a puzzled glance. "The bookmobile," Josh said patiently. "Everybody knows about it."

"They . . . do?"

"Well, yeah," Holly said. "It's famous all over the place."

"You're like a mobile billboard." Josh held up an imaginary sign and chugged around the room with it. "No other library in this part of the state has a bookmobile at all, let alone one as cool as ours."

Ours, he'd said. And Holly had nodded. A warm happiness flooded through me. For months, the bookmobile had been, in Stephen's words,

"Minnie's little project," but it had already become part of the greater library family.

"The bookmobile," I said, "isn't exactly what I'm worried about." I looked around. Saw no one but the three of us, but motioned them to move in, just in case. "I think he knows about"—I lowered my voice to a whisper—"Eddie."

Josh and Holly both sat up straight.

"How could he?" Holly asked.

Josh shook his head. "No way. What makes you think that?"

"Nothing for certain," I said, "but you've heard that little laugh he makes sometimes?"

"Yeah." Josh grinned crookedly. "He sounds just like a cat would if it laughed right before it jumped on a mouse."

It was an apt description, but I could have done without the feline reference. "When I said it'll work out and he said he hoped so, he looked right at me. I mean *right* at me." Using my index and middle fingers, I pointed at my own eyes.

"Whoa." Josh sat back. "Stephen never looks straight at you. Through you, maybe, but never at you."

Holly laughed. "I think maybe I'd turn to stone if he did. Stephen as Medusa."

"So, something's up, right?" I asked. "I'm not imagining things?"

"Not a chance," Holly said. "The fact that he laughed and looked you straight in the eye?

Two signs that something weird is going on."

Josh smirked. "Or the end of the world is coming."

"There's not much we can do about that," Holly said briskly, "but we can help Minnie find out if Stephen knows about Eddie."

I'd kept Eddie's presence a secret even from Holly and Josh for months. Back in August, though, when it had become crystal clear that Eddie was a part of the bookmobile whether or not I wanted him to be, I'd made them raise their right hands, put their left hands on an ancient green *Readers' Guide to Periodical Literature* that I'd hauled out of the library basement, and swear to keep the Eddie Secret.

"Okay," Josh said, popping open his second soda can. "I'm in. But how are we going to figure this out? I mean, anyone could have said something on Facebook."

Holly laughed. "There's no way Stephen does Facebook. He says social media is a waste of time."

Which was true. We'd all heard Stephen pontificate on the time-wasting properties of the Internet in general and social media in particular. It had gotten to the point where we could recognize the signs of a pending lecture and slide away with some excuse before he really got going.

Josh shrugged. "Doesn't mean he wouldn't use it, not if he could see some advantage."

Which was also true.

"Well, I don't think Stephen has any idea about Eddie," Holly said.

"Maybe. Maybe not." Josh tipped his head back and studied her through narrowed eyes. "How sure are you?"

"Sure enough to bet a double batch of my peanut butter fudge."

"You're on." Josh held out his hand.

"Not so fast, buster," she said, pulling back. "What do I get if I'm right? You're about the worst cook in the world, next to Minnie."

"Hey!" I protested, but neither one of them paid any attention to me.

"Gift certificate to Cookie Tom's?" Josh asked.

Holly rolled her eyes. "Like I need more baked goods."

"Gift certificate to Shomin's, then."

Shomin's was a new deli in town, and the library staff members were enthusiastic supporters.

Holly put out her hand, then jerked it back. "Gift certificate big enough to buy two lunches."

Josh pursed his lips, but we all knew it was a done deal. Holly's peanut butter fudge was arguably better than her cookies. "Two lunches," he agreed.

This was all well and good, but I had a question. "So, how are you going to do this without making Stephen suspicious?"

"Easy," Josh said. "I was going to update some

software on his computer on a Saturday, but I'll come up with some reason to do it on a weekday. I can just rattle off some IT words, and he won't know the difference. I mean, it's not like he's going to leave his office when I do the updates. I could kind of ask him about the bookmobile, maybe act like I think it's a bad idea, and see what he says."

"Now you're talking." Holly raised her hand for a high five, and we slapped all the way around. "First off, I'll see if I can find him on Facebook. Then I can check LinkedIn, Pinterest, and Twitter. I'll even look at Google Plus, Tumblr, and Instagram. If he's not on any of those, he probably isn't doing social media at all. And where else would he hear about Eddie? It's not like he goes anywhere but here."

"You two are awesome," I said.

"Ah, it's nothing." Josh upended his soda can and slugged down half the contents. "We'd do this for any assistant library director who got the library a bookmobile and had her cat stow away on it."

"It'll be fun," Holly said. "Sleuthing around, trying to find out what's really going on with Stephen—it'll be a kick. We should have started doing this years ago." She grinned.

I looked at them. My coworkers, my companions, my friends. I didn't know what I'd do without them. "There's one thing, though."

"What's that?" Josh asked.

I hesitated. They'd think I was silly and a worrywart, but it had to be said. "Be careful, okay? Just . . . be careful."

Chapter 3

Thursday and Friday passed without any major incidents, assuming you didn't call the Thursday delivery of six boxes for the Cheboygan Area Public Library to our library and the delivery of our books to Cheboygan a major incident.

Stephen had summoned me after taking one look at the stack of boxes. "Minnie. Take care of this." He'd spun around and left me standing there.

I'd squinted at his retreating figure, shrugged, and called Cheboygan's library director. That noon, we'd met at a restaurant near the halfway point between our two fair cities, had a nice lunch, shared some library stories, and left with the appropriate boxes.

Aunt Frances had enjoyed the story immensely, and even Eddie had seemed amused.

Friday morning arrived with a forecast that could excite only small children and die-hard skiers.

"Snow," Kelsey said, frowning at the front-desk computer screen and shaking her head so hard that her short blond hair flew around her head. "It's only the middle of November. They should not be predicting eight inches of snow for tonight. That's just wrong."

Kelsey was a part-time clerk and my most recent hire. Well, sort of. She'd worked at the library years before, but had left when she'd had her first child. The kids were older now, and Kelsey didn't mind leaving them with her mother a couple of times a week. One of our part-timers had relocated to Arizona in July, so it had all worked out.

"What about you?" Kelsey asked. "Have you driven anything like the bookmobile in winter?"

I smiled. "It'll be fine. The heavier the vehicle, the easier it'll go through the snow. Besides, the roads should be plowed by the time we get out."

Her eyebrows went up. "On that route? You're kidding, right?"

For the first time, I had a moment of pure panic. What was I thinking? Surely driving an incredibly expensive vehicle out on snow-covered and slippery roads was misguided at best, and dangerous at worst. I was going to put the bookmobile, Eddie, and Denise in danger, and for what? To say that the bookmobile always made its appointed rounds? For the sake of my pride?

Then my common sense asserted itself. *You're not stupid,* it told me. *If the weather is truly horrible, you won't go out.*

"No need to make that decision now," I said.

"We'll see what happens overnight. If it looks bad in the morning, I'll call the sheriff's office for a report on the road conditions."

Kelsey shook her head. "You're a braver woman than I am, driving that big bookmobile beast all over the county. There's not even cell-phone reception in a lot of places, you know."

Beast? I puffed up a little at hearing my beautiful bookmobile called a beast. The only beastly thing about the bookmobile was Eddie, and he slept a lot of the time. Maybe hiring Kelsey hadn't been such a wise decision.

"Hey," she said, snapping her fingers. "I keep meaning to tell you. A friend of mine lives over in Peebles—you know, one of those little towns where Stephen shut down their library a couple of years ago? Anyway, you have a bookmobile stop there, and my friend says that getting the bookmobile is the best thing that's happened to that town since the grocery store reopened. Pretty cool, right?"

Then again, Kelsey wasn't so bad.

I had dreams that night of freezing rain and howling winds, and woke up to the smell of bacon cooking.

My shower was fast, and I hurried down to the kitchen just in time to see Aunt Frances filling two plates with eggs and bacon and hash browns.

"Wow," I said, bumping Eddie to the floor and sitting in my chair. "What's the occasion?"

Aunt Frances nodded to the wide kitchen window. "Thought you could use a hearty breakfast before going out in that."

I half stood so I could see outside. Nothing but white and more white. "Huh," I said, sitting back down. "That's, um, a lot of snow."

"More than six inches," she said cheerfully. "Let's eat."

While downing crisp bacon glazed with maple syrup, my aunt regaled me with tales of winters long, long ago. "And then there was the blizzard of 1978," she said almost wistfully. "Remember?"

I didn't, since that had been two years before I was born, but I nodded anyway, figuring it counted if I remembered seeing the pictures Mom had stuck into the photo album.

Our plates were soon empty. I thanked Aunt Frances for the wonderful breakfast, and as soon as the table was clear, I fetched my cell phone and dialed the sheriff's office.

"Deputy Wolverson," said a male voice. "How may I help you?"

"Oh, uh." I hadn't expected someone I knew to answer the phone, let alone a man who was about my age, with a muscular build, short brown hair, and a squarish jaw. *Hot* was what Holly called him, and I supposed she was right. "Hi. This is Minnie Hamilton. From the library. I didn't expect you to be answering the phones."

"Hey, Minnie," he said. "I don't usually, but I'm

covering for someone this morning. What can I do you for?"

The old-fashioned phrase made me smile. "Today is a bookmobile day, and I was wondering about the road conditions."

"Hey, that's great that you called to check," he said. "Not many people think to ask. Where are you headed?"

I gave him the road names and heard the click of a few computer keys. "You should be fine," he said. "Those are primary roads, so they'll be clear by nine o'clock."

I thanked him and hung up. Aunt Frances was at the sink, doing the dishes against my objections. "We're on," I said, and looked around for Eddie. He was nowhere to be seen. "Hey, Eddie," I called. "Ready for a bookmobile ride?"

Though he hadn't been in the kitchen half a second earlier, there he suddenly was, sitting in the middle of the floor as if he'd been there the entire time.

"Mrr," he said.

Half an hour later, the bookmobile was out of the garage, warming up while I made sure all was ready for the day's adventure.

I'd run through the outside checklist and was halfway through the inside list when there was a knock on the door. This was strange, because people rarely knocked at the door at stops, let alone while the bookmobile was sitting in the library's back parking lot, but maybe the handle had frozen shut with the snow and Denise couldn't get it unlatched.

Mentally shrugging, I went to open the door.

Outside, a man in jeans, work boots, and a brown Carhartt jacket stood with his back to the bookmobile. He was doing what I often did in the mornings, drinking in the view of the downtown Chilson rooftops and Janay Lake. Even on this snowy day, with a sky still morning gray, it was a sight worth taking in, and I was already liking the guy, whoever he was.

"Hi," I said. "Can I help you?"

He turned. He had a salt-and-pepper beard, weathered skin, and a cheerful expression. "Morning. I'm Roger Slade. My wife sent me over."

"Your . . . wife?"

"Denise."

This was making no sense whatsoever. "She sent you?"

He nodded. "Didn't she call? She said she was going to."

"Haven't heard it ring." And I knew for a fact that my cell was charged up and raring to go. I always made sure of that on bookmobile days.

"Oh. Well." He shrugged. "She meant to, but you know how she gets. Anyway, she can't make it today on the bookmobile."

"She what?" My eyes thinned to mere slits. I'd known this was going to happen. Just known it. Denise was capable but not dependable, no matter how many promises she made. Why had I ever thought this time would be different?

"But she sent me," Roger said. "She said it'll work out fine."

Oh, she did, did she? I opened my mouth . . . but then shut it. I would deal with Denise later. Right now there was a bookmobile run to embark upon and a new volunteer to train.

I smiled at Roger. "Come on in."

Ten minutes later we were on our way. I'd introduced Roger to Eddie and Eddie to Roger, given him a quick tour of the bookmobile, handed him the necessary paperwork, given him a fact sheet on the Dewey decimal system, and asked him whether he'd brought food.

He shook his head. "Denise didn't say anything about it and I didn't think to ask."

I stopped in the middle of buckling up my seat belt. "Do you want to stop to pick up something on the way out of town?"

"I'll be okay," he said. "I'm used to not having lunch."

It was then that I was struck with the realization that I knew absolutely nothing about the man I was going to be traveling with for the next eight hours. "So," I said, dropping the transmission into gear, "what do you do when you're not riding with the bookmobile?"

"Lately or normally?" he asked.

I was starting to like this guy. I grinned. "Both."

"Normally I work construction for a company in Petoskey." He gave a name that rang a vague bell in the back of my brain. "We specialize in old structures. Bridges, barns—whatever. Do projects all over the state. Did your library here," he said, nodding at the brick building.

No wonder the name of his company had sounded familiar. I'd moved to Chilson on the happy end of the school-turned-library renovation. While I'd helped plan the move from the old building to the new, my only dealing with the construction project itself was to marvel at the finished product.

"So, you're off for the winter?" I asked.

"Off until the doctor gives me the thumbs-up." He pointed at his midsection. "Had hernia surgery three weeks ago and I need the doc's sign-off before I can swing a sledgehammer again."

Wonderful. Not only had Denise bailed on her bookmobile promise, but she'd sent me a walking wounded for a replacement. I braked to a stop, right in the middle of the empty road. "If you're recovering from surgery, I'm afraid I—"

"Minnie, I'm fine." He looked at me with serious gray eyes. "I wouldn't put you or the library in any jeopardy. After two weeks, I was fine to lift things up to ten pounds, so as long as you don't make me tote any big boxes of books, there won't be any problems."

I studied him, thinking hard.

What did I know about this man? Next to nothing. The fact that I'd already mentally moved him into the friend category meant zip where the bookmobile and the library were concerned. I had to do what was best for the library and not be swayed by a kernel of friendship.

Then again, what were the risks if I brought him along?

"It was laparoscopic surgery," he said, "and it was three weeks ago. All I can't do is lift heavy things, which is why I'm here instead of out hunting."

That was right: It was the first day of deer season. I tried to remember what people said about snow for hunting, whether that made it easier or harder, but since I wasn't a hunter, I didn't try very hard.

I drummed my fingers on the steering wheel. "Let me make a phone call. There's this doctor I know." I dug into my backpack for my phone and called Tucker. Having an emergency-room doctor boyfriend was coming in handy. "Hey," I said. "Got a quick question for you."

"You're not canceling our date tonight, are you?" he asked.

"Not a chance." It had been weeks since our

schedules had synced to where we could have a weekend night together. "My question is a general one, about hernia surgery."

"Don't do it," he said promptly.

I laughed. "Not in my future, as far as I know. But I'm wondering about recovery time."

He started asking all sorts of questions. What kind of hernia surgery, had there been a mesh installed, who was the surgeon, how healthy was the patient, and on and on.

Okay, maybe having a doctor for a boyfriend wasn't so handy. I waited until he paused for breath, then asked, "If the guy is around fifty, fairly fit, and had laparoscopic surgery three weeks ago, do you think it's okay for him to work at a desk job?"

"Well, what I'll tell you," Tucker said, "is most guys are back at work inside of a week if they don't have to do any lifting."

I breathed a sigh of relief. "Excellent. Thanks."

Tucker went on about possible complications, said he couldn't make any real recommendations without seeing the guy, that every case was different, and to get a solid answer the guy should consult with his surgeon.

"Sure," I said. "I understand. Thanks." I tucked the phone away. "Well, it sounds like you're good to go."

" 'Fairly fit'?" Roger quoted me, lifting one eyebrow.

I grinned and checked the vehicle's mirrors. The road was still empty, so I took my foot off the brake. "Well, I don't know your best mile time, do I?"

"Last summer I ran a half marathon in under two hours."

I tried to do the math. Gave up fast. Anyone who could run 13.1 miles at all had to be a lot healthier than I was. One of these days I'd start eating better and get into working out. This spring, maybe. Winter was no time to start an exercise program.

We spent the ride out to the south central part of the county working through the pros and cons of over- and underestimating people and came to no conclusions. We talked about the library's renovation project on the way to the second stop, wherein I learned that my office had previously been part of a fifth-grade classroom, and talked a lot about the weather on the way to the third stop.

This was because although I'd already lived through three northern Michigan winters, I'd spent most of those months in town or on highways that had priority for snow clearance. I had never quite realized how varied the snowfall amounts could be in different parts of Tonedagana County.

"Oh, sure," Roger said, nodding. "Over by Chilson, that's what we call the banana belt."

"Bananas?"

"It's a joke. But over there we got—what?—six,

maybe eight inches? Which is a lot of stuff to shovel, sure, but look at that." He gestured at the snow-laden trees. "That's ten to twelve inches, easy."

As Deputy Wolverson had predicted, the roads had been cleared nicely and the driving was fine, but there was indeed a lot of snow. Cedar branches were weighed down with great clumps of the stuff, the few houses were thickly blanketed with white, and the only bare ground to be seen was the roadway in front of us.

"Why?" I asked.

"Does it snow more over here?" He shrugged. "Ask a weather guy. All I know is that it does. Always has."

Something to do with the Great Lakes, no doubt. That was always the stock answer for any odd weather up here. And it was probably true. Having multiple vast bodies of water—Lake Superior, Lake Michigan, and Lake Huron— smush themselves together in basically one location was bound to create strange weather patterns.

At the third stop, I continued what I'd done at the first two and kept an eye on Roger to make sure he limited himself to desk-job duties. No way was I going to allow him to hurt himself on my bookmobile, and even though he seemed like a very nice man, he was still a man and would undoubtedly try to do more than he should.

"Mrr."

I turned from where I was showing the picture books to a young mother and her small child and saw Eddie jump onto Roger's lap. Eddie, who had slept most of the morning in his carrier, was typically not a cat to rush to judgment, but he had obviously decided that Roger was his new buddy.

"He's more than ten pounds," I cautioned Roger. Thirteen-point-five, to be exact. "If you want him to move, please don't lift him. Just give him a gentle shove."

My toddler patron squealed with delight to see a kitty cat. "Mommy, Mommy, can I pet the kitty?"

Mommy looked at me.

"Sure," I said. "He has claws, but he's great with kids. Of course, he does tend to shed a lot, so . . ." I spread my hands and shrugged. "Up to you."

The mom gave the go-ahead, and the child rushed forward to pet Mr. Ed. The kid kept petting Eddie, Eddie kept allowing it, and poor Roger was stuck, caught between a cat and a kid.

Not that he seemed stuck. He seemed to be enjoying himself while Mom selected books, I checked them out, and we chatted as she slid them into a tote bag. When all was ready, Mom turned to her child and said, "Okey-dokey-kokey, kiddo. Zip up your coat—it's time to go."

The kid immediately started to wail. "I don't wanna go! I wanna pet the kitty some more!"

The kitty in question didn't look as if he cared

for the wailing, but he didn't move a muscle, submitting, with bizarre acceptance, to the kid's clutching of his fur. If I'd done such a thing, he would have howled and taught me a quick lesson with his extended claws.

"Now, now," Roger said calmly. "There's no crying on the bookmobile."

The kid's wails slowed. "I ca-can't cry?"

Roger shook his head. "Not here. We have rules about it, right, Miss Minnie?"

"Absolutely," I said. "Bookmobile rule number one is No Crying." I visualized an imaginary list of rules and saw that the second rule was No Cats. Well, at least we weren't violating rule number one. "The books don't like to hear crying," I added.

The kid's eyes went wide. "They . . . don't?"

Roger nodded seriously. "They don't like crying a single bit, so you see why we have a rule against it."

Sniffing, the kid patted Eddie's head. "Okay." *Sniff.* "Will the bookmobile kitty be here next time?"

Roger looked at me. So did the kid and the mom. "Count on it," I said.

A few minutes later, Eddie was back in his carrier, and Roger and I were buckling our seat belts.

"Now where?" Roger asked.

I glanced over at him. "You were really good

with that kid. Do you and Denise have children?"
It seemed odd that I didn't know, but conversations with Denise tended to focus on whatever her current project might be.

"Two," Roger said. "Girl and a boy. Both are grown and gone. One lives in Texas; the other's in Arizona."

I started us rolling forward, heading back north in the direction of Chilson. "Not fans of the snow?"

"More like they're fans of getting jobs," he said, smiling. "But, yeah, neither one seems interested in moving back. They come up in the summer; we visit them at Christmas. It works out."

We headed to the next stop, chatting idly about topics from Thanksgiving (he and Denise were eating with her extended family, while my parents were headed to my brother's in Florida, and I was staying with Aunt Frances and an assortment of guests) to the chances of the Detroit Lions making it to the Superbowl (slim to none, we agreed) and the annoyance of political signs cluttering up the roadsides a week and a half after the November election.

"Just look at that." He pointed through the windshield.

I glanced at the busy cluster of signs that included people running for a variety of offices, from seats in the US Congress to the state legislature, local townships, and even one for the

Chilson City Council. VOTE FOR ALLISON KORTHASE, it proclaimed with a professional design in red, white, and blue. Why there was a Chilson sign all the way down here, I wasn't sure, but it must have worked, because I remembered that she'd won the seat.

"It's as bad as seeing Christmas advertisements after Christmas," I said.

"Take another foot of snow to cover up those buggers," he said morosely. "Bet most of them are still there come spring."

I laughed, but he was probably right. "Lunch stop coming up. I usually pull in at that township park, but I'm sure it's not plowed. There's that gas station over on the county highway. I was thinking about stopping there. We can use the facilities, and you could grab something to eat."

"You don't have to stop for me," Roger said. "I'm fine."

For the zillionth time that day, I wondered how this laid-back, easygoing, no-cares-whatsoever man had stayed married to the high-frequency, pay-attention-to-my-problems-because-they're-more-important-than-yours Denise for so many years. But, as my mother had once told me, every marriage is a mystery.

"Well," I said, "I could use a break, and we have a little time."

I'd cut each stop short by a few minutes, just in case of slippery conditions on the way to the next one, but the roads were fine. One car, a dark blue multi-bumper-stickered SUV kind of thing, had even passed us a few miles back.

Roger shrugged. "Works for me. I can grab a sandwich, if they don't look too scary."

"Eddie?" I peered into the cat carrier. "Is there anything you want?"

He opened his mouth to say "Mrr," but no noise came out.

"Nothing, you say?" I asked. "I had no idea you could be so accommodating. You're okay, pal, no matter what Aunt Frances says about you."

"Mrr."

Roger laughed. "It really does seem like he knows what you're saying."

It was frightening, actually, how Eddie and I could carry on conversations. Almost all of my brain knew there was no way a cat could understand human speech, but I had a few brain cells, tucked somewhere in a back corner, that were convinced Eddie understood everything I said, and even some of the things I didn't say.

We pulled into the gas station—with two wide entrances, it was my favorite kind of place—and came to a stop in a vast parking lot behind the building. I went in first, while Roger stayed on the bookmobile.

In short order, I returned, laden with a bottle of water and a PowerBar, because I would have felt guilty about using the restroom without purchasing something. I clambered up the steps and said, "It's colder over here. Wind's up, too."

"Told you," Roger said. "Chilson's the banana belt. Warmer near the lake and all that, just like they say."

The weather folks said it was cooler near Lake Michigan in the summer, when that great mass of water acted as a big refrigerator, but in the winter the big lake kept the lakeshore warmer than the rest of the state. Not always by very much, but every degree counts, especially in January.

Roger gave the side of Eddie's face a scratch, stood, and zipped up his coat. "I'll just be a minute." He took two steps, then stopped, muttering, "Almost forgot."

I started to turn, assuming he was talking to me, but he was moving again and out the door. "Talking to himself," I told Eddie, nodding. "They say that can be the first step toward insanity. Of course, they say the real danger is when you answer yourself."

"Mrr."

I shrugged. "Yeah, I don't know who they are, either. Sounds like a bunch of hooey, doesn't it?"

Eddie rubbed his face up against the door of the cat carrier. The wire caught on his kitty lips, pulling them back to reveal sharp, pointed teeth and pinkish gums.

"Not a good look, bud," I said. "You're cute and adorable in many ways, but your gums are just not attractive." I thought about that. "Then again, probably no one's are. Maybe a periodontist would have an opinion on good-looking gums, but I bet everyone else would just as soon—"

Bang!

Eddie and I both jumped as the echo of a rifle shot bounced back and forth across the hills.

We blinked at each other; then I remembered. "It's the first day of hunting season," I said, nodding authoritatively. Of course, it was technically the first day of the Michigan's two-week-long deer rifle season, but nobody called it that. It was Opening Day, spelled with capital letters, and if you didn't know what that meant, you were either from the depths of a large city or from another solar system. There were other deer seasons—bow season, black-powder season, and who knew what else—but rifle season saw the most action.

All day long, Roger and I had seen trucks and SUVs parked in odd places; on the sides of roads, a short ways down narrow dirt trails, and in parking lots of long-abandoned homes. Hunters. Some of them, no doubt, were looking for that elusive trophy buck with a huge rack of antlers, but for the most part, hunters—male and female— were trying to fill their family's freezers with venison.

I'd grown up in the Detroit area, where the only thing I'd learned about hunting and fishing was that it was something my family wasn't ever likely to do. "A lot easier to buy meat and fish at the store," my mother had said more than once.

My city-bred father was more likely to sprout feathers than he was to venture into a boat (the poor man couldn't even watch *Titanic* without getting seasick), and he had so little sense of direction that he could get lost in a large wooded park. Basic survival arts weren't something my older brother and I had ever been taught.

"Not that it's likely I'll need to build a fire out here," I said to Eddie. "All I need to know, I learned from Jack London, which is to stay out of the wilderness if you don't know what you're doing." I smirked, but I didn't think Eddie got the joke.

I started to explain the short story, but my cat yawned at me. "Fine," I said, sitting back. "I can take a hint. What should we talk about instead?" I hummed a few nonsense notes. Eddie looked at me sideways, then closed his eyes.

The perfect topic presented itself. "I know. Let's discuss the rising price of cat food. It's going up fast, so you might want to consider getting a job."

The idea of Eddie becoming part of our household revenue stream amused me, and I considered the possibilities. What could a cat do to earn money? The most likely possibility was pest control, but since Eddie hadn't seemed the least bit inclined to do anything about Aunt

Frances's basement mouse problem, why would he do the job at someone else's house?

"I'll take any suggestions," I said.

One feline eye opened, then it shut again.

Right. I was on my own. What else could Eddie do to earn a paycheck? I tapped the steering wheel and tried to think. Bookmobile-goers of all ages seemed to like him, but the idea of renting him out was just too weird. And although he was photogenic, since there were so many free pictures of cats available on the Internet, I couldn't see much of a market for Eddie photos.

"Too bad you don't really talk," I said. "Now, that would make us some money. Just think if—"

Bang!

I sat up straight, feeling a tingle crawl up the back of my neck. "That one was close," I said, staring out the window, looking up into the woods. Every hunter was required by law to wear bright orange, but I couldn't see a hint of it anywhere.

I'd heard there was a law about how far you had to be from a house to shoot, but I had no idea whether that law included other kinds of buildings. Or how much time was spent enforcing the law.

"It was probably a lot farther away than it seemed," I murmured. At least I hoped so. While my knowledge about firearms was limited, I had a pretty good idea that the bookmobile's walls wouldn't be able to stop a speeding bullet.

"Mrrr."

I looked at Eddie, trying to decide if he'd been agreeing or disagreeing, but he wasn't paying any attention to me. He was on his feet, pacing around the interior of the cat carrier like a caged tiger.

"What's the matter, pal?" An agitated Eddie wasn't a good thing. Because if he was upset, the next thing he was likely to do was—

"MMRR!"

My ears tried to plug themselves, but, as usual, it didn't work. The howl of an agitated Eddie could probably pierce the thickest sound protection, anyway. Maybe the muffs that airport workers use would work, but I doubted it. His mouth started to open again, and this time I slapped my hands over my ears.

"MMRR!"

I leaned over the console and unlatched the carrier's door. "Are you okay? You're not sick, are you?"

He shouldered the door open, jumped onto the passenger's seat and then up onto the wide dashboard. "Mrrr! Mrr! Mrr!"

"Hey, come on." I half stood to pet him. "What's wrong?" I was tempted to ask him if Timmy had fallen down the well, but figured he wouldn't get the reference to the old *Lassie* shows.

"Mrr," he said. "Mrr!" He pulled out of my reach and paced the length of the dashboard.

I eyed the paw prints he was leaving behind. "I

cleaned the dash with that special spray just last week, you know."

"Mrr!" Eddie pawed at the windshield, scraping at it, really, with his claws extended. He howled and he whined and he pushed the side of his face against the glass, leaving marks that would be hard for a person like me, who had distance-challenged arms, to clean without crawling up onto the dashboard itself.

"Get down from there." I grabbed at Eddie's back end and gently pulled him toward me. "What is with you? You've never acted this way." He'd done a thousand other odd and unusual things, but crawling up on the bookmobile dashboard and howling out his little kitty lungs was not one of them.

"I'm glad you weren't acting like this in front of Roger," I told him. "Talk about bad first impressions. So far he seems to like you and—"

And then I realized that Roger had been gone for a long time. If he didn't get back soon, we'd risk being late for the next stop. I glanced at the dashboard clock, but couldn't remember what time he'd left. It had been a while, though, and I'd been in that gas station on a regular basis since starting up the bookmobile; their sandwich offerings weren't so numerous that it would take long to make a decision.

"Ham, turkey, or egg salad," I told Eddie. "Sometimes roast beef."

"MRRR!" Eddie slid out of my hands and started whacking the top of his head against the windshield. It made a loud and hollow thumping noise that made the inside of my skin cringe.

"Cut it out already, will you?" I grabbed for my cat, but he whipped out of my reach and kept bonking his head. "What is your deal? Have you bonded with Roger so quickly that you're lost without him? I didn't know I could be so easily replaced."

Eddie glanced over his shoulder and stared me straight in the eye. "MMMRR!"

I glared back. "Fine. I'll go see what's keeping your new best friend. I'm sure he just got talking with the guy running the cash register."

"Mrr." Eddie jumped down to the passenger's seat and sat, prim and proper and not looking at all like a cat who'd been beating his skull against thick glass.

I zipped up my coat, muttering about manipulative cats and their enabling humans. Shutting and locking the door behind me, however, I came to the not-so-profound realization that the term "manipulative cat" was redundant. "They're all manipulative," I said. Which made me grin, for some reason. I waved at Eddie, who opened his mouth in a "Mrr," that I couldn't hear, and trudged my way through snow to the front of the store.

Inside, I saw no sign of Roger.

"Hey," said the thirtyish guy behind the counter. "Need something else?" He picked up his fountain soda, which was large enough to hydrate a family of nine, and slurped.

"Looking for Roger," I said. "He came in after me. Brown Carhartt jacket, jeans, work boots."

The guy looked at me like I was an idiot. "He left five minutes ago. Bought an egg-salad sandwich and a bag of chips, then left."

This wasn't making sense. "He didn't come out to the bookmobile. You're sure he's not in the bathroom?"

"No way. He left out the front door. I saw him."

Not that I thought the guy was lying, but maybe he'd been distracted by a phone call or another customer. "Do you mind if I check anyway?"

The guy shrugged. "I'm telling you—he's not there."

And he wasn't. Not in the men's room and not in the women's. He also wasn't in the back room (I made the counter guy look).

I stood in the middle of the store, turning in a small circle. "Did anyone else stop?" From where the bookmobile was parked, I hadn't been able to see the traffic. I couldn't think of any reason for Roger to leave with someone else and abandon me, but it was the only explanation I could come up with.

Counter Guy shrugged. "An SUV with a couple of hunters from downstate stopped for gas, and an old couple in a beater sedan came in to get some food. Other than that, there's been nobody."

Then where the heck was he? I wanted to stamp my foot, but made a grunting noise instead.

The counter guy smirked. "Maybe he's got early Alzheimer's or something. Maybe he got lost getting back to your rig."

I started to say that was ridiculous, but I stopped myself before getting further than "That's ridic—" Because maybe it wasn't. After all, I hardly knew the man. You'd have thought Denise would have said something if Roger had that sort of issue, but who knew?

"Thanks," I said, and headed back out into the cold, snowy world. "Now what?" I muttered. Well, first thing was to make sure Roger wasn't standing outside the locked bookmobile, waiting for me.

I hurried back around the way I'd come, but there was no Roger. I did see Eddie pawing at the windshield, so I gave him a friendly wave and, suddenly hurrying, kept going around to check the other side of the building. If Roger had been struck down by a heart attack and I'd done nothing but dawdle, I'd never forgive myself.

A wide variety of possibilities suddenly popped into my brain, and none of them was good.

Stroke.

Brain aneurism.

He fell on an icy spot and whacked his head.

He fell and broke a leg or a hip or an ankle or wrist, or any combination thereof.

An icicle fell off the roof and hit him in the head.

I swallowed and went even faster. Why hadn't I thought about any of these things earlier when I was messing around with Eddie, waiting? With the bookmobile's engine running, I wouldn't have heard any calls for help. I should have paid more attention to the time. I should have paid more attention to the potential dangers. I should have done everything differently. Why had I been so complacent? Why had I assumed that everything was fine?

All this went through my mind in a flash. I broke into a run and rounded the corner of the building, breathless with worry, because I knew with a sick and sudden certainty that something was deeply wrong.

Fast as I could, I ran through the snow, dodging around the back of the tall wood fence that screened the Dumpster, hoping to see Roger standing there, talking on his cell phone to a buddy about hunting, having lost all track of time.

But there was a primal part of me that knew there would be no easy explanation.

So when I saw a man lying on the ground, I was almost expecting it. When I recognized Roger's jeans, work boots, and canvas jacket, I was almost prepared. When I saw that he wasn't talking, wasn't moving, wasn't doing anything, I was almost ready to accept that something horrible had happened.

Almost.

"Roger!" I rushed to his side and dropped to my knees in the snow. "Roger, what's wrong? Are you okay?"

But in spite of all my fears and all my mental preparations, I wasn't anywhere near ready for the vast spread of crimson that stained the left side of his jacket.

And I could never have prepared myself for his open eyes, staring sightlessly at the gray sky.

In a flurry, I yanked off my gloves, felt for a pulse at his neck, pulled my cell phone out of my pocket, and pushed those three short numbers that could sometimes help, that could sometimes make all the difference.

But I knew nothing was going to help Roger.

He was dead.

Chapter 4

Many, many hours later, I knocked on the door of a condominium in Charlevoix, a small town in the next county. It was a very quiet knock, one that lacked energy or interest or much of anything except an overwhelming sense of fatigue.

Tucker opened the door. He was barefoot and

dressed in his typical posthospital wear of jeans and a black zip sweatshirt. "Minnie. I wasn't sure if I heard you or not." He stood aside. "Come on in."

"Can I . . . ?" I paused, not sure what I wanted, not sure I had the strength to move.

"What?"

"Can I have a hug?"

Then he looked at me. Really looked at me. I don't know what he saw—if it was my red-rimmed eyes or the fatigue that drooped at my shoulders or what must be my woebegone face—because he immediately swept me inside, shut the door, put his arms around me, and embraced me fully and completely.

I clung to him, needing his strength, needing his comfort, wanting him to make everything better. Which he couldn't do, of course, but maybe he could keep the sadness at bay for a little while.

He released me and kissed the top of my head. "Any better?"

Sniffing, I nodded. "A little." *Sniff.* "Thanks."

"Let me take your coat." He unzipped it and turned me around, then pulled on the cuffs, de-coating me fast and easy.

As he hung it on the coat tree, he said, "I'm guessing you need a couple of things." He held up one finger. "Food." He held up another finger. "A nice, long talk. You go get settled," he said, gesturing toward his living room. "I'll order the pizza. Mushroom and sausage on your side?"

When I nodded, he picked up the phone and started to order.

I shuffled over to the beige couch and flopped down, exhaustion dragging at me. In the months I'd been visiting Tucker in his condo, I don't think I'd once sat down before standing at the window for a few minutes, enjoying the view of the channel that connected Charlevoix's Round Lake to Lake Michigan, but today I couldn't bring myself to stand any longer than I had to. Self-preservation, really, because it was only sensible to sit before I fell down.

"Now." Tucker sat down in a leather chair that matched the couch. "Talk to me."

I wanted to protest, to say that what I wanted most was just to have him hold me, but held back. He was probably right. If we snuggled, I might break down into a bucket of tears. What I really needed was to talk, and I could do that best if he wasn't within arm's length.

"Okay." The word came out so slowly, it was almost pitiful. I told myself to buck up, and, according to my mother, the best way to start feeling better was to sit up straight and put your shoulders back.

So I did.

"Okay," I said again, and felt my spirits rise. Not by much, but anything was good. Once again, Mom was right, and maybe one day I'd call and tell her so. Not today, though. Monday, maybe. Or Tuesday.

"Okay," I said, this time with feeling. Only . . . I wasn't quite ready to talk.

I let my gaze wander around the room. Beige furniture, hotel room–quality art on the walls, and bland carpet. The only Tucker-type things in the room were the bookshelves he'd bought and the books he'd filled them with. Knowing he'd be too busy at the hospital to equip even a small house properly, he'd leased a furnished two-bedroom condominium. It was nice enough, but no more than that. A wise choice for a busy bachelor, I supposed, but there was no life in the room, and I suddenly couldn't bear it.

I stood and went to the window. The sun had set long ago, but evenly spaced lights illuminated the wide walkway that ran adjacent to the river channel, all the way out to the pier. While I couldn't see the lighthouse itself, I could see the reflection of its circling light on the water. Around and around and around and . . .

"Minnie?" Tucker asked gently. "What's the matter?"

And, just like that, I was ready to talk.

I told him about what had happened that day. Told him about Roger. "He was dead," I said quietly, watching the water ripple in the glow from the lights. "I called nine-one-one, but I knew he was dead before they showed up." There had been no chance he'd still been alive. Not with no pulse, not with his skin growing so terribly cold.

"He'd been bleeding?" my doctor boyfriend asked.

I laid a hand flat against the left side of my chest. Over my heart. "Yes," I whispered.

Tucker stirred, and I figured he wanted to ask medical questions, but there was no way I'd be able to answer them. "The ambulance came and took him to the Petoskey hospital," I said. "A sheriff's deputy came out, but there wasn't much I could tell him." There hadn't been much to tell my boss, either, though I'd dutifully called Stephen and told him what had happened.

"It was those shots you'd heard earlier?" Tucker asked.

I nodded. Shrugged. Nodded again. "Hunters are all over the place today. Poor Roger was in the wrong place at the wrong time, I guess. Just a stupid hunting accident." They happened. Rarely, but they happened often enough to stay in everyone's minds.

"It's not your fault, you know."

I put my forehead against the cool of the window. Part of me knew he was right. It wasn't my fault; it was the fault of the guy who'd held that gun. Then again, if it hadn't been for me, there wouldn't have been a bookmobile for Roger to have been on.

Did that make me partially to blame? Not in a

court of law, but what about the court of public opinion? How about my own opinion? With my own self blaming me, how would I ever sleep tonight—or any other night in the foreseeable future? And even if I did sleep, what sort of dreams would I be likely to have?

I shivered and wrapped my arms around myself.

Tucker got up and put his hands on my shoulders. "Repeat after me: It was an accident."

I managed a smile. "It was an accident."

"It's not my fault," Tucker prompted.

"It's . . ." I shook my head and blew out a breath. "It's not my fault."

"I will spend the rest of the evening eating pizza and breadsticks and watching old movies, and will not think about this again until tomorrow."

Somehow, magically, I laughed. Not a big laugh—a very small one, actually—but still a laugh. It was good to have a boyfriend who could make me feel better when all I'd wanted to do half an hour ago was wrap my arms around my knees and bawl. "I'll do my best."

"That's my girl." He reached around me to begin a serious hug, but a knock on the door stopped him. "Must be the pizza guy."

He went to the door, and I went to the kitchen for plates, napkins, forks (two, even though Tucker wouldn't use his), and drinks.

"Movie time?" he asked, holding the two boxes

aloft. "I recommend something with a happy ending."

"Can we watch *The Sting* again?" I carried my stack of food-related items to the living room and piled them on the coffee table.

One of the first things Tucker and I discovered we had in common was a love of movies. One of the second things we discovered we had in common was a love of staying up late watching movies.

"Only if we can watch *The Andromeda Strain*, too," he said.

I smiled. There weren't that many movies that featured medical research, but Tucker had all of them on DVD. He also had many of my favorites, from *The Wizard of Oz* to *The Princess Bride* to *Shakespeare in Love*. He didn't have *Ghostbusters*, but I was planning on giving it to him for his birthday.

We settled in, immersed ourselves in Depression-era Chicago, and when the food was gone I was content to sit back with Tucker's arm around me.

Five minutes later, his cell phone rang. It was the ring tone for the hospital.

I tensed. "I didn't think you were on call tonight."

He was pulling the phone from his pocket. "Had to switch with somebody," he muttered, then into the phone said, "Dr. Kleinow."

There was a short pause when he didn't move,

but when he sat forward to listen with that intent expression on his face, I knew our evening together was over. I should have been sad that some patient at the hospital was in such bad shape that they needed Tucker to come in, and on most days I would have been, but tonight I needed him. Needed his comfort, his calm, his voice, his kiss, his presence. And he was going to leave.

"Okay," Tucker said. "I'll be there in ten minutes."

I was already on my feet and reaching for my coat.

"Minnie, you don't have to leave," he said. "I won't be long."

The last time he'd said that, I'd waited in the car while he went to check on a patient. I'd reached into my purse for my e-reader, opened up *The Hunger Games*, and was wondering how much rest Katniss was actually going to get sleeping in a tree, when Tucker returned.

"No, thanks," I said now, a little shortly.

"I'm sorry." He grabbed his own coat. "This wasn't how this night was supposed to end up."

"I'm sure it wasn't. And I'm sure that person in the emergency room needs you a lot more than I do." My words came out a little childish and a lot whiny, but they were said and I couldn't take them back. Besides, they were true. I sighed. "You'd better get going. I'll be fine."

"Minnie, please don't go. Stay, at least for a

little while. I'll be back as soon as I can—you know I will."

But I couldn't stay, not here alone in this room that had no life. "I'm sorry, Tucker. It's just . . ."

I shook my head and left.

Late that night, up in my room, lying on my side with Eddie curled up next to me, I wept the tears I'd been keeping in, the tears I couldn't shed in the bookmobile for the sake of rule number one. I wept for Roger, for Denise, for their children, for their entire extended family. I cried for all his friends and neighbors and coworkers.

At the end, I finally wept a little for myself, gulping down sobs of sorrow and loss for a good man I'd barely known.

Then, with Eddie purring comfort into my bones, I fell into a dreamless sleep.

Chapter 5

The next day Aunt Frances insisted on indulging me. She brought me breakfast in bed, dug around in her extensive bookshelves for the entire Mrs. Tim series by D. E. Stevenson, and only let me come down for lunch when I promised I wouldn't try to help with the cooking.

I sat at the kitchen table, watching while she sliced bread off the loaf she'd baked the day before, then watched while she made grilled cheese sandwiches at the same time that she put together a salad of spinach, mandarin oranges, and walnuts.

"Some people," I said, "say that cooking is therapy."

Aunt Frances raised one sardonic eyebrow. "Obviously those people haven't seen you at work in the kitchen."

"Hey, I can cook." I thought about that and amended it a little. "If I have to."

"And how often do you have to?"

She had a point, and I was not about to argue with a woman who said she loved me too much to let me eat my own cooking while I lived under her roof. In the summer, I lived on breakfast cereal, peanut butter and jelly sandwiches, and take-out meals, along with a healthy dose of leftovers from Kristen's restaurant.

I grinned at my aunt. "Often enough to remind myself that I'd rather wash someone else's dishes than cook my own food."

"Not today," she said. "After what happened yesterday, you're going to let me take care of you from sunrise to sunset." She glanced out the kitchen window at the backyard. "So to speak, anyway."

I looked out at the gray sky. It was one of those days of low, thick cloud cover, a day during which it would be hard to wake up completely. The temperatures had risen, and the white world was turning into a dripping, sodden mess. It was a day made for reading in front of the fireplace and maybe watching a movie or two. *Movies* . . . I sighed.

"What's the matter, my sweet?" Aunt Frances asked. "You never did say why you got home so early last night."

I shook my head, not wanting to talk about it. Tomorrow, maybe. Or the next day, after I got things figured out.

"Mrr." Eddie jumped onto my lap, pushing aside my elbows on his way up. He turned once, twice, and flopped down into a tidy meat-loaf shape, his chin resting on my arm. "Mrr," he said quietly.

"Don't we have a rule about no cats at the table?" my aunt asked.

I rested my hand on Eddie's back. "You do, and I do, but I'm not sure he's signed the agreement."

"Well." She put the bread onto the sizzling griddle. "He can stay until the food's ready. We have to draw the line somewhere."

I looked down. "Did you hear that, pal? You'll have to—" My cell phone, which I'd laid on the table after texting Kristen, buzzed and rattled. I picked it up and read the screen. A text from Tucker. I blinked, looked out the window at the soggy afternoon, then steeled myself to read the text.

You were right, it said. *Got back at two a.m. I was wrong and I'm sorry.*

I texted back, *I'm sorry, too.*

Tucker: *Can we be sorry together sometime soon?*

Me, smiling: *I'll have my secretary get with your secretary.* This was our code for saying we'd check our schedules and make plans for a date as soon as possible.

Tucker: *On it. See you ASAP.*

My observant aunt eyed me and said, "Good news, I take it?"

I wrapped my arms around Eddie and hugged him until he gave a squeak of protest. "Very good."

The next day I donned my bright red, hooded raincoat and squelched my way over to the library. The grayness of yesterday had evolved into an even grayer today, complete with a rain that, if it continued, would melt the weekend's snow within a few hours.

"November at its finest," I said to the wet sidewalk. The sidewalk didn't answer, which was okay, and perhaps even preferable, because I wasn't sure I wanted to know what a sidewalk would have to say.

It probably wouldn't be concerned about its hair, which would make it different from me. Curly hair and rainy weather are not good friends. By the time I got to the library it would be Frizz City, and there was nothing I could do about the situation except drive instead of walk, and that seemed silly for a commute of less than a mile.

I kept my head down and my attention fully focused on stepping around the puddles and what remained of the snow. Happily, that took a lot of concentration, and I barely had time to think about what the day would inevitably have in store for me.

Just outside the library, I shook a gallon of water off my coat and onto the sidewalk, then went in, keeping my mind firmly on the tasks ahead.

There would be phone calls to make to reschedule the stops I hadn't been able to make on Saturday afternoon, there would be the book returns from Saturday morning to reshelve in the bookmobile's separate circulation room, and that was just the start of it.

I started a pot of coffee and purposefully headed to my office. Lots to do, all sorts of things to do, and I needed to get to work. Focus—that was the thing. *Stay focused.*

That plan worked fine until the next staff member arrived.

Donna rushed into my office, her arms wide open. "Minnie, oh, Minnie. I'm so sorry!"

I took a deep breath. *Here it comes,* I told myself, and stood.

She wrapped her arms around me, enfolding me

into a great big grandmotherly hug, the kind of hug at which she excelled, since she had (at last count) seven grandchildren. "How are you holding up?" she asked. "What a horrible, horrible thing. That poor man. Poor Denise. And their children—they'll be devastated." She sounded as if she was about to cry.

I gave her some calming pats and started to say something, then realized I didn't know what to say. So I just patted her some more.

"Oh, look at you." Donna sniffed. "Trying to comfort me when you're the one who should be getting comforted." She gave me one last squeeze and stepped back, reaching into the pocket of her cardigan sweater for the tissue she always kept there. She wiped her eyes and blew her nose. "Do you want to talk about it, or would you rather not?"

I knew I'd have to say something, and, while eating my fortifying Aunt Frances–made bowl of oatmeal, I'd actually planned what that would be. But right at that moment I couldn't remember a word of it.

"Minnie—oh, my gosh—how are you?" Kelsey rushed in. On her heels was Holly. Donna backed away as the two younger women took their turns at giving me hugs. They were being nice, being supportive, being the best coworkers anyone could want, but I really wished they'd go away and leave me alone.

"I'm fine," I said, returning their hugs. "Thanks, but I'm fine."

"We should do something," Donna said. "I'm sure he'll be at Scovill Funeral Home. Should we send flowers?"

The three of them started talking about the pros and cons of cut flowers versus live plants, and I breathed a sigh of relief. I'd already decided to send my own card and flowers, and here at the library it was far preferable to talk about floral arrangements than to repeat the details of Saturday's events. Telling the story to anyone would be like reliving it, and that was the last thing I wanted to do.

"What about the bookmobile?"

We all turned. Josh was standing in the doorway, with his hands making knobby bulges in his pockets.

"What about it?" I asked.

"It's okay, right? I mean, it didn't get shot, did it?"

I wasn't sure whether to be appalled or touched. Appalled, because Josh was concerned about the bookmobile when the loss of a man's life was what really mattered, or touched because he cared about the bookmobile so much that he could consider its status in a situation like this.

"It's fine," I said, deciding to go with *touched*. He was a guy, after all, and there were lots of people in the room on the edge of weeping over Roger. It was only reasonable that Josh would be the one to ask about the car. Not that the bookmobile was a car, but it had an internal combustion engine, and that was close enough.

"And how about . . . ?" Josh glanced over to the women, who were talking about fern varieties. He used both hands to give himself what could only be cat ears.

"Fine," I said quietly, glad that I'd chosen the touched option.

The phone on my desk rang with the short ring of an internal call. I took a quick head count. Everyone who was scheduled to work this morning was in my now-crowded office. Everyone except the library director.

I picked up the receiver. "Hello?"

"Minnie, I need to see you in my office right now." There was a short *click,* and then nothing.

Though I'd known this was going to happen, I'd hoped it wouldn't take place for a few hours. At least until after I'd finished my first cup of coffee. I put down the receiver and looked at my coworkers. "That was Stephen," I said.

The conversation that had been going on around me stopped in its tracks.

"He wants to see me right now." I picked up my mug and got down a few healthy swallows.

"Oh, dear." Donna wrapped her arms around herself. "Oh, dear, dear, dear."

"What does he want?" Kelsey asked, her eyes wide open. "Is he going to yell at you?"

Holly bit her lower lip. "He won't make you get rid of the bookmobile, will he?"

"He won't fire you," Josh said confidently. "I'm sure of it. Who else would he get to work so many hours for so cheap?"

I rolled my eyes. "Gee, thanks for the pep talk."

Josh snorted. "Like you need one of those to talk to Stephen."

"Yeah," Holly said, smiling. "You're the one who gives them to us whenever we have to talk to him."

"Which is hardly ever, now that we have an assistant director to run interference." Josh cuddled an imaginary football and shouldered away an invisible attacker.

"For which we thank you very much." Donna patted my shoulder.

My relationship with Stephen was, of necessity, very different from everyone else's. For one thing, I was his assistant director, and took my marching orders directly from him. For another, I'd learned very young that bluster and size were things to ignore. I was five foot nothing. Most people were bigger than me, and by the age of ten I'd become more or less immune to the subtle coercions of size, gender, and voice timbre.

I gulped down the rest of my coffee and headed up the stairs.

Stephen had the only office on the second floor. The rest of the space was occupied by conference rooms and the book-sale room, and Stephen's aerie wasn't anywhere I would have liked to work. Sure, he had a corner office with windows that gave a great view of Janay Lake and even Lake Michigan when the leaves were off the trees, but in spite of the heavy drapes and the auxiliary heating unit, to me it still felt like a cold and unwelcoming place.

Of course, that could have been due to the nature of the occupant.

Stephen looked up from his computer when I knocked on the doorjamb. "Ah, Minnie. Come in and shut the door behind you."

The action seemed pointless. It wasn't as if anyone was going to be following me up the stairs to eavesdrop, since they all knew I'd soon be sharing everything Stephen said, but I shut the door anyway and stood in front of his desk, my hands clasped together lightly, my head slightly bowed. It was my Penitent Pose, and I'd perfected it as a child. I hadn't been a bad kid, but I hadn't always seen the need to do exactly what my parents told me to, especially when it came to putting my book down and going to sleep at my prescribed bedtime. I mean, how could I when I was in the middle of a chapter?

I stood there waiting, and eventually Stephen sat back in his chair. He took off his glasses and rubbed his eyes. If I hadn't known he'd been at his desk fewer than thirty minutes, I would have guessed he'd been laboring for hours. And, judging from past history and the general emptiness of his desk, all he'd been doing was reading online newspapers.

He put his glasses back on and looked up. "Minerva, you do seem to have a knack for finding trouble," he said, sighing. "Roger Slade was a good man. He will be missed by many."

A commonplace platitude that held a deep truth. I tried to swallow a sob, but it got stuck halfway down and I had to cough it away. "I didn't know him very well," I said quietly. "He seemed like a great guy."

Stephen peered at my face. "Do you need some time off?" he asked. "Although Roger wasn't a relative and the bereavement policy wouldn't apply, I'm sure you have vacation time accrued. I can approve a day, should you need it."

I murmured my thanks, but said I'd be fine. I'd never used all of my annual vacation hours; why should I start now?

My boss nodded, clearly approving of my ability to keep a stiff upper lip. "But do you realize," he said, putting his elbows on his desk and folding his hands, "that you have placed the library at risk?"

"I . . . what?"

"Under your direction and care," he said, "a bookmobile volunteer was killed while on the bookmobile."

I wanted to point out that Roger hadn't actually been on the vehicle, but I managed to keep quiet.

"How," Stephen asked sadly, "could you have let this happen?"

My jaw dropped. "*Let* it happen? Stephen, it was an accident. A horrible, tragic accident."

"On your bookmobile. This makes it the library's problem."

"It was an accident," I repeated, this time a little louder. "Awful as it was, it was an accident. We could have an accident here." I waved at the walls. "A library Friend could be carrying a box of books, trip on the stairs, and fall. Or—"

"Roger Slade is dead," Stephen said, cutting into my theoretical list, "and his sister is suing the library for negligence."

"His . . . sister?"

"Tammy Shelburt."

The name thudded into the middle of the room. Tammy Shelburt was Roger's sister? My spine lost its starch. I wanted to flop into Stephen's uncomfortable guest chair and put my head in my hands.

Tammy Shelburt had made a name for herself as one of the region's most energetic business owners. She'd taken an unsuccessful fast-food restaurant in Gaylord and built it into an extremely lucrative regional franchise. She was known for making hard decisions and for not backing down from any fight she deemed necessary. And there were a lot of them.

My first year in Chilson, Tammy had brought suit against a commercial property owner over a driveway easement adjacent to one of her properties. Two days after she won the lawsuit, a monstrous fence went up that forced her neighbor to rework the entrance to his ice-cream shop. It had been a financial hardship for the well-loved, yet not terribly lucrative, business and Tammy had lost much local goodwill over the incident. Rumor had it that she'd said, "So what? I make my money from the tourists, not the locals," which had, of course, only made things worse.

On a personal basis, I knew that Tammy had a tendency to return books late and then try to argue her way out of the fines. This didn't endear her to me, but I tried to look on the bright side. At least she was borrowing books. But what bright side could there be in this case? Roger was dead, and Tammy was looking for someone to pay the price.

"Stephen, I . . ." No words came to fill the empty space. I looked at my boss. I had no idea what expression was on my face, but he softened the slightest bit.

"Minnie, I will have to inform the library board of the recent events."

Of course he would. He probably already had.

"The board will also be made aware of the progress of Ms. Shelburt's lawsuit," Stephen said.

"The library's attorney has already been contacted and has said that there is little doubt that the library will eventually be cleared of any wrongdoing, but Ms. Shelburt will undoubtedly make sure no stone is left unturned."

I swallowed. The library attorney was eminently qualified for this kind of thing, but his hourly rate was higher than my first out-of-college paycheck. Once again I wanted to say something, but there still wasn't anything I could think of to say. "I'm sorry." The words came out in a whisper.

"Yes." Stephen adjusted his glasses. "Your reaction speaks well for your character, but you cannot let your emotions interfere with what needs to be done. Duties still call, Minerva." When I nodded slowly, he returned his attention to the computer screen.

I knew, from long experience, that this was my cue to retreat, but halfway down the switchback stairway, I stopped stock-still.

If Tammy was suing the library, was she also going to sue *me?*

All through the morning, I brooded over the question. Sure, every volunteer on the bookmobile signed a waiver of responsibility, and the library's insurance covered bookmobile-related incidents for those on board, but did any of that truly mean anything when something so horrible as a death had happened?

I debated contacting the Association of Book-mobile and Outreach Services to ask whether anyone had any experience in such matters, but decided to wait. Maybe I was worrying unnecessarily. And maybe Tammy had only threatened to sue. Maybe when she got over the shock of her brother's death, she'd drift away from the need to make the library pay for what had happened.

Maybe all that would happen.

And then again, maybe it wouldn't.

I fidgeted away the rest of the morning, and at lunchtime I donned my almost-dry coat and headed out into the rain.

By now the morning's dripping had rendered the weekend's snow almost invisible. What little remained was in the piles tossed up by plows and under the shelter of building eaves and trees. It was the time of year when, if you didn't have a calendar handy, you wouldn't know for certain whether it was November or early April.

Keeping my head down, I walked quickly through the mishmash of downtown architecture, past the county building, and to the adjacent sheriff's office.

"Hi," I said, pushing back my hood and smiling at the deputy at the window. "May I please speak to either Detective Devereaux or Detective Inwood?"

"Detective Devereaux is out on medical leave." The deputy eyed me. I tried to look tall and confident. This was a hard thing to do when faced with a high counter that reached almost to my chin, but I could, and did, meet the deputy's gaze with a calm assurance.

"Is it serious?" I asked. The detective and I weren't what you might call friends, but we had a relationship that was working, more or less, and I hoped whatever was wrong was fixable.

"He won't be back until after Thanksgiving," the deputy said.

"Then how about Detective Inwood? Is he around?"

"Let me check." He asked for my name, reached for his phone, and dialed. Though he spun away from me to talk, he glanced at me once over his shoulder.

I smiled brightly, and he turned away. My interior self, which was not nearly as polite as my exterior self, snorted. I could just imagine that conversation. The detectives and I had a history, some of it positive, much of it not. They saw me as impatient and interfering. I saw them as slow and stolid, especially when it came to law-enforcement issues involving people whom I knew were law-abiding citizens of the sort who would never be late returning a book to the library, let alone anything as violent as—

"Ms. Hamilton? He says you can go back." The deputy pushed a button, the door to the inner sanctum unlocked, and I went on through.

Inside, Detective Inwood was waiting. "We thought we'd be seeing you."

I squinted up at him. It was a fair ways up. The first few times I'd met the two detectives, they'd always been together. You'd think that I'd have been able to keep their names straight, considering that one was tall and thin while the other was shortish and round, but it hadn't been until a sympathetic deputy had told me that Detective Inwood, the tall and thin one, looked like a letter *I* and that Detective Devereaux looked like a letter *D* that their names got stuck properly in my head.

"We?" I asked. "I heard Detective Devereaux is out on medical leave."

Detective Inwood nodded and ushered me toward another door. "Knee replacement."

I winced. My primary cold-weather activity was downhill skiing, and I'd heard enough tales from former mogul jumpers to make me want to avoid the surgery at all costs. "He's doing okay?" I asked.

"Says he's getting bored watching so much TV."

I made a mental note to put together a selection of suitable reading materials, and entered the small meeting room that held a table, four chairs, and nothing else. It pained me on a deep level to see a room without a single book, but I kept my thoughts to myself and pulled out a chair.

"When I said 'we,'" the detective said, "I meant

myself and Deputy Wolverson. You might recall that he's training to be a detective."

As if on cue, the man himself walked into the room. "Sorry," he said. "I got caught with a phone call." He slid into the seat diagonally across from me and smiled. "Hi, Minnie. Sounds as if you had a rough time on Saturday."

I glanced at Detective Inwood, who was settling into the chair opposite me. I wanted to tell him that his much-younger coworker here had the right attitude, that a little kindness could go a long way, but once again I kept my thoughts inside. Which probably wasn't an entirely good thing, because someday they might come hurtling out of me in a manner I wouldn't be able to control. But why color today with the pending doom of tomorrow?

"It was a lot worse for Roger Slade," I said. "Do you have any idea who shot him?"

Deputy Wolverson glanced at his senior officer, so I knew what was coming. "I know, I know," I said. "This is only the beginning of the investigation, all avenues will be explored, and you won't rest until you get the right guy."

A small grin formed on the deputy's face. Detective Inwood, however, simply nodded.

"Exactly right, Ms. Hamilton. I'm glad you understand our position. All possibilities will indeed be considered."

Something in the phrase sounded off to me. "What do you mean, 'all possibilities'?"

He steepled his fingers and stared at them intently. "The obvious is, of course, the most likely answer: a tragic hunting accident. We are interviewing property owners in the area about hunting permissions and we're talking to other parties who might have knowledge of poachers. However, there is another possibility."

"What do you mean?" I asked, frowning.

Detective Inwood's eyebrows rose. "Surely, Ms. Hamilton, with your recent experiences, you've thought about the one other thing that could have caused Mr. Slade's death."

I shook my head slowly, ever so slowly. I didn't want to hear this. Not today, not tomorrow, not ever.

"It could have been murder."

The possibility that Roger's death could have been something other than an accident hadn't entered my head until Detective Inwood shoved it there.

"Thanks a lot," I muttered as I squelched my way back to the library. An accident was horrible enough, but murder? Roger was the nicest possible guy. He worked for a construction company that had a fantastic reputation. He'd helped his kids build tree forts and volunteered his time with Habitat for Humanity. How could anyone want to kill a guy like that?

With my thoughts not on what was in front of

me, I stepped straight into a puddle deep enough that I felt wetness across my instep. Sighing, I trudged onward.

An accident seemed much more likely than murder. We'd been out in the middle of your basic nowhere, and it had probably been a bullet from a deer hunter with very bad aim that had struck poor Roger. Then again, maybe there'd been some wacko up in those hills who'd felt like using a human for target practice. Things like that made you think there was no safety anywhere.

My breath sucked out of me, and I stopped in the middle of the sidewalk. I turned in a small, damp circle, suddenly seeing threats where seconds before I'd seen only a quiet downtown.

What was behind that fence?

Was someone lurking around the corner of that building?

Had I heard someone following me?

"Of course not," I said loudly, but my voice came out much thinner and weaker than I would have liked. I cleared my throat and almost said it again, but decided that would sound like I was talking to myself.

Not that there was anyone to hear.

Was there?

I stood for a moment longer, willing myself to not be a scaredy-cat, then squared my shoulders and walked briskly back to the library.

Once inside, I shut myself in my office. "Think,

Minnie," I told myself. If I was ever going to get to sleep that night, I needed to reassure myself that Roger's death was an accident. Only . . . how?

Everything I knew about guns came from an in-depth series of self-defense classes I'd taken last summer, and most of what I'd learned had been about handguns. Up here, deer hunters used rifles, and my extremely limited experience with those—an hour on the range with a .22—wasn't going to help much. What I needed was to talk to a hunter.

I picked up the phone and dialed. "It's Minnie. Do you have a minute?"

Rafe Niswander clucked at me. "You say a minute, but is that what you really mean?"

"No."

"That's women for you," he said. "Never saying exactly what they want, always leaving us poor men to guess at what's going on up in their heads. No wonder there's such a communication gap."

I put my feet up on my desk. "You're making assumptions about my entire gender based on a single colloquialism?"

"Oooh, big college word."

"The right word," I said firmly. "And you have as many degrees as I do."

"Don't remind me." He sighed. "It's embarrassing sometimes."

I snorted. For whatever reason, Rafe liked to pretend he was a country bumpkin, fresh off the farm and clueless about almost everything. It was an act that his middle-school students ate up.

"Fifty seconds already," he said.

Whatever. "I take it you heard about what happened Saturday?"

"Yeah." Rafe's voice was quiet. "I meant to call you, but . . ."

Rafe was good at many things, from being a school principal to home improvement to boat repairs, but handing out sympathy wasn't part of his skill set. "I know," I said. "It's okay. Anyway, I wanted to ask you a couple of things."

"Fire away." He paused. "Um, I mean, go ahead."

"You remember where that gas station is, right?" I asked, my heart suddenly pounding hard. "Do you know any guys who hunt around there?"

"Nope. There's no state land in that part of the valley. Most of the property out there is owned by a timber company, and they don't like guys hunting, because of liability reasons."

"What about poaching?" I persisted. "Do you think there'd be much of that going on?" A guy hunting illegally—it would make sense for someone like that to have killed Roger.

There was another pause. "Minnie," Rafe said slowly, his voice sounding suddenly serious. It was an odd way for him to sound and I wasn't sure I liked it. "Why are you asking?"

"I just . . . I just want to know who . . ."

This time the pause lasted a lot longer. "Tell you

what," he finally said. "I'm going to give you two phone numbers. One is a guy who lives out there; the other is the conservation officer for that part of the county. And, for crying out loud, don't tell them who gave you the numbers. I have a reputation to keep up."

"Thanks," I whispered. Coughed, then said more loudly, "You're not so bad for a misogynistic, prejudiced redneck wannabe."

"And you're not so bad for an uptight know-it-all."

His voice was sounding normal again, which was a small relief. I wrote down the numbers as he read them off, thanked him again, and started dialing.

Dinner that night was an Aunt Frances–inspired creation of seafood, coconut milk, and who knew what else. My contribution was washing the baby spinach for the salad.

"Another outstanding meal," I said, dipping my soup spoon into the hearty mix. "I don't know how you find the energy."

"Oh, it comes and goes." She covered her mouth to hide a yawn. "And right now it's going. Tell me a story to keep me awake."

Normally I would have a funny library story for her, but not today. So I told her about Stephen's tale of a pending lawsuit and I told her about my trip to the sheriff's office. I also told her about my phone calls to Rafe, plus my calls to the guy who lived near the gas station, and the conservation officer.

"The sheriff's department had already talked to both of them," I said. "The guy who lives there was gone that weekend, and the conservation officer, the CO, is already following up on some leads." It was an active investigation, the officer had said, so he couldn't talk about it. Though he was nice enough, I hadn't learned much.

"I'll keep asking around," I said, "but with the sheriff's office and this CO working on it, I'm not sure I'll be able to find out anything they don't already know." I looked at her hopefully. "Unless you have some ideas?"

My intelligent and thoughtful aunt frowned. I waited, anticipating words of wisdom or reassurance, or both. Preferably both. Both would be excellent.

"That Deputy Wolverson," she said. "Is his first name Ash?"

I blinked at her. "Sounds right." I knew it had something to do with fires, but couldn't remember exactly what. "Do you know him?"

"Not him." Aunt Frances ground more pepper onto her salad. "I know his mother. She lives in Petoskey." She yawned again.

I looked at her fondly. She was too tired for niece reassurances, and, besides, I didn't really need them. Wanted them, sure, but that was different.

After dinner, I encouraged her toward the living room couch and started a fire. I brought her a book, a blanket, and an Eddie, and asked whether there was anything else I could get her. "I could open the TV if you'd like."

Throughout the summer, my aunt's television was hidden away in a clever cabinet that looked so much like an extension of the fireplace mantel that the summer boarders didn't even know it was there. "Summers aren't for television," Aunt Frances always told them. "Go outside and play." Even in winter, we didn't use the TV much except for watching movies and the weekly episode of *Trock's Troubles*, the cooking show that was sometimes filmed in Chilson.

"Not tonight, thanks." Aunt Frances smiled down at Eddie as he settled on her legs. "You sure you don't want him?"

I did, but I was trying to learn how to share. Plus, the rain had stopped while we were eating dinner. I'd even seen a few stars while I was doing dishes, and I felt the need to get outside and see some open sky.

When I told Aunt Frances as much, she pulled the blanket up to her neck. "Have a nice time, dear. I'll be here when you get back."

I looked at Eddie. "How about you? Will you still be here?"

He closed his eyes at me and didn't even bother to say "Mrr."

Outside, the air had shot up at least ten degrees since my walk home. Hard to believe that two days ago we'd been swimming in snow, but these things happened in November. I stood on the porch steps for a moment, enjoying the warm air that must be at least fifty degrees. It wouldn't stay this way, and I didn't really want it to, but there was no reason not to enjoy it while it lasted.

The front door of the house across the street opened and shut. I peered into the dark, but I couldn't see if Otto Bingham had come outside or if he'd been out and gone in.

I came down the rest of the creaky wooden steps and headed across the street. It was just plain weird that neither Aunt Frances or I had ever talked to the guy. He'd lived there for weeks, and at this time of year he was our only neighbor for a block in either direction.

"Mr. Bingham?" I crossed the street, looking for nonexistent traffic both ways because I couldn't make myself not check. "How are you tonight?"

The man, because there was indeed a man standing at the bottom of his porch steps, looked straight at me. But as I got closer, I could see that he wasn't smiling the polite neighborly smile I'd expected. Instead he was giving me a look that was more deer in the headlights than anything else.

Which was weird, but now that I was standing in front of his picket fence, I was already committed to a conversation. "I'm Minnie Hamilton." I considered holding out my hand, but eyed the distance and decided against it. There were unwritten rules about handshake distances, and I was pretty sure the gap between Mr. Bingham and me was outside the appropriate range.

Then again, since he hadn't said anything, it was getting awkward even without the handshake. "Um, you are Mr. Bingham, aren't you?"

He nodded in a vaguely friendly way. Well, it wasn't unfriendly, anyway.

"Okay, good. Like I said, my name is Minnie. I live at the boardinghouse in the winter, with my aunt, Frances Pixley."

Mr. Bingham jumped visibly when I said my aunt's name. I frowned. A mention of my aunt usually made people smile, if anything. What was with this guy? I studied him a little closer. Well dressed, handsome enough—if you didn't mind a cleft chin—with salt-and-pepper hair, and, judging from the distance between porch railing and the top of his head, tallish. He had "retired successful professional" written all over him. So why was he jumpy?

Puzzled, I went on. "I work at the library here in town and"—I paused for my coup de grâce—"two or three times a week I drive the bookmobile." I waited for his reaction. If this guy didn't respond to the mention of a bookmobile, he was a lost cause.

He wasn't. His lips started to curl up at the corners, curving into what ended up as a very attractive smile.

"Minnie?"

I turned. Aunt Frances stood on the porch, waving a cordless phone at me. "Phone call for you, dear!"

"Be right there," I called, turning back to Mr. Bingham.

But his front door was already closing with a soft *click*.

I squinted at it, then shrugged and trotted across the street.

"Who is it?" I asked, taking the phone from my aunt's hand.

She started doing what generous people might have called a hula, so I knew it was Kristen on the other end of the line. Not that anyone did the hula in Key West, but, then again, I'd never been to Key West, so what did I know?

"Do people do the hula down there?" I nodded a thanks to my aunt, who had opened the front door for me.

"Da dah dah daaaa," Kristen sang.

"Seriously?"

She snorted. "No idea. Us locals don't pay attention to that touristy stuff. We're too busy enjoying the sunshine and warm air."

"It was warm here today," I protested.

"I can Google your weather reports, you know.

Plus, that webcam the city has downtown showed all sorts of snow on Saturday. And now rain."

That darn Internet. "I like snow."

"Yeah, and I like beating my head with a hammer because it feels so good when I stop."

With our standard opening greetings done, there was a pause. "So, what's going on down there?" I asked. "Anything fun?"

"Not really," she said, but instead of launching into her usual litany of snorkeling, sunset watching, bike riding, and hammock napping, she hesitated, then said, "Just wanted to make sure you're okay. After Saturday and, all that."

That was Kristen, crusty on the outside, tender on the inside, just like the sourdough bread she loved to make. I couldn't imagine a better best friend. I started to tell her so, but stopped just in time. She'd be embarrassed, I'd feel bad for making her feel embarrassed, and why clutter up our conversation with that kind of thing?

"Yeah," I said, slipping off my coat. "I'm okay."

"More or less?" she asked.

Less, really, but I'd been doing well at faking it since Saturday night. "More?" I suggested.

"Bzzz!" Kristen said. "Wrong answer. Try again."

So I hung up my coat, headed to the bright lights of the kitchen, and told her everything.

It's good to have friends, and it's really good to have a best friend.

Chapter 6

The next day ended up busy with meetings, an evaluation of the staff's holiday-decoration plans, and a workshop directed toward senior citizens on how to order gifts online. All of these tasks were made more complicated by my efforts to avoid Stephen while trying not to look as if I were avoiding Stephen.

I knew the longtime library employees had perfected the skill years before, and once or twice I was tempted to ask for tips when Stephen came down for his twice-a-day walkabouts, but I stopped myself just in time.

Bad enough that I was trying to stay out of Stephen's way in the first place; the possibility that my friends would learn about my lapse in fortitude was one step past what I was willing to endure.

So I kept busy keeping my head down. The overcast Tuesday (during which I'd received another postcard from Kristen: *Key West, warm and sunny. Chilson, cold and cloudy. Silly you.*) eventually turned into a sunny Wednesday, and as the sky cleared, so did my head.

Research. What I needed to do was research, and lots of it.

I worked nose to the grindstone all morning and

finished off the things that had to be done. After a quick lunch of leftovers (Aunt Frances–made lasagna from the night before), I settled into an afternoon stint at the reference desk, hoping for once that there wouldn't be many questions to answer.

"Hey, Minnie. I got a question for you."

I looked up, then up some more. Looming in front of the desk was Mitchell Koyne, one of the tallest men I'd ever met in my life. He was also one of the oddest men I'd ever met.

Though he was clearly intelligent, he'd never seen any need to get more than a high-school diploma, and I wasn't absolutely sure he'd bothered to do that. And even though he was about my age, he seemed to have no desire to move out of his sister's attic. And, judging from the amount of pizza boxes piled in the bed of his beater pickup truck, his diet was that of a teenager's.

Plus, he was what my coworkers called a library fixture. Mitchell, in his baseball cap, jeans, and flannel shirts, spent more afternoon and evening hours in the library than most of the staff did. Never mornings, though. As far as I knew, he'd never once set foot inside the library in the a.m. hours. Josh's current theory was that Mitchell spent his nights poaching deer; Holly and I believed he stayed up late playing video games.

But despite his lack of education or even a permanent job, Mitchell's mind had been cast in an inquisitive mold, and hardly a day went by when he didn't come in with a question for whoever was staffing the reference desk.

Hardly a day until a couple of months ago, rather, because that was when Stephen had come down with a new edict for me: Get rid of Mitchell. Or at least make sure he didn't spend so much time in the library, asking pointless questions of the library staff, who had much better things to do.

Though I'd tactfully pointed out that answering questions was one of our main functions as a public library, Stephen hadn't cared. He wanted fewer Mitchell hours in the library, and that was what he was going to get—or it would be my fault, forever and ever.

For a while I'd hoped Stephen would forget the issue, but I should have known better. Instead of the edict fading away to nothing, my procrastination only fanned the flames of Stephen's determination.

Happily, a little more procrastination on my part had solved the problem. Well, actually, Mitchell solved the problem himself. He'd hovered on the edges of two recent murder investigations and had managed to convince himself that he'd been a critical part of the solution. Ergo, his latest career move was to set himself up as a private detective.

At the end of the summer, he'd spent a lot of time handing out business cards fresh from his sister's laser printer. NORTHERN DETECTIVE

AGENCY. MYSTERIES SOLVED BY MITCHELL KOYNE.

His pride had been so self-evident and he'd been working so hard telling people about his new business—it was a lightning-striking-twice rarity to see Mitchell work hard at anything—that I'd waited a couple of weeks to burst his bubble. I'd pulled him into my office, shut the door, and said, "Mitchell, did you know that the State of Michigan has licensing requirements for private investigators?"

I'd rarely felt so sorry for anyone as I did for Mitchell at that moment. If I hadn't been sitting behind my desk, I would have . . . well, probably not hugged him, but I definitely would have patted his shoulder. Librarians need to have boundaries, especially with people like Mitchell.

He'd pulled his business cards out of his shirt pocket and stared at them. "Licensing?" he asked dully. "Like a fee or something?"

Classic Mitchell. So very smart in so many ways, yet completely clueless in so many others.

I'd shown him the list of requirements.

"Huh," he said. "I've got everything except this."

He pointed to the necessity for a licensee to have a bachelor's degree in criminal justice or the alternative of three years working either as a private detective in another state, three years as a police officer, or three years as an investigative employee of a licensed private-detective agency. I was sure he also didn't have the required ten-thousand-dollar bond, but first things first.

"You think there's a detective agency around here anywhere?" he asked. "With my experience, I bet I can get a job with them, easy. Get my three years, then I can go out on my own."

"Um . . ."

He'd nodded to himself. "Yeah, that'll work. Thanks, Min!"

For two weeks, Mitchell didn't darken the door of the library. When he returned, he'd changed his business cards to NORTHERN INQUIRIES. PROBLEMS SOLVED BY MITCHELL KOYNE.

I'd breathed a sigh of relief. While there was no telling what kind of messes he might get himself into, at least he wouldn't get into trouble with the licensing authorities. And Stephen had checked Mitchell off Minnie's to-do list, because whatever Mitchell was doing with his time these days, he wasn't spending as many hours at the library.

However, things just weren't the same without a daily dose of Mitchellness. Josh said it wasn't the same—it was better—but Josh was a guy and therefore couldn't be counted on to be truthful regarding matters about another guy.

So now I looked at Mitchell, trying to guess what was going on inside his head. But that was an exercise doomed to failure, so I gave up and smiled at him. "Hey. What's up?"

Grinning, he scratched at his stubbly face and hefted a bulging plastic bag. "Look what I scored from the sale upstairs."

"That's a lot of books."

"Yeah. I'd heard there were a bunch of donations last week, so I wanted to get in here before anyone else."

Because clearly there was such a rush at the Friends of the Library book sales in November. "What did you get?" I asked.

He dumped the contents of the bag across the reference desk. "I got *The Anansi Boys*, *The Hitchhiker's Guide to the Galaxy*, and a whole bunch of books by Dean Koontz. What I really wanted was George R. R. Martin's Game of Thrones books—you know, the ones on TV. They said a boxed set came in a week ago, but what's-her-name got to it right away, that Allison who married a Korthase. You know."

Not really. Mitchell was forever talking about people he knew that I didn't, so I did as per usual and just nodded.

"And," he said proudly, "I got four of Dan Brown's books. Say, do you know which one comes first?" He pulled out *The Da Vinci Code*, *The Lost Symbol*, *Angels & Demons*, and *Inferno*.

As I sorted them into chronological order, Mitchell craned his neck around to see my computer screen. "What you working on, any-way? Hey, that looks like—"

My hand moved as fast as if Stephen had been approaching when I'd been checking my Facebook page. I minimized the Web site I'd been reading and said, "Never mind what I'm doing."

Mitchell half winked at me and nodded slowly, then leaned forward. "I won't tell," he whispered. "I can see why you'd want a gun after what happened Saturday."

"No," I said. "That's not—" But then I stopped, because there was no need for Mitchell to know what I was really doing.

"Yeah?" He adjusted his baseball hat to what looked like the exact same position it had been preadjustment. "Hey, I bet I know! You're trying to figure out what kind of gun someone used to . . . well, you know."

The idea that Mitchell was trying to be considerate of my feelings made my heart go a teensy bit mushy. "Sort of," I said. What I was actually doing was looking up the specifications for the typical hunting rifle, trying to figure out how careless a hunter would have needed to be to hit Roger. I was quickly learning, however, that there was no such thing as a typical hunting rifle, so I might as well have spent my time trying to guess what Mitchell's question of the day might be.

"Sure, I get it," Mitchell said. I wasn't sure how he could, since I hadn't told him anything, but it wasn't wise to get between Mitchell and his conclusions. You'd end up spending far too much time trying to correct him, and he'd still walk away with the wrong idea. "Say, now that I'm a detective, or training to be one, I can help you, you know. Just say the word, okay?"

The idea of straight-on Mitchell assistance was more than a little frightening. "Thanks," I said. "I was just doing some research on guns for someone, that's all."

"Oh." Mitchell deflated. "You sure?"

"Absolutely." He looked so disappointed that I took pity on him. "Say, you're a hockey fan, right? Can you explain what icing is?"

He puffed right up again and launched into what was undoubtedly going to be not only an explanation that wouldn't made sense to me but also one that I wouldn't remember.

I was okay with that, though. A distracted Mitchell was better than a helpful Mitchell any day of the week.

On the other hand, when Holly was helpful, she was helpful with a capital *H*. If you asked Holly to do something, you never had to follow up to make sure it got done. Most times she'd probably finish the job before you remembered to ask her how it was going. This made her a tremendous employee, a dependable friend, and a mother to be reckoned with.

So when she approached me that afternoon in a

stealthlike manner, I steeled myself to hear what I'd titled in my head as the Eddie Report. Maybe it would be good news, but I had to be ready to deal with the fallout if Stephen had heard anything about Eddie.

What that fallout might be, I wasn't sure, other than my being fired. I supposed I could take an extended trip to Florida, and though I could shuttle between my brother's house in Orlando and Kristen's apartment in Key West for a while, neither Eddie nor I would care for summers in Florida.

"Sorry, Minnie," Holly said shaking her head, "but I can't find him anywhere."

I yanked myself back from the heat and humidity. "Can't find who?" I was pretty sure my cat was, at this moment, making a big, Eddie-sized dent in my pillow.

"Stephen. Remember?" Her eyebrows went up. "On Facebook."

Oh. Right. "Well, that's good, isn't it?"

"Maybe, but maybe not. I checked every variation of the name Stephen Rangel I could think of. Stevie, Steve—all that—but I didn't find anything. But he could be using a different name, an avatar, you know?"

"If he's using a different name, how are you going to find him?"

"Through his connections," she said promptly. "Even if he's calling himself the Northern Star, he'll still have some of the same Facebook friends I do, some of the same links to the same public groups. Restaurants, nonprofits." She snapped her fingers. "I should be checking the library's own Facebook page. There's no way he could keep from liking that one."

I squinted at her. "So you think Stephen is on Facebook? In spite of what he's said about it being a waste of time."

Holly looked left and right, then leaned forward. "I figure Josh is probably right. There are advantages to Stephen for being on Facebook, and even more if he can be on there incognito. All I have to do is figure out what name he's using."

"But won't his privacy controls keep you from seeing his posts?"

She grinned. "On his own page, sure, if he's set them that way, but I bet he's leaving comments on pages that don't have the same settings."

It sounded like a lot of work. "Thanks for going to all this trouble," I said.

"Hang on," she warned. "Like I said, I haven't found him yet. And if he's posting on snowbird pages, it might take me longer to find the comments, because a lot of them are in transit right now."

I'd always thought the term for the seasonal folks a misnomer. Shouldn't we really be calling them *sunbirds?* You don't give something a name for the thing it doesn't do; if we did, cats would be called swimmers and men would be called worriers.

I yanked my attention back from the flight of fancy it wanted to take. "Well, let me know if there's anything you want me to do."

Holly shook her head. "No, I can take care of this. If I see anything about Eddie—" She stiffened at the sound of a man's footsteps crossing the tile in the lobby. We both turned to look, saw Jim Kittle, a regular library patron, and heaved small sighs of relief.

"Right," Holly went on. "So, that's where I am. I have a couple of leads already on connection names. I just wanted to give you an update."

Leads? Update? She was starting to sound like the last visitor to the reference desk. I almost said so, but stopped myself just in time. Holly would not appreciate being compared to Mitchell.

"I appreciate all your work on this," I said. "If I was any good at baking, I'd make you cookies."

"Please don't." She grinned. "Anyway, it's kind of fun. You can start calling me Trixie anytime now."

I knew she was referring to Trixie Belden, the amateur sleuth who starred in many juvenile mysteries. "Not Nancy Drew?"

"Nah. I'm a small-town girl." She laughed and headed off.

I watched her go, wondering what I'd ever done

to deserve such good friends. It was enough to make you believe in past lives, because there was no way I'd done enough good things in my thirty-three years to have earned what I had.

Then again, what had Eddie ever done to earn what he was getting?

"Negative-income stream, for sure," I said to myself. Not only was Eddie using cat food and cat litter on a daily basis that he apparently had no intention of paying for, but he also had that habit of destroying paper products.

Plus, I bought him cat treats. And cat toys. Sometimes I even bought him things that weren't cat toys but were things I knew he'd enjoy playing with. Bath puffs, for one. Felt Christmas-tree ornaments, for another. He seemed especially fond of one I'd found at the thrift store: a Santa Claus head. To me it was a little disturbing to see Eddie fling Santa's head around the living room, but Aunt Frances found it hilarious.

"All that," I murmured, "and no financial return. Huh." I'd have to have a talk with Eddie when I got home. Maybe he'd have some ideas about how to boost his earning potential.

Then again, Eddie's suggestions probably wouldn't be very useful, even if he had any. At best he'd look at me, say "Mrr," rub up against my leg, and purr until I picked him up and snuggled him.

Smiling, I went back to work.

Sure, he was a negative-income stream, but what did you need with money when you had an Eddie?

I was in my office, rearranging the piles of paper on my desk in the vain effort to convince myself that I'd made some progress in figuring out what to do with them, when my desk phone rang.

"Ms. Hamilton, this is Deputy Wolverson from the Tonedagana County Sheriff's Office."

I squinted at the ceiling. As if I'd know a Deputy Wolverson from any other sheriff's office. "Hi. What's up?"

"We were wondering if you'd have time to drop by for a short meeting."

A meeting? What could they have to say in a meeting that the deputy couldn't tell me over the phone? Did they have more questions for me? Or had they found something? Better yet, had they arrested someone for Roger's death?

But none of that necessitated a jaunt by me to the sheriff's office. Conversations like that were why phones were invented. So why the summons?

Huh.

"Sure," I said. "I haven't had lunch yet." It was almost two, but I'd been busy. "I can walk over right now."

"I'll see you in a little bit, then."

I hung up the phone and stared at it for a while, wondering. Then I got up, grabbed my coat and purse, and headed out.

. . .

According to the clock on the wall of the same small meeting room I'd been in two days before, it was exactly nine minutes after the phone call that Deputy Wolverson came in and sat across from me.

"Good afternoon," he said.

"Hey." I glanced at the open doorway. "No Detective Inwood?"

The deputy opened the notebook he'd carried in and didn't look up. "Hal had to leave."

So I was left with the junior officer, a guy who wasn't even a detective yet. Did that mean anything? If it did, I had no idea what it might be.

I sat up straight and clasped my hands on the table. "So, what's the news?"

Deputy Wolverson looked up at me, and I was suddenly reminded that he was a very good-looking guy, especially if you had an attraction for men in uniform. Which I'd never had. But that didn't mean I couldn't acknowledge that particular type of handsomeness.

"Most people call me Ash," he said. "My first name."

I blinked. "Okay. Sure." I could do that. Maybe. But there was no way I'd ever be calling Detective Inwood by his first name. I tried it out in my head. *Morning, Hal. How are you today, Hal?* Nope. Wasn't going to happen.

Deputy Ash Wolverson was still paging through

his notebook with one hand and tapping the table with the pen he held in the other. I mentally *tsk*ed at him for not being prepared for a meeting he'd set up. "So, you've figured out something about Roger's death?" I asked.

"In a way." He flipped another page, paused, flipped another, then went back three pages and poked at it with his pen. "Detective Inwood and I have conducted extensive interviews with Roger Slade's friends, family, neighbors, and coworkers."

That sounded like a lot of work to have accomplished in two days, and I said so.

Ash smiled, and it almost took my breath away. I must not have ever seen him smile before, because I would have remembered how it changed him from a good-looking member of the male species to a drop-dead-gorgeous man that no woman would ever tire of mooning over. How could something so simple as a smile make such a dramatic difference to a person's appearance? I had no idea, but there the evidence was, right in front of me.

"I had help," he said, and it took me a moment to remember what he was talking about.

Oh. Right. The interviews. I nodded for him to go ahead. As quickly as possible, because if he talked, he'd have to stop smiling.

"Detective Inwood and I talked to the key people," he said, "but we enlisted the aid of other deputies. Anyway, I—we—wanted to let you know that as of today we've found no motive for Roger Slade's murder." He tapped at his notes. "But while we have no reason, at this point, to believe it was murder, if someone did kill Mr. Slade intentionally, it's clear that this is a very dangerous person."

It was such an obvious point that I couldn't think of a response that didn't drip with sarcasm, something my mother had always warned me against. "I think I might have been able to figure that out on my own," I said. *Sorry, Mom.*

Ash colored. "Minnie, if there is a killer out there . . ." He stopped, then started again. "I just want you to be careful out on the bookmobile. That's all."

I squinted at him. "Are you saying I'm in danger?"

"It's a very small possibility. Please keep your eyes open and give us a call if you see anyone suspicious."

While it was refreshing to have someone in the sheriff's office who was concerned about my well-being, I was pretty sure it was because no one would want the job of figuring out how I'd gotten myself killed. "Thanks," I said. "I'll make sure to keep an eagle eye out for rifles pointed in my direction."

He looked down, and it was my turn to flush. Once again, my mother's admonition to think first and be sarcastic in privacy at a later time had gone unheeded. This time I did start to thank him, but he ignored me.

"As we told you before," he said, "we'll do our best to find the person who killed Mr. Slade."

"Sure." But I couldn't help thinking how hard it might be. What if the shooter had been a guy from downstate? From out of state? No matter how hard they tried, Ash and Detective Inwood might never catch the guy who was responsible. And if this someone might actually have taken a shot at me . . . ? The skin at the back of my neck prickled.

Nah. There was no way.

Ash flicked at his notepad. "Well, I guess that's all I wanted to tell you."

Really? Why on earth hadn't he just called? Maybe this was part of the reason he was still a deputy and not a detective. Inwood wouldn't even have bothered to call. "Thanks." I started to stand. "I appreciate your time." Even if he had raised the hairs on the back of my neck with his silly remote possibility.

The deputy scrambled to his feet, notepad in hand. "You're welcome, Minnie. And, uh, if you don't mind, I have another question for you."

"Fire away." I grabbed my purse from the chair upon which I'd tossed it and slung the strap over my shoulder. I smiled at him. "Librarians have the best answers, you know?"

He paused, then looked down at his notebook. "Well, I—"

From deep in my coat pocket came the sound of Wagner's approaching Valkyries. Stephen. I reached for my cell phone. "Sorry. It's my boss. I should probably answer this."

Ash nodded. "Sure. No problem. I'll talk to you later." He opened the door for me.

"Thanks," I said, thumbing on the phone. "Hello, Stephen. What can I do for you?"

"I'm told you were in the sheriff's office," he said. "I'd appreciate an update."

How Stephen managed to hear about things was a complete mystery. "Walking out the door right now," I said, doing that very thing. It felt good to be able to tell him the complete truth every so often. "They told me that Roger Slade's death was most likely an accident." More or less.

Stephen gave a *hmmph*ing sort of grunt.

"So that's good news," I prompted him. "Right?"

"No. As far as Roger's sister is concerned, her brother is still dead. Her lawsuit doesn't speak to the manner of death; it simply casts the library as negligent."

Which didn't make a lot of sense to me, but maybe that was part of the reason Tammy Shelburt was a wealthy business owner and I was treading financial water as a bookmobile librarian.

By now I was outside, standing on the sidewalk in front of the sheriff's office. I started to ask about the lawsuit, then realized that no one was there, because my boss had, in his Stephen-like manner, ended the call with no good-bye.

I slid the phone into my pocket and stood there, thinking.

As far as Stephen was concerned, until Tammy's suit was resolved to the benefit of the library, I was still on the hook. Also at risk, by virtue of my close personal relationship with a very large vehicle, was the bookmobile.

Not to mention . . . well, my life.

Something my dad had once told me about financial planning floated to the top of my brain. "No one," he'd said gravely, "will care as much about your money as you do." The police were no doubt doing their best to figure out who killed Roger. But if someone was after me, unlikely as that possibility might be, would anyone care as much as I did?

There was only one answer to that: nope. Which meant it was time for me to get some answers.

I stood there for a moment, thinking, then called the library. Kelsey answered. I coughed and told her I felt like I might be coming down with a bad cold. "Sorry," I said, trying to sound weak and pathetic and pushing away all feelings of guilt. "But I think the last place I should be this afternoon is the library."

Kelsey made murmurs of sympathy and told me to get some sleep.

"Good advice," I said, and it was, for someone who was sick. I could have used some advice regarding finding anyone with a reason to kill Roger Slade, but that wasn't something I was going to ask Kelsey.

As I walked back to the boardinghouse to get my car, I thought about who I could talk to about Roger. Coworkers. Neighbors. People from his church. Anyone he'd grown up with, except his sister, Tammy, of course. Golfing buddies, if he had any. Poker buddies. Fishing buddies. Roger had been a likable guy; there were lots of people who might be able to tell me something.

It was time to get busy.

"My first attempts at finding a motive for murder were a complete bust," I told Eddie that night. "No one had anything but nice things to say about Roger. Everyone looked truly upset that he's dead." More than that, there was a lot of anger at the guy who'd killed him; if I'd wanted to get up a posse, it would have been easy. But I'd only talked to a fraction of the people I wanted to, and maybe at some point I'd turn over the right rock.

Eddie yawned at my face, whiffing out a distinct odor of cat food.

"What was that?" I asked. "Did you say 'Tomorrow is another day,' or 'Good things come to those who wait'? Neither is useful, just so you know. Do you have anything else to share?"

Eddie stared straight at me. "Mrr," he said.

"Well, I knew that."

"Mrr!"

"You're right," I told him. "You're always right. I don't know why I ever doubt you."

"Mrr," Eddie said, and curled up on my lap, purring.

Chapter 7

The next day was a bookmobile day. With Denise out as a volunteer, I had dragooned Donna into being my temporary assistant.

"You'll get all the benefits that the regular volunteers do," I'd promised her the day before.

She'd made a rude noise that was very ungrandmotherly. "And what's that? A pat on the back?"

"Cookies from Cookie Tom's," I'd said. "Still warm." Last summer Tom had set me up with a deal on cookies and, even better, let me pick them up from the back door rather than making me stand in line.

That had perked her up a little. "Do I get to pick?"

I'd hesitated. Donna had a penchant for licorice flavor, something I wasn't fond of. I wasn't sure whether Tom had a licorice-flavored cookie, but did I want to risk it? "Sure," I said bravely. "Anything you want."

She'd laughed and shoved at my shoulder a little. One of the reasons Donna worked part-time instead of full-time was her hobbies of marathon running and long-distance snowshoeing. She was only a couple of inches taller than me, but she was much stronger and fitter.

So, when I staggered backward from her shove, I didn't feel incompetent at having been physically bested by a woman more than thirty years my senior. At least not completely.

"Get me a few of those coconut chocolate chip, and I'll be your slave for the day," she said. "Anything special I should bring?"

"A lunch," I'd said. "And don't wear anything black."

She'd winked. Donna knew all about Eddie. "Or white," she said, nodding. "I have just the thing."

Now I glanced over at her, still not quite believing what she'd chosen as appropriate bookmobile wear.

She caught my glance and waggled her eyebrows. "It's what all the best-dressed bookmobile volunteers are wearing, don't you know?"

I laughed. Donna, from her many years as an athlete, had a closet full of nylon running pants, jackets, shirts, shorts, and, for all I knew, nylon hats and underwear. Today's clothing of choice included a bright pink jacket over bright pink pants. Her socks were a shocking color of yellowish green, and her shoes had so many fluorescent colors that I couldn't count them.

"Watch this." She leaned down, reached through the wire door of Eddie's carrier, and rubbed her fingers over the blanket that lay on the carrier's floor. The blanket also happened to be pink, but that had nothing to do with Donna. A boarder of Aunt Frances's had knit it from an especially soft yarn, and Eddie had instantly bonded with the soft fuzziness. I suspected it was because he shed so much hair on it that it felt like a long-lost sibling, but maybe he just liked pink.

"See?" Donna held a small cluster of cat hair over her pink-clad thigh and let it drop.

Any fabric, from cotton to polyester, would have sucked Eddie hairs tight into its weave, making them near to impossible to extract. With Donna's running attire, however, the former bits of Eddie fell away, to settle who knew where.

"That's amazing," I said, wide-eyed. "I wish I could wear an outfit like that."

"Why can't you?" she asked. "Seems like reasonable attire for a bookmobile."

"Stephen," I said succinctly. My boss had made it clear that since the bookmobile and I were representing the Chilson District Library, I must always present myself in a professional manner. To Stephen that meant dressing two steps more formally than necessary. It had taken me a month and a PowerPoint presentation to convince him that my typical library wear of dress pants, a jacket, knee-high nylons, and low heels wouldn't make sense on the bookmobile. Dress pants, a tidy sweater, and loafers were eventually deemed acceptable bookmobile clothes for Minnie.

Donna snorted. "That man needs a serious dose of lightening up."

I didn't disagree, but I also wasn't going to enter into a let's-beat-up-on-Stephen discussion. Stephen might not be the easiest person in the world to work for, but he was our boss and so deserved our respect.

Most of the time, anyway.

The bookmobile rolled happily over the hills and dales of the glacier-carved terrain. November could be a drab month of rain and unrelentingly gloomy skies, but today the sun was popping through puffy white clouds, sending down slanting light onto bare tree branches.

Donna groused a little. "Perfect day for a nice, long run. What am I doing here, anyway?"

"Participating in the outreach activities of your favorite library," I told her.

"Really?" She sounded puzzled. "I didn't know the Grand Haven library had a bookmobile."

My chin went up. "Hey, that's—"

Her laugh stopped my outrage. "Joke, Miss Minnie. Joke."

My chin went down. "Not funny," I muttered, although it actually was, and Donna knew it.

"I wouldn't have moved up here from Grand

Haven," she said, "if the Chilson library weren't the best in the world."

"That's laying it on a little thick." I considered the point. "Although if we had a better collection of local history books and had the staff to hold a few more evening events, we might come close."

Donna laughed again, and then we were driving into the parking lot of a white-steepled fieldstone church, our first stop of the day.

The first bookmobile stop since Roger died, I thought, and experienced a quick clutch of fear. The feeling took me by surprise. I hadn't realized I was nervous about going out again.

I braked gently and parked the bookmobile on the far side of the gravel parking lot, leaving plenty of room for the vehicles that would soon be arriving. That were already coming, since I saw two cars slowing, with their blinkers on.

Donna, unbuckled and out of her seat, laid a hand on my shoulder. "You okay, Minnie?"

I reached up to pat her hand. In spite of the pink running gear and the hardcore hobbies and the determinedly black hair, she had the soul of the most comforting grandmother ever. "I'm fine, thanks."

And, as it turned out, I was. By the time I recommended *My Father's Dragon* by Ruth Stiles Gannett to a gentleman who was trying to find a book that would give a young boy a lifelong interest in reading, I was feeling much better. And by the time Donna and I had worked through the morning stops, spreading entertainment, knowledge, and Eddie hair (though not necessarily in that order) across the land, my small attack of whatever it had been was gone.

I ushered Eddie back into his carrier at the end of a stop. "Do you think cats have any concept of time?" I asked.

"Absolutely," Donna said. "When I bought my first house, I adopted a gray tabby. If I went anywhere for more than a day, he'd break something. When I was gone for a week on vacation, he pushed a Native American pot I'd purchased on my last trip onto the floor, shattering it into tiny bits." She sounded more entertained than angry.

I got into the driver's seat and buckled up. "Do you think . . . ?" *Nah.* No way could a cat have connected her new vacation to the pot.

Donna slid, in a whispery nylon way, into the passenger's seat. "I think it wouldn't be a good idea to underestimate what a cat might know. Maybe they're not as smart as we might think they are, but, then again, maybe they're smart enough to hide their conclusions. Why take the chance?"

I put the transmission into gear and we rolled out toward the county road. We had to wait for a car to go past, and I looked over at Eddie. He'd put the side of his head up against the wire door, which meant half of his whiskers, one of his ears, and most of the fur on that side of his face was sticking out.

Shaking my head, I pulled out onto the asphalt. If that cat was supersmart, he was doing an excellent job of hiding it.

The next few stops were deliveries to home-bound patrons. The day before, I'd pulled the requested books, checked them out with a specialty one-month due date, and popped them into plastic bags, all set to go for fast delivery.

In my push to set up this system, one thing I hadn't happened to mention to Stephen was how road conditions might interfere with the deliveries. Not just snow, but the driveways themselves. Our bookmobile was thirty-one feet long and it wasn't exactly easy to turn around in tight quarters. I'd become quite good at backing up, but if a driveway was snowy, slippery, hilly, and curvy, I might have a problem.

On the plus side, there was a thing called Google Earth, and I'd been able to take an aerial look at the driveways in advance. So far they'd been easy enough, and I dearly hoped the trend would continue.

Donna had handed out the bags at the drop-off locations while I'd carefully turned the book-mobile around. The last delivery, however, was at a farmhouse with a wonderful circular driveway. "Go ahead," Donna said, putting her feet up on Eddie's carrier. "Your cat and I will commune silently with each other in your absence."

"You think so?" Laughing, I picked up the last plastic bag. "That noise you hear isn't the engine; it's Eddie's snores."

She gave me a startled look, then leaned around to stare at my furry friend. He'd turned himself around and was doing a face-plant into the pink blanket. His snores had been a quiet, resonating drone for the last fifteen minutes.

Still laughing, I went out into the fresh air, across the yard, and up onto the wooden porch. I knocked on the back door and poked my head in. "Mr. Hadlee? It's Minnie Hamilton, from the library. I have your books."

"Come on in," called a strong male voice. "Did you bring them all?"

I pulled off my shoes and followed the voice, walking in my stocking feet, hefting the bag. "And then some."

In the living room, I found Mr. Hadlee— a farmer, volunteer firefighter, and freelance photographer—lying on the couch with his legs propped on pillows. He'd fallen off his barn roof the week before, broken two of two ankles, and now had multiple screws in both. His wife, a registered nurse, worked the afternoon shift at a nursing home, and between her job, taking care of him, and taking care of the farm animals, she didn't have time to make sure he got his desired reading material.

I sat in a nearby chair and pulled each book out of the bag like a magician pulling out rabbits. "*The Guns of August, The Peloponnesian War, The Coming of the French Revolution, Imperial China 900 to 1800*, and, for a special treat, a brand-spanking-new copy of *Battle Cry of Freedom*." I created a pile on the table next to the couch and grinned at him. "You have them for a month."

He laid his hand on the tall stack with what looked almost like reverence. "You are the answer to my prayers, Minnie."

I started to make a joke along the lines of good things coming in small packages but stopped. The man was serious, and making light of his feelings was completely inappropriate. "Glad we could help," I said, suddenly getting a little teary. "What do you want next time?"

When I got back to the bookmobile, I must have had an odd expression on my face, because Donna smirked. "Got you, didn't it?"

"What do you mean?"

"The delivery." She jerked her thumb in the direction of the Hadlee's house. "They're so grateful, it makes you want to cry."

"I didn't cry," I said indignantly.

"No?" Her eyebrows went up. "Then why are you sniffling?"

"That's from . . . from going in and out of the cold. It's hard on the nasal passages."

145

Donna grinned and made a *hmph* sort of noise. I ignored her, and we headed out.

"Um, Minnie?" Donna asked ten minutes later. "I have a problem the size of a large coffee and two bottles of water. Any chance of a restroom anywhere close?"

When I'd set up bookmobile stops, I'd made sure there was an available bathroom at every other location. With the home deliveries, though, I hadn't considered the issue. Most people probably wouldn't mind if we asked to use their facilities, but it didn't seem right.

"Okay," I told Donna, thinking hard, trying to see a map of this part of the county in my head, and mainly seeing places that were closed for the winter. There was one place that wasn't too far, but it was the last place I wanted to be.

I sighed, shaking the map out of my head. It was the only place, and it had to be done. "Hang on," I said. "We'll be there in a jiffy."

"Sorry," Donna murmured.

"Don't be," I said. "Eddie and I will commune silently with each other in your absence."

She laughed, and in a few minutes we were driving around the back of the gas station where, less than a week ago, I'd waited for Roger Slade. I didn't know if Donna knew that, but I wasn't about to bring up the subject. "Go around this side," I told her, pointing to the side of the building where I hadn't found Roger.

"Thanks," she said. "I'll be back as soon as I can."

"Take your time." I unbuckled and stretched. "We're a little ahead of schedule."

"Mrr," said Eddie.

Donna laughed, and as I heard the door open, I leaned over to unlatch Eddie's carrier. "You been in there a while, haven't you? Sorry about that. From now on, when we do a bunch of home deliveries in a row, I'll have to—"

In a flash of black-and-white fur, Eddie zipped past me.

"Hey," I said. "That's no way to thank the person who—"

There was a small *thump,* and all was quiet.

I scrambled to my feet. Donna must not have shut the door Eddie-tight. He'd pushed his way outside and could already have . . .

I kept my thoughts away from the road out front, and ran to follow my troublesome cat. Outside, the world was brown and gray, nothing like the whiteness of last week. I looked left, the way I'd directed Donna, and didn't see anything catlike, or even Eddie-like. I looked in the direction I didn't want to, toward the side of the building where I'd found Roger, and saw a flash of a tail.

"Eddie," I muttered, and hopped up into a fast trot. When he wanted to, Eddie could run rings around me at speeds that made me dizzy. The trick was to convince him that he didn't want to run.

"Here, kitty, kitty!" One of these days I'd remember to put a can of cat treats on the bookmobile. Shaking a cardboard can of treats was my best tactic for attracting a runaway Eddie. "Here, kitty, kitty, kitty!"

I ran around the building's corner, swung wide to avoid the Dumpster's wood screen, and skittered to a halt. There, nestled up against the building, as if he'd been sleeping for hours, was Eddie.

"What are you doing?" I asked.

He opened his mouth in a silent "Mrr."

"Once again," I said, "we have solid proof that you are the weirdest cat in the universe."

Eddie stood, shook himself, and picked up something in his mouth. It was a fairly large something, and he ended up dragging the thing more than carrying it.

I squatted down to see. "A hat. You've found yourself a nice winter hat." I looked at him. "But you're a cat and you already have a fur coat. What do you need with a hat?"

He ignored me and continued to prance his way back to the bookmobile, towing his new prize.

"Hang on." I picked up my cat and the hat, almost wishing that the cat had been in the hat, because if you squinted, Eddie could pass for the Dr. Seuss character. "Since you like it so much, I'll check inside and see if anyone lost it. Maybe they'll let us keep it." The hat in question looked to be handmade, with ear flaps and braided yarn lengths that tied under the chin. It was a fun blend of colors—red and yellow and blue and orange—but not in such bright shades that they hurt your eyes. Though it was a little damp from being outside, it was clean enough. With a washing, it would be good as new.

I slid it over Eddie's head. "We can keep it on the bookmobile," I told him. "You never know when someone will need a hat."

"Mrr," he said, and that seemed to settle it.

When Donna returned, I secured permission from a shrugging convenience-store employee to take the hat, which both Donna and I agreed was hand knit, and we headed off to finish the day's bookmobile schedule.

These were the among the first stops I'd ever scheduled, and the first thing all the regulars—especially the family with six children, which was comprised of the statistically impossible three sets of twins—wanted to do was greet Eddie.

"Hi, bookmobile ladies!" Each of the six kids greeted Donna and me as they breezed past on their way to the front of the vehicle, where Eddie had ensconced himself on the top of the passenger's seat headrest. It was his current preferred position for receiving visitors, and he accepted their pets and coos of admiration with great tolerance.

"Hey, Minnie," said the children's father, Chad Engstrom.

In their bookmobile visits over the months, I'd learned that Chad's wife worked for Tonedagana County as an accountant, that Chad worked from home as a designer of educational video games, and that he homeschooled the children with the help of a retired neighbor who'd once taught high school biology.

I'd also learned that the youngest Engstrom girl's favorite color was orange, that her twin brother's was red, that the middle girl was learning to play chess, that her twin brother didn't like peas, that the oldest girl wanted to get a pony, and that her twin brother had already decided he was going to be an archaeologist when he grew up. It was amazing what you could learn about people on the bookmobile.

"Nice day out there," Chad said, stomping his feet and blowing on his fingers. "Can't wait for winter."

"Do I detect a note of sarcasm?" I asked.

"A note?" He snorted. "More like an entire symphony. One of these days I'll convince my wife to move to a climate that doesn't hate people."

I laughed, knowing he didn't mean it, but his children heard his comment and clustered around.

"Dad, we can't move!" pleaded nine-year-old Cara.

"But, Dad, I just planted daffodils," said twelve-year-old Rose. "If we move now, I'll never see them come up. And I really, really want to."

Her twin brother, Trevor, frowned at his father. "If we move out of state, what colleges am I going to apply to? In-state tuition is a lot cheaper, but I don't want to go to a school that doesn't have a good archaeology program."

"Well, I'm not going." Six-year-old Ethan kicked at the carpet. "I'll run away. I'll come back here and I'll stay with Granny Engstrom."

"Me, too," said his twin, Emma. "She loves us. She won't make us move."

The last child to be heard from, nine-year-old Patrick, spread his arms wide. "We can't leave the bookmobile. We just can't!" He looked at my cat. "Right, Eddie?"

"Mrr," said Eddie, right on cue.

Chad laughed, a great, loud, uproarious sound that turned his children's worried expressions to smiles. "All right, Eddie, you've convinced me. We'll stay. But only because you asked so nicely."

I shook my head. Eddie as a chamber of commerce representative. The world was truly a strange, strange place.

When we got back to the library, I asked Donna to help me haul the returned books into the building, then said she could go.

"Are you sure?" she asked. "I can help with the rest."

I grinned. "Careful. If you keep showing this much interest in the bookmobile, I might ask you to volunteer again."

"Well, we wouldn't want that, now, would we?" She cast a last look at the vehicle, hesitating. "See you tomorrow," she said, still looking at the bookmobile, and shuffled off across the parking lot to her car.

I climbed back aboard, and the second I started doing all the closing-down chores, Eddie started pawing at his wire door.

"Mrr," he said. "Mrr."

"Oh, you want out, do you?" I sat on the console and looked down at him. "Well, you have been stuck in there for a while. Tell you what. I'll let you out if you promise to go back in easy-peasy when it's time to leave."

He blinked. "Mrr," he said quietly.

It was clearly a promise. Of course, what a cat's promise was worth, I didn't know, but there was only one way to find out. I opened the door. Eddie jumped up next to me and bumped his head against my shoulder.

"Yeah, yeah. Save it for your adoring fans." I kissed the top of his head and stood. "I have a few chores, pal. Why don't you do something productive while I take care of business?"

But instead of straightening the bookshelves or doing a little dusting or even working through the intellectual exercise of figuring out where to squeeze in a few more books, Eddie jumped to the small front desk, stretched out one paw, and snagged his new hat from where I'd stashed it behind the computer.

He pushed it off the edge of the desk, watched it drop to the floor, and promptly jumped down to flop on it.

"Fine," I told him. "Just don't think it's yours forever." Eddie ignored me, which was typical when I was telling him something he didn't want to hear. It was the cat equivalent of sticking your fingers in your ears and saying "La, la, la."

"It's not big enough for a cat mattress, for one thing," I said, eyeing him. "Your back feet aren't even on—"

The door to the bookmobile opened. Donna, no doubt, coming back to sign up for a lifetime of bookmobile volunteering. I turned, a big smile on my face.

Only it wasn't Donna. Not even close.

"You," Denise Slade said, pointing a shaking finger at me. "It's your fault."

My arms dropped to my sides. I swallowed. "Denise, I am so sorry about your husband. If there's anything I can do—"

"Do?" she asked shrilly. "Don't you think you've done enough?"

Gray sorrow raked at the inside of my chest. I wanted to protest, to say that I'd done all I could, to say that I'd done all anyone could, but how could I when I wasn't sure that I had?

Denise's hair was unkempt. She wore a perky spring coat of lime green over cropped pants, with short white socks and plastic clogs that looked like something she'd gardened in for decades. Never once had I seen Denise look anything but tidy and ready to take on the world's to-do list.

"More than anything," I said quietly, "I wish that your husband was still alive. I am so very sorry for your loss."

"Sorry?" she shrieked. "What good does 'sorry' do me now? 'Sorry' isn't going to shovel the driveway this winter. 'Sorry' isn't going to fix that leak under the kitchen sink. 'Sorry' isn't going to finish the landscaping that never got done last summer."

She was right, but what else could I say? Nothing that would make any difference, so I stood there and took the abuse.

"Sorry!" She tossed her hair back out of her face. "'Sorry' isn't going to keep me warm at night. 'Sorry' isn't going to fix my Sunday breakfast. 'Sorry' isn't going to help me rake the leaves next fall, and 'sorry' isn't going to help me one little bit when the car breaks down."

I wanted to ease her pain, to make her feel even a tiny bit better, but I had no idea how. Maybe there wasn't a way. "Denise . . ."

"Don't 'Denise' me!" She took a step forward, her face mottled red with fury. "All you had to do was drive the bookmobile around and bring my husband back home. Instead you got him killed. This is all your fault!"

I gasped, feeling as if I'd been punched in the stomach. I tried to talk, but nothing came out.

"Rrrrr," Eddie said from the floor—not exactly a growl, but not the friendly sound he usually made, either.

"And that cat!" Denise transferred her focus to Eddie. "How can—" She made a soft mewling sound and fell to her knees, her hands reaching out toward Eddie's new mattress. "The hat," she whimpered. "This is where he left it."

"This is Roger's hat?" I stared at one of the tasseled ends, the one Eddie had been chewing on.

"It was mine," she whispered. "My sister made it for me, but I wanted him to take a hat on Saturday. All that snow—I thought he might need something, he just had surgery, and it was the first one I found. He laughed and said he'd wear it. He said . . ."

I crouched down, rolled Eddie off the hat, and handed it to Denise.

Slowly she stood, holding it to her cheek, stroking it. She stared at nothing, her lips moving, and though no sound came out, I knew what she was saying.

"Roger. Roger. Roger . . ."

Without another word to me, she turned and left

the bookmobile, her footsteps on the gravel parking lot slowly fading away to nothing.

I sat down on the console. Eddie jumped up beside me.

"Mrr."

"Yeah, pal," I said absently, "I hear you."

I would have bet money—and lots of it—that Roger wouldn't have worn that feminine hat unless he'd been in danger of having frostbite take his ears off.

Then a flash of memory came back to me: Roger giving Eddie one last scratch, taking a couple of steps, then stopping and saying, "Almost forgot." Had it been the hat? Had he been taking it out of his pocket so he could tell his wife he'd kept his promise to her and worn it out in the cold?

The bright design would have been visible to anyone with a scoped rifle.

A unique design made especially for Denise.

Had Denise been the killer's real target?

I dug through my purse and found the business card Ash Wolverson had given me. "Hi. Minnie Hamilton here. Are you at the office? Because I have something you might want to hear."

Chapter 8

Half an hour later, I was sitting in what I was coming to think of as My Chair. I even knew to avoid catching my pant leg in the tiny crack on its front right edge. But if I was going to keep spending so much time in here, something needed to be done about the ceiling tiles. Even if those stains had been from something as completely innocuous as a roof leak, they weren't at all appealing. In some areas—right by the door, for instance—the pattern was downright scary.

Detective Inwood, tall and skinny like the letter *I*, walked in, followed closely by Ash. Deputy Wolverson, not at all shaped like the letter *I*, was in a tidy uniform of dark brown shirt and lighter brown dress pants that exactly matched his tie. The detective, with evidence of morning coffee on his white shirt and what might have been mustard stains on his gray pants, bore more resemblance to the ceiling tiles.

"Something amusing, Ms. Hamilton?" Detective Inwood asked, sitting in the chair directly across from me. Ash, who was being as quiet as a detective in training should probably be, sat to the detective's right.

I brushed the back of my hand across my face,

getting rid of the smile. "Just trying to be pleasant, Detective." I looked at him brightly. "How was your day?"

He sat back, crossed one of his legs over the other, and clasped his hands around his raised knee. "The usual mix of miscreants and trouble-makers. How about you?"

Over in Ash's direction, I sensed a small movement that might have been a smirk, but I kept my gaze focused on Inwood. "I convinced a nine-year-old boy that reading wasn't a complete waste of time and might even be fun, given the right book."

The detective smiled. "Then I think you had a much more productive day than I did."

For a moment I considered what the daily life of a law-enforcement officer must be like. Putting bad people in jail had to be rewarding, but, after a while, it must feel like most of the people in the world are, well, bad. Coworkers and family members would be the only ones you could assume were on the side of the angels, and on dark days, maybe not all of them.

I felt an unexpected wave of sympathy for the two men. "If there's an opening at the library, I'll let you know."

They shared a glance, which I interpreted as a mutual expression of *Is she insane?*, and my sympathy dried up.

"Let me tell you what I found," I said in an

exquisitely polite tone. From there I launched into the Tale of the Hat, starring Eddie and the bookmobile, costarring me, and featuring the supporting character of the bereaved widow.

"So, I'm thinking that maybe it was really a murder attempt," I concluded. "And that Denise was the real target."

The detective released his hands from around his knee and reclasped them. "The hat is in the possession of Mrs. Slade?"

I nodded. Maybe it was evidence, and maybe I should have told her to take it to the police, but after seeing her put it against her cheek like that, there was no way I'd suggest such a thing.

Detective Inwood made a noise that wasn't quite a grunt. "And where at the convenience store did your . . . cat find the . . . hat?"

I studied him, but he didn't appear to be laughing, even on the inside. Then again, if anyone could conceal laughter, it had to be the man sitting in front of me. "Just past the northeast corner."

"Hmm." The detective squinted at the ceiling tiles. He had to be looking straight at the stains, and I wondered what pattern he saw. Probably not the fire-breathing dragon with the big talons that I kept seeing, but you never knew.

"Wolverson," Inwood finally said, "why don't you drive out there? When you come back, you can let me know why you didn't find that hat on

Saturday." He gave Ash a straight look that made me sit back flat in my chair.

"There was a lot of snow," I said. "Anyone could have missed it."

The detective's gaze slashed at me. "The average person, yes. But what would you say about a deputy who is training to be a detective? You'd say that if the snow was six inches deep, if it was *sixty* inches deep, he shouldn't have missed it." Detective Inwood stood and almost shouted right in Ash's face. "And you'd be right!"

He banged the table with his fist, glared at both of us, and stomped out. I winced in anticipation of the door being slammed, but he shut it in a surprisingly gentle fashion.

I looked at Ash. "Sorry about that," I said. "If I'd known . . ."

He shook his head. "You did the right thing. I should have found the hat the other day, no matter what."

"Well, I'm still sorry. He didn't have to yell at you like that."

Ash shrugged. "It's just Hal. He doesn't mean anything by it."

Which made no sense to me, but whatever. I stood, made good-bye noises, and started to leave.

"Hey, Minnie?" Ash asked.

When I stopped and turned back to face him, he started to say something, then stopped. Started again. "Thanks for bringing the hat." He grinned, revealing his extreme good looks once again. "Even if it did get me in trouble."

I smiled back. "Anytime."

That night, I told Aunt Frances about the cat, the hat, and the detective. The phrase didn't quite scan, but I couldn't think of a rhyming word that would fit Detective Inwood. Brat? Drat? Mat?

"So you think Denise was really the target?" Aunt Frances asked. "That it really was murder?"

I didn't want it to be. Though tragic accidents are a hard thing to make sense of, at least you could do your best to make sure they didn't happen again. But murder? An uncomfortable prickle went up the back of my neck. I shivered, which made the cat on my lap twist his head around to look up at me.

"Sorry about that," I murmured, scratching the tip of Eddie's nose.

Murder made everything different. In a general sort of way, people are pretty nice to each other, at least when they're face-to-face. Sure, there's the occasional incident, but on a daily basis our lives are made up of coworkers saying "Good morning," and things like the person heading into the post office three steps ahead holding the door open for you. If people started being nasty to each other as a matter of habit, where would we be?

"Minnie?" Aunt Frances asked.

I blinked out of my dark reverie. My aunt was

sitting on the couch across from me, a crocheted blanket covering her legs. A cheerful fire burned in the fieldstone fireplace, and there was a mostly empty plate of cookies on the low table between us. Two empty mugs that had formerly held hot chocolate stood nearby.

"If it was really murder, the police will find out." I'd meant the words to sound confident, but they came out as almost a question.

"Hmm." Aunt Frances leaned forward and took the last peanut butter cookie, leaving the chocolate chip for me. "You don't have any inclination to find out for yourself?"

"Of course I do." If it had been murder, I wanted the killer put in prison so he couldn't kill ever again—not me, not Denise, not anyone.

The cat-oriented weight on my legs was starting to cut off the circulation to my feet. I shifted and though I tried not to move Eddie, the movement made him unhappy enough to stop purring and give me a look. "Sorry," I said. I was pretty sure I'd made more apologies in the few months I'd been a cat caretaker than I had in the entire decade prior.

"So, what are you going to do?" my aunt asked. "About Roger?"

I thought about that and came to a fast conclusion. I was a librarian. Research was one of my favorite things in the whole wide world, so it only made sense to—

My cell phone, which I'd flopped on the table next to the cookies, started vibrating. I picked it up.

Aunt Frances gave me a quizzical look. "Tucker?" She made getting-up movements, but I waved her back down. Making her leave the comfort of her own couch was ridiculous.

"Give me a sign if it gets too personal," I said, "and I'll go upstairs." I thumbed on the phone. "Hey."

"Hey, yourself," Tucker said.

There was a long beat of silence. Another one. Two seconds later we were sliding deep into the uncomfortable-pause phase, because in spite of our exchange of text messages on Monday, I'd never heard back from his nonexistent secretary. We'd done more texting, but none of it had to do with his schedule, and I was getting a little annoyed.

Eddie purred.

"Are you still there?" Tucker asked.

"Still here," I said. "What's up?"

"Sorry about not getting back to you, but we've had a couple of staffing issues that made a huge hole." He sighed. "We're not even close to having December nailed down."

I squinted at the fireplace. "But it's almost Thanksgiving."

"Thank you, Minnie," he said. "I wasn't aware of that."

The starch in his voice made me stiffen. Eddie turned his head sideways and almost upside down to look at me. I started petting him, long, gentle strokes from head to tail, creating a small mound of loose Eddie hair at the end.

"Until we get this straightened out," Tucker was saying, "I won't be able to make any plans."

"Oh," I said.

"Look, Minnie, I'm sorry about this—I really am—but there's nothing I can do. This is what being a doctor can be like. You know that."

Not really, but I was learning. Fast. "So, you'll let me know when you have some free time?" I asked.

"Sure. We'll work it out, Minnie."

If he'd sent me those words in a text I might have believed him; as it was, I could hear the doubt in his voice.

"Tucker . . ."

"It'll be fine," he said. "Don't worry."

But it was hard not to. After we said limp good-byes, I pulled Eddie close and buried my face in his side.

"Minnie?" Aunt Frances asked. "Is everything all right?"

I rubbed my eyes against Eddie's thick fur, which absorbed my half tears easily. Aunt Frances was a matchmaker of the first order; if she knew Tucker and I were having troubles, she'd be rolling up her sleeves and getting to work.

"I'm fine," I said, looking up at her with a painted-on smile. "It'll be fine."

That night I didn't sleep well. Every time I felt myself start spiraling down into the darkness, my thoughts would jerk me back awake.

Well, either my thoughts or Eddie. It was one of those nights he thought I should be awake and attending to his every need. The first hint I had of this was a wet nose on my cheek. That was my cue to roll onto my back so his front half could lie across my shoulder and his back half could cozy up into the inside of my elbow.

After a while, though, this position didn't suit him. He stuck out a paw and pushed on my nose. This was my cue to turn onto my side so he could snuggle up against my chest with my arm around him.

But he didn't stay that way very long. A few minutes later, he slid out from underneath my arm, stood, stretched, and walked down the length of me to flop on my feet. This, of course, kept me from moving the rest of the night, since it Just Doesn't Do to disturb a sleeping cat. Cats have amazing powers, and if they ever decided to take over the world, it wouldn't be long before they asserted their control over us.

The next morning, as I picked an Eddie hair off my pant leg, I again considered the possibility of cats controlling the world. "It's possible," I muttered to myself as I dropped the hair into a wastebasket, "that they already do."

"Sorry?" The woman standing at the library's checkout desk was eyeing me cautiously.

I considered gifting her with the Eddie Hair of the Day, but decided against it. Judging from the look of her winter-white jacket and pants, they were dry-clean only, which meant they were pet-hair magnets, and I knew I wouldn't appreciate a gift of cat hair if I'd been wearing them. Not that I would have been. Dry-clean-only clothing wouldn't be in my budget until I paid off my college loans.

"Just talking to myself," I told the woman. She looked a little older than my thirty-three years and she also looked familiar, yet I could have sworn I'd never met her. "That's a pretty necklace you're wearing," I said, nodding at the simple yet elegant pendant of fused glass in multiple colors.

"Thank you," she said, smiling. "I designed it myself."

It was noon, and I was covering the front desk while Kelsey took her lunch. It had been awhile since I'd done this, and I was remembering how much fun it was. On the bookmobile, I knew the likes and dislikes of the patrons inside and out, but here I typically didn't know people's preferences, which left me free to imagine why they checked out certain books. I also had a regrettable tendency to recommend the books they should be checking out, but I kept those recommendations in my head. Mostly, anyway.

I took her card and ran it under the reader. *Allison Korthase.* The name was familiar, but I couldn't put her into any of my frames of reference. Mentally I zipped through all the places I was likely to run into people. The library, the sheriff's office, downtown, grocery store, post office . . . but none of them jingled anything in my memory.

The only other place I went on a regular basis was on the bookmobile, and I was sure I'd never seen this woman on—

My brain took a big bounce and the answer came to me. *Bingo!*

I started beeping her checkouts through the computer. Every book in the pile was a biography of a prominent woman, with a concentration on women in politics. Eleanor Roosevelt, Margaret Thatcher, Emily Murphy, Indira Gandhi. It suddenly all made sense.

The checked-out books went back across the counter to her. "So, how's it going at city hall?" I asked, smiling.

Because I'd finally remembered that Allison was newly elected to the Chilson City Council. Her political signs were among the signs Roger and I had wished gone from the landscape. I thought about recommending another book for her, *The Wartville Wizard*, but held back. "Righting all the wrongs? Forging a new path to a brighter future?"

I spoke in jest. She'd been elected barely two weeks earlier; I wasn't sure there'd even been a council meeting since the election. And I knew many of the other council members; they were thoughtful, well-intentioned people who were doing their best for the city. How much could there possibly be to fix?

"There's a lot of work to do," she said earnestly, turning her stack of books to face her and aligning all the edges. "I have a number of items I'd like to see implemented as soon as possible. Changes need to be made, and if there's a little pain involved, well, sometimes that's what has to happen."

"Changes?" I didn't know—or care—much about politics, but I did know that making changes, even in a small town like Chilson, could be fraught with the kinds of things that would make even the strongest want to whimper.

Allison smiled wide. "If we keep on doing things the same way here in Chilson, at the state level, and in Washington, we can only expect to get the same results. Improving our lives and the lives of our children and grandchildren is worth working toward, don't you think?"

It was a question that guaranteed a positive response, the kind of manipulative question that I found annoying. I gave her a polite smile. "Good luck," I said.

Watching her go, I marveled at her enthusiasm for her new position. Working with Stephen and the library board was as much politics as I ever wanted to deal with. I tried to remember what she did for a living. A council member's job wasn't anywhere near full-time, at least not in Chilson. Meeting pay and a small annual stipend were the extent of the compensation. Not even the mayor got much more than that.

Realtor? No, I would have recognized her name a lot faster. Attorney? Maybe. Or a—

"Hey, Minnie. Are you in there? I been standing here half an hour."

I looked up. Mitchell was standing at the desk, flapping some papers in my direction. "Half an hour?" I asked.

"Well, it felt that long."

He grinned, and I found myself smiling in return. A large part of what charm Mitchell possessed lay in the fact that he didn't take himself seriously. Of course, he didn't take much seriously, so maybe there wasn't much virtue in it.

"What do you have?" I nodded at the papers.

"Oh yeah." He pushed the small stack over to me, then readjusted his baseball hat. "This is what I been working on the last few days. What do you think?"

The pages were a long listing of names, phone numbers, and addresses. It was a nice list, and I was proud of Mitchell for such a professional presentation. Clean white paper, alphabetical by last name, correctly formatted; it was very well done. The only thing was, it lacked a title, and I had no idea what it was all about.

I looked through the names, many of which I recognized. Men, women; young, old. Mostly local addresses, but not all. No pattern to it, as far as I could tell, but there had to be a reason Mitchell had gone to the trouble. There was always a reason for something, even if we didn't know what it might be. Even if we thought the reason was dumb.

"You must have spent a lot of time on this." I was fishing for an explanation, but Mitchell was oblivious. "Okay, I give up. What is this?"

He grinned. "The start of my investigation. You wouldn't believe how many people I talked to in the past couple of days. I started with the easy ones, like the neighbors all down that short road he lived on. Then I did the guys he worked with— you know, that construction company."

The lightbulb over my head went on with a loud *click*. Mitchell kept talking, but I pretty much stopped listening to him. What he had so laboriously—and probably unnecessarily—done was assemble a list of everyone Roger Slade had ever known. Mitchell was describing his efforts to track down the names of Roger's fifth-grade classmates when I rudely interrupted him.

"You know what you should do with this?" I

tapped the papers and internally smiled a small, evil smile. "Take it down to the sheriff's office."

"Yeah? You think so?" Mitchell's eyebrows went up, disappearing into brown hair that badly needed cutting. "Because last time I tried to help, when that woman was killed last summer, they didn't seem real happy to see me coming."

I tapped the papers again. "But this time you have something concrete, something they really might be able to use."

Mitchell was nodding. "You mean I got something to bring to the table this time."

"Exactly." Beaming, I returned the papers. "Make sure you deliver these to Detective Inwood. Tell him I sent you."

"Sweet." Mitchell tidied up the small stack. "You're all right, Minnie, no matter what Chris Ballou says." He saluted me with the papers and made his long-limbed way toward the front door.

Smiling, I leaned back and put my hands behind my head, laughing inside, knowing that Detective Inwood would soon be getting a Mitchell-sized surprise. It was a lovely day, and I didn't see a single cloud on the horizon. Yes, I needed to figure out the whys and wherefores of Roger's death, but for the moment, everything was—

"Hey."

I turned around. Josh was standing in the doorway between the back offices. Lurking, almost. "What's up?" I asked.

"Well." He fiddled with the doorjamb. Not that it needed fiddling with; it was relatively new woodwork, having been put in place barely three years prior, when the old school was converted into our present library facility, but whatever.

"It's about, well, you know," he said.

"Not a clue," I said cheerfully. "Give me three guesses?"

Josh ran a hand through his dark curly hair and kept not looking at me. Clearly he wasn't going to play my game. "It's that stuff we talked about earlier," he said. "About, you know." He glanced up and sideways.

I looked in the same direction Josh was gazing and realized he was looking toward Stephen's office.

My second mental lightbulb of the day went *click* and I remembered that Holly and Josh were trying to help me work out if Stephen knew about Eddie.

"When I went up to do those software updates on Stephen's computer," Josh said, "he left for a meeting with some software vendor down in Traverse City. Said he wouldn't be back until late afternoon."

Riiiight. I knew for a fact that there was no software vendor. Stephen never met with vendors until I'd vetted the sales reps first. What was far more likely was that he wanted to see what was going on at the Traverse City library. I made a mental note to check their programming schedule.

"You think he knows about Eddie?" I asked, and was embarrassed to hear a catch in my voice.

"Nah," Josh said. "The other way around. I bet he doesn't know at all. If he did know, he would have thumped you for keeping things from him. He hates it when that happens."

Which was true. Stephen was always talking about the need for more communication. However, I'd long since figured out that what he really meant was that *we* needed to tell *him* more things, not that he needed to share things with us.

"Thanks for trying," I finally said.

Josh nodded. "I don't think you have anything to worry about, but I can go back in a couple of days. I'll ask him how the upgrade is doing, then sneak in a couple of questions about the bookmobile."

I eyed him. He hated going up to Stephen's office. He'd said more than once it was like going up to the principal's office after you'd been caught sneaking a look through the window of the girl's locker room.

"You're okay," I said, "for a geeky IT guy."

His smile flashed bright. "And you're okay for a nerdy library girl."

We bumped fists and went back to work.

That evening, my loving cat greeted me when I walked in the front door.

173

"Mrr," he said, then yawned to demonstrate the enthusiasm he so deeply felt upon my return.

"You don't fool me." I picked him up from the back of the couch and gave him a good snuggle. Since I was still wearing my winter coat, my library clothes were relatively safe from a new influx of Eddie hair, which was the main reason I was still wearing it. I loved an Eddie snuggle when I got home, but the subsequent half hour of picking the cat hair off my clothing wasn't how I preferred to spend my time.

"I bet you did nothing today except pine for my return." I patted the top of his head. "Yep, I bet all you did was—"

Suddenly I noticed that something in the living room was different. Something was missing . . . wasn't it?

Eddie squirmed out of my embrace and his feet double-thumped to the floor.

I turned in a small circle, trying to figure it out. The furniture was the same, the drapes were the same, the picture frames on the mantel were the same . . .

"Eddie!" I shrieked. "What have you done?"

"Mrr," he said calmly.

"Don't *mrr* at me!" I stomped over to the low bookcases that stood against the far wall. They held games and puzzles and scrapbooks and other things that the summer boarders used to while away rainy afternoons. For as long as I could remember, there had been local maps hung above two of the three bookcases, and snowshoes above the third.

Now, thanks to what must have been Eddie Interference, the snowshoes were on the floor.

I tried to hang them up the same way they'd hung for decades. "Nice work, Mr. Ed. Did you not get enough exercise yesterday, running around the bookmobile, getting pats from everyone on board? Don't look at me like that—I saw you sucking up to that guy who always gives you cat treats."

"Mrr."

"I did, too."

"Mrr."

"Did, too."

"Mrr."

"Did—" I stopped and looked at my cat, who had reduced our conversation to that of two seven-year-olds. "Just leave the snowshoes alone, okay? They're antiques and are definitely not cat toys."

Eddie stalked off toward the kitchen, his tail straight up in the air, obviously sure he'd won the battle.

I couldn't decide whether to laugh or to roll my eyes, so I did both. And somehow the act of doing so reminded me that I'd promised Aunt Frances I'd pick up some groceries on the way home.

"Hey, Eddie," I called. "If Aunt Frances gets

back before I do, tell her I'm getting provisions for the weekend."

There was a pause; then I heard a faint "Mrr."

"Thanks, pal," I said, and headed out for the short walk to the grocery store.

The unseasonably mild weather of the past few days was on its way out, and I kept my head down against the rising wind and chill air.

Yes, winter was coming, no doubt about it. I took one mittened hand out of my pocket and zipped my coat up all the way to the top. Technically winter wouldn't arrive for another month, but I judged the presence of winter more by the clothing I wore than by what the calendar said.

Thoughts of the upcoming season occupied me as I stepped into the sudden moist warmth of the grocery store and picked up a small basket. As I debated between red and green peppers, I wondered how well the bookmobile's heater would combat the deep cold spells we'd get in January and February. Below-zero temperatures were not uncommon, and thirty below wasn't out of the question.

While I looked at the rice choices, I wondered how the bookmobile would handle in the snowy road conditions. The icy road conditions. And, worst of all, the slushy road conditions. The commercial driver's course I'd taken had taught me techniques to handle every possible condition, but driver's-course knowledge was different from true road experience.

I stood in front of the freezer section—ice cream wasn't on the list, but it never hurt to look—and told myself to stop being such a worrywart. There were numerous bookmobiles all across the country that drove through harsh winters, probably worse winters than this part of Michigan ever got. Everything would be fine. I just needed to relax and—

"Did you hear what happened to Denise?"

Though I couldn't see the woman, her voice was loud and piercing enough to carry from the adjacent aisle. I gave a last, longing look at the quart of Cherry Garcia and started toward the registers.

"You mean Denise Slade?" another woman asked.

I stopped cold. Retreated a few steps. Kept listening.

"She left early this morning," the loud-voiced woman said. "Headed downstate to visit her—Oh, I'm not sure. Her mother or aunt or some sort of relative." There was a pause. "Or was it a relative of Roger's? I don't remember. Anyway, she'd gone over to the interstate since she was going to the Detroit area, when her engine just stopped."

"You mean it turned off?" The other woman sounded puzzled, which was the same way I would have sounded if I'd asked the same question. And I almost had.

The loud woman said, "That's what my husband said, and he's a car guy, right? He said that the engine seized up."

Sadly, I knew exactly what that meant. It had happened to the car owned by my best friend from high school. She'd started the engine, heard some horrible noises, smelled some terrible smells, and then the thing had simply stopped running. The fix had been horrendously expensive.

"Anyway," the loud woman said, "this happened when Denise was on the expressway, going seventy miles per hour. When the engine seized, it made so much noise and scared her so much that she kind of ran off the road."

The woman's friend gasped. "Is she okay?"

"She didn't hit anything, is what I heard, but when she went off the road . . . You know how much rain we've been having? She drove right into this deep ditch that was filled with water." The loud woman's voice dropped, and I had to strain to hear. "She almost drowned, is what they said."

The woman talked on, but I made my way to the front of the store, head down and thinking hard about things I really didn't want to think about.

About circumstances, about cases of mistaken identity, about crimes of planning and patience.

About murder.

Chapter 9

The next morning I did my best to sleep late, but the combination of my aunt's jovial singing and Eddie's ongoing efforts to find a comfortable sleeping position on my head woke me long before I'd hoped.

"It's mostly your fault," I told my furry friend as I toweled my hair dry, post shower. "I've heard Aunt Frances sing the theme song to *Gilligan's Island* so many times that it's something I've learned to sleep through. But I don't see how I'm going to ever learn to sleep through you flopping yourself across my face. You might suffocate me, you know."

Eddie, however, was playing Cat Statue. In this mode, his ears didn't work, which was often very convenient for him.

"Then again," I said, "if Aunt Frances ever sang anything other than theme songs to old television shows, who knows what it might do to my sleep habits?"

The thought humored me, mostly because there was little chance she'd ever sing anything different. Her brain, she'd said seriously, didn't maintain a hold on any other song lyrics. I was very grateful her brain didn't stick on Christmas songs, because the idea of hearing "Frosty the Snowman" every

Saturday morning October through April made me want to scratch out the insides of my ears. Hearing "Frosty" in December was fine, of course, but, in my opinion, a little went a long way.

"You know," I told Eddie, "I almost feel like singing myself." Because it was a beautiful day for the Saturday before Thanksgiving. Clear skies and no wind, and what more could you really hope for at this time of year?

"Any requests?" I pulled an almost-cat-hair-free sweatshirt over my head. " 'Cat's in the Cradle'? 'The Lion Sleeps Tonight'? No, wait, I have it: 'Stray Cat Strut.' "

Laughing, I looked around for Eddie, but all I saw was the end of his tail as it whisked out the bedroom door.

"How about 'Cat Scratch Fever'?" I called. " 'Honky Cat'? And don't forget 'What's New, Pussycat?' " I waited for a positive response to at least one of my suggestions, but all I heard was the thumping of his feet on the stairs.

Cats.

I smiled a Saturday-morning-that-I-didn't-have-to-work smile, and headed down the stairs after him.

After a breakfast of slow-cooked oatmeal and orange juice, I decided to go for a walk while the sunshine lasted. "Do you want to come with me?" I asked my aunt.

Aunt Frances turned the page of a cookbook. It was one of many that were scattered around the kitchen table. "I'll go later," she said absently. "I want to try a new stuffing recipe for Thanksgiving, and I know I saw something in one of these books last summer. All I have to do is find it."

I looked at Eddie, who was lying Sphinx-like on the newly installed padded shelf underneath the window. "How about you?" I asked. "A walk would do you good."

He turned his head and closed his eyes.

"Well, it would," I said, but all I got in response was a tighter closing of his eyes and another page turn from my aunt. Smiling, I headed for the outside world by my wild lone.

Once there, though, I wasn't sure I'd made the correct decision. Last night's wind had been a north one, and it had brought air so cold that it belonged more in January than in November.

I didn't see another soul out and about on this chilly morning, and I felt almost as if I were the only person on the planet. For a moment I played with that idea, and decided that I would be a gibbering madwoman within a month. Maybe less.

Just as I was starting to feel what that might be like, I heard a distant noise. Mechanical, and in no rhythm whatsoever. It was clearly human in origin, and I felt as pulled to it as a child being led by the Pied Piper.

A few blocks later, I figured out where the noise was coming from: Bryant's Repair, the garage that helped me take care of the bookmobile. Darren Bryant, mechanic extraordinaire, had willingly done a vast amount of research so he could do whatever maintenance and trouble-shooting the vehicle would inevitably need. He'd even developed an e-mail network of bookmobile mechanics across the country. "If one bus has something going on, odds are good another one has already had the same problem," he'd said.

Darren was a treasure, one of those mechanics who could talk car stuff both to enthusiasts and to people like me, who just wanted their vehicles to function. He was patient and he never used that annoying, condescending voice, and if he hadn't been a little too old for me and married to a very nice lady who regularly checked historical fiction out of the library, I might have wanted to marry him.

I opened the shop's door, and the noise, which had been muffled from without, was extremely loud within. Darren was standing on the front bumper of a large white pickup, leaning over the engine with what I now knew was an impact wrench in his hand.

He looked over at me. "Hey, Minnie. What's up?" He triggered the wrench one last time while I put my fingers in my ears; then he jumped down and put the tool on the bench.

At most, Darren was an inch taller than I was, which had created a bond between us that we would never, ever, discuss. He grabbed a dirty rag and wiped his hands. "Anything wrong with the bookmobile?"

I shook my head. "Just my normal worries about the generator." From everything I'd heard and read, generator issues were the bane of a bookmobile librarian's existence. A generator was critical to the bookmobile's operations, since it powered the lights and heat when the engine wasn't running.

Darren switched to a slightly cleaner rag. "And I'll tell you again, there's nothing to worry about. It'll be fine."

I looked at him askance. "Are you saying that just to make me feel better or do you really mean it?"

"Don't ask questions," he said, grinning, "unless you really want to know the answer."

I laughed. "I need to remember that. I've run into trouble more than once, because . . ." Something on the other side of the garage caught my attention. I couldn't remember what I was saying, so I let the sentence trail off.

"Are you okay?" Darren frowned.

"Um, sure," I said, peering at a crumpled SUV in the far bay of his shop. "Is that Denise Slade's?" I pointed.

"Got it in yesterday morning. The insurance

guy's coming in to look at it on Monday. They'll probably total it." His face went from friendly and cheerful to thoughtful and considering. Maybe even troubled.

"Is something wrong?" I asked.

He redirected his considering look from Denise's SUV to my face. I don't know what he saw there, but he gave a small nod and said, "If you were anyone else, I wouldn't say anything, but you were there when Roger was killed."

That didn't make sense to me, but maybe things would become clear if he talked a little longer.

"Yeah." He tossed the rag he was still using on his hands onto the workbench. "I know I don't need to tell you to keep quiet about this, so I won't. Denise's SUV over there? I was poking around at it, seeing how much damage there was to the front end, and I think . . ." He stopped, sighed, and shook his head. "I think someone intentionally sliced the radiator hose. That's why the engine seized up—I'm sure of it."

The world around me tilted. I wanted to grab onto something, anything, to help steady me, but there was nothing that wasn't scary, expensive, greasy, or all three, so instead I pulled in a deep breath and waited for the tilting to stop. "Did you tell the sheriff's office?"

Darren laughed shortly. "I'm not telling those yahoos anything I don't have to. I talked to Scott from the Chilson Police."

I looked at him curiously. "You have a problem with the sheriff?"

It was the wrong question. He immediately launched into a long story involving an open trailer, a pile of metal he was hauling to the scrap yard, and an overeager deputy who ticketed him not only for an unsecured load, but also for driving too fast for conditions. And for having expired plates.

Darren, red-faced, was waving his arms and saying that his birthday wasn't until the end of the month, and why should he pay for registration any earlier than he had to? But I wondered how quickly Detective Inwood would learn about the cut in the radiator hose.

Because he needed to know.

He needed to know that Roger had been murdered, that Denise had been the intended victim all along, and that Denise's life was in danger.

I burst into the sheriff's office. "I know it's Saturday," I said breathlessly, "but is there any chance that either Detective Inwood or Deputy Wolverson are here?"

The heavyset woman behind the counter nodded. "Both. You want to talk to them?"

I nodded, gave her my name, and I was soon admitted to the back, into the interview room.

A short time later, the detective came in. "Ms. Hamilton, what brings you to see us on a Saturday morning?"

I looked at him suspiciously. "You're smiling."

"My wife tells me I should do it more often," he said, sitting at the table.

"She's right." His face transformed completely when he smiled. And in a good way. He didn't look nearly the dour everyone-is-guilty-of-something cop when he did. "Why are you so happy about being at work on a Saturday morning?"

His smile went even wider. "You'll be glad to know that we have a solid lead on the person responsible for Roger Slade's death."

"You . . . do?"

"No arrest, but with the help of the area's conservation officer, we have a very good idea about what happened out there."

"You do?"

Detective Inwood's smile slipped a bit. "Don't look so surprised, Ms. Hamilton. We may not solve crimes in an hour, but we actually do know what we're doing."

"It's not that," I said quickly. "It's just that Denise, Roger's wife, she had a car accident a few days ago, and her mechanic just told me that the radiator hose had been cut."

I waited for the light to dawn, but instead he simply nodded. "Yes, we know about that. The city police notified us."

"And?" I asked. "Does that fit with the guy you think killed Roger?"

His smile took on a polite cast. "Ms. Hamilton,

anyone truly trying to kill Denise Slade would have cut her brake lines. A slice in a radiator hose?" He shook his head. "She's been known to call nine-one-one and report loud parties. Most likely she left her car in the drive, and one of the neighbor kids took the opportunity."

"What if it wasn't?" I leaned forward. "What if Denise was the target all along? What if Roger was killed by accident, because he was wearing her hat? What if Denise is still in danger?"

The detective stood. "Thanks for the information, Ms. Hamilton. We'll consider what you said, but please let us do our jobs."

I started to protest, to try to convince him that he was wrong, but he was already gone.

When I left the sheriff's office, it was past ten o'clock and the stores were opening. The Round Table, our local diner, had been serving food for hours, but now the signs on the retail stores were being flipped from CLOSED to OPEN, lights were being turned on, and there was an overall feeling that the town was stretching its arms, yawning, and waking up to another day of business.

"Good morning, Minnie!"

I looked around for the origin of the voice and saw a woman waving at me from the entry of an antiques store. It was Pam Fazio, the owner of Older Than Dirt, and I didn't understand why she was there.

"And a fine morning it is," I said, smiling at her as I crossed the street. "But aren't you going to be late for the Friends of the Library meeting?" For decades, Friends meetings had been held once a month on Saturday mornings.

Pam scowled. "Funny, Minnie, really funny."

I blinked at her. "It was? I wasn't trying to be."

She blinked back. "Oh. Sorry. You must not have heard."

No, I hadn't, and whatever it was, I was getting a bad feeling about it.

"It was at the last Friends meeting," Pam said, wrapping her arms around herself. She'd stepped outside to talk to me, and the cascading purple cardigan she wore over black pants and ankle-high shiny black boots wasn't keeping out the cold.

"I guess you were out on the bookmobile that day," she said. "By the time you got back it was all over."

Yep, I was getting a very bad feeling. "What happened?"

"Denise Slade happened," Pam practically spat. "I know I should feel sorry for her, with Roger being killed and her crash and everything, but that woman is impossible! Why Roger stayed married to her is a huge mystery."

"What happened at the meeting?" I asked.

Pam rubbed her upper arms. "Typical Denise,

really, but something about that day just sent me up the wall. Just because she's the president doesn't mean she has executive privilege to make decisions. She told us—told us!—that from now on the Friends were going to open the used bookstore on Wednesdays and Saturdays and not have it open any other time." Pam's face was a fierce scowl. "No vote, no nothing—just Denise changing the way we've done things for years because she thinks she knows the best way to do things."

That sounded like Denise, all right.

She clutched at her arms, her fingernails digging deep into her sleeves. "No one else said a thing. Denise has them beat down to nothing. I said something like we should have a vote, or at least a general consensus. Denise gave a smirk—you know the one, right?"

I did, and my expression must have shown how much it annoyed me.

Pam nodded. "Yeah, well she gave that smirk and said there already was consensus, and if I didn't like it, that I knew where the door was." She stopped. Smiled a little. "So you know what I did?"

An uneasy feeling crinkled around in my stomach. "Do I really need to know?"

She grinned. "I lit into her the way I've been wanting to do for months. And you know what? It felt great."

"Minnie? Minnie!" A woman was waving from the passenger's window of a dark sedan.

"Surprised to see us?" she asked, laughing. "We're headed to the gallery, if you have a few minutes."

I stared at the mid-fiftyish couple in the car, who were both smiling broadly.

They weren't supposed to be here. They should have been long gone. Why were they still in Michigan?

"Please say you can stop by," the woman said. "We have a lot to tell you."

I bet, I thought grimly. *And I have a thing or two to tell you.*

I turned back to Pam. "Sorry, but I have to go."

"That's okay," she said, smiling. "All I was going to do was complain about Denise, and I'm sure you get enough of that without me."

"Even the most tolerant of people have their breaking points," I said. "And though I understand how you feel about Denise, I hope you'll consider rejoining the Friends someday."

Pam laughed. "Not as long as *she's* there, but you're a sweetie for trying. Anytime you want morning coffee, just let me know and I'll bring an extra mug onto the porch."

She ducked back inside to the warmth of her store, and I hurried the three blocks to my new destination.

By the time I burst in the front door of the

Lakeview Art Gallery, I'd built up a nice head of steaming outrage. I shut the door firmly behind me and faced my good friends Barb and Russell McCade with my hands on my hips and my chin up. Behind them was a middle-aged woman I assumed was the new gallery manager, but introductions would have to wait.

"Why are you still here?" I asked, glaring at the smiling McCades. They were standing next to a large canvas, the back of which was to me. Though I was excited to see the painting, I didn't move. There were things that needed to be said.

I kept glaring. "You promised you'd be gone before the first snowfall. You took solemn vows that you'd be in Arizona before there was any danger of driving on snowy roads. You promised me—"

Russell McCade, known to most as Cade, an internationally famous artist, grinned and turned the painting around. His left hand lost its grip, but Barb caught the painting before it hit the floor. "What do you think?" Cade asked. "Not bad for an old man still recovering from a stroke, yes?"

Oh, yes. I drank in the glorious colors, the uneven brushstrokes, the shapes and images and impressions taking me straight back to the end of summer, to dark blue evenings on the lake, to cool air and the knowledge that winter was coming. It was powerful and beautiful and haunting, and I didn't want to look away.

"Sentimental schlock," Cade said, quoting one of his few critics.

"But well-done sentimental schlock," Barb added, quoting one of his thousands of supporters.

"I couldn't finish this painting in Arizona," Cade said. "I had to work on it here, and I couldn't leave until it was done."

He had a point, and a good one at that. It wouldn't have been easy for him to visualize the greens and blues of summer in northern lower Michigan in the middle of the reds and browns of southern Arizona. Still, there had been a promise made, and I wasn't letting them off the hook that easily.

"You promised," I said, trying not to sound like an eight-year-old. "You said—both of you said—that you'd leave before snow, and if you didn't, you'd call me instead of driving yourselves anywhere. It snowed ten inches barely a week ago, and did I get a phone call? No."

I crossed my arms and waited for their answer. It wasn't long in coming, and it was about what I'd expected.

Cade laughed, and Barb made a noise that sounded suspiciously like a giggle.

"My dear Minnie," Cade said. "I know you've taken a proprietary interest in my health since you and your bookmobile rushed me to the hospital, and there is no question that your rapid response is what helped me recover from the stroke so quickly, but Barb and I aren't exactly elderly. Neither one of us is even sixty."

Barb took her husband's hand. "Besides, we didn't drive anywhere while there was snow on the roads. We just stayed home. I read some of those wonderful books you've recommended, and Cade finished his painting." She nodded at the canvas.

"Plus," Cade said, "our bags are packed and we're headed for the airport the moment we leave here."

I gave a mock sigh. "So you're on the way out of town?"

"Decidedly," Cade said, smiling a little.

I couldn't help it; I started laughing. Last summer the McCades and I had become acquainted over Cade's hospital bed, and it had solidified into a permanent friendship over the use of words that started with the letter *D*. To have him pull one out now was a top-notch use.

"You're incorrigible," I said.

"Are we doing *I* words?" Barb asked. "Because I've always wanted to use the word 'irrefragable' in a sentence."

"You just did," Cade said. He smartly stepped out of the way of her elbow and smiled at me. "How is that fuzzy feline of yours?" Cade and Eddie had become good friends over the past few months, but I finally had to forbid Cade from bringing him any more treats or cat toys until next spring. Even Eddie could only eat and play so much.

"Fuzzier than ever," I assured him.

"You can expect the portrait by Valentine's Day," Cade said. "I'll have it crated and freighted direct to you."

"Oh, wow, you don't have to do that. Really, you don't have to—"

Barb cut into my babbling. "Minnie, dear, hush. We've been through this before, and you're accepting Eddie's portrait. If you don't, Cade will paint *you*."

The threat had been made before and it still sent a shiver of unease down my back.

"Ha," Cade said. "Look at her face. You'd think I did abstract art with a nasty twist, the way she's looking."

"Distraction is in order," Barb said. "Give her the other news."

Grinning, Cade rubbed his hands together. "It's all set, Minnie. The painting the Radles have chosen to donate is scheduled for auction the week after Thanksgiving."

"It . . . is?" After Cade had been involved in a murder case last summer, he'd told the parents of the murder victim that he'd donate a painting to a charity of their choice. And even though the victim hadn't been a patron of the Chilson library, her parents had said her favorite times as a child had been spent in their local library. I hadn't expected the grieving parents to choose a painting until next year, though. "They're still willing to donate the money to the library?"

Cade nodded. "Every cent."

I wanted to thank him, to thank Barb, to thank everyone and everything in the whole wide world, but all I could manage to do was nod.

"Look at her." Cade nudged his wife. "Now, that's a face worth painting."

I tried to smile. Couldn't quite, thanks to the emotions clogging my throat. "You're irredeemable," I managed to say.

"Incurable," he agreed.

"But not irrefragable," Barb said.

We all laughed, and if I wiped away a tear or two, the McCades were polite enough to allow the fiction that it was from the laughter.

Chapter 10

The rest of the weekend flew past with a number of Aunt Frances–directed trips to the grocery store for Thanksgiving preparations, which included a trip to Mary's Kitchen Port in Traverse City for whole nutmeg ("You want me to go where? For what?" "You heard me. Get going.") and an attic search for a box of extra pie plates. There were numerous text exchanges with Tucker, ranging from stilted to friendly to warm, and a Sunday-afternoon phone conversation with Kristen during which I listened to her enthuse about the beach conditions and she listened to me talk about grant possibilities.

Monday was such a busy library day that it wasn't until Tuesday, a bookmobile day, that I had time to wonder whether I really was spending too much time on the bookmobile. Which was high irony, but I wasn't sure Eddie saw any humor in it. Donna didn't, either.

She sat with her feet on either side of Eddie's carrier and pooh-poohed my angst.

"The reason you didn't hear about Pam's hissy fit is because you weren't in the building. You could have been gone for any reason. It didn't have to be the bookmobile."

True, but still. "I should have known."

Donna yawned, stretching. "You really want to know all the goings-on of the Friends? Maybe get a personal monthly update from Denise?"

I blanched at the thought, and Donna laughed. Then we were at our first stop of the day, Moulson Elementary, and things got busy fast.

Moulson was a new stop for us. The school was on the east side of the county, out in the flatter land where potatoes were grown. There were no other bookmobile stops for miles, but it had taken only a single request for me to justify the mileage.

As soon as Donna lowered the steps, a parade of five-year-olds marched out of the building. At the head of the line was Brynn Wilbanks, the little girl who had called with the stop request.

She bounced up the stairs, smiling widely, energy practically oozing out of her skin. "Where's the bookmobile kitty?" she asked. "I said they'd get to meet Eddie."

Recognizing that my place in Brynn's life was secondary to my cat's by far, I bowed and made a grand wave toward the front, where Eddie was sitting like an Egyptian statue on the console.

It had been for the sake of Brynn, whose leukemia was now in remission, that I'd brought Eddie onto the bookmobile after his first stowaway episode. And it had been for Brynn that I'd just rearranged the bookmobile's every-other-Tuesday route to make sure she got her fill of Eddie during the school year.

A young man came up the steps, herding the last of the kids aboard. "Hi. I'm Andrew Burrows. Brynn's teacher." He had a stocky build and such a complicated arrangement of facial hair that it made me wonder if he was trying to hide something. He also looked barely old enough to have graduated from high school, let alone college.

I introduced myself and Donna. Andrew kept a close watch on his small charges as we talked. I knew there were supposed to be fourteen of them, but it was hard to be sure, since they moved around so much. "You'll do a quick introduction?" Andrew asked. "About the book-mobile?"

"Sure," I said. "I'll show them—"

I stopped, because Andrew's polite smile had suddenly turned into an expression of horror. He started to lunge past me. "Brynn! Put him down!"

Before I even turned, I sensed what was happening. "Don't worry," I said. "Brynn and Eddie—"

"See, everybody?" Brynn called. She was grasping Eddie around his middle, his front legs draping stage right, his back legs draping stage left. His head was dangling loosely, and the tip of his tail beat the air lightly. "This is my friend, the bookmobile kitty cat. You can come and pet him if you want, but you have to do it one at a time," she cautioned.

"Brynn," Andrew said in an anguished voice. "Please put the cat down."

The little girl looked up at him with her big brown eyes. "Why?"

I grinned. Eddie, who would send me an if-looks-could-kill expression if I so much as gave him one pat more than he wanted, had always allowed Brynn to toss him around like a stuffed animal. But I also didn't want Mr. Kindergarten Teacher to have a heart attack, so I edged forward around the line of small children that was forming to Brynn's command.

"Sit up here," I told her, patting the console,

"and Eddie can sit right next to you. That way you can keep petting him."

She frowned, obviously considering my statement as a suggestion, then nodded. I took Eddie from her, she jumped up, and I nestled Eddie appropriately.

"This is a good idea." She patted Eddie between the ears, making his head bounce a little. "Okay," she said, pointing to the youngster at the head of the line. "You can pet him first."

I backed away, but not too far away. Eddie had always been beyond tolerant of children, but you never knew, so I made sure I was close by, just in case.

"So that's Eddie," Andrew said.

I laughed. "You've heard stories?"

"Looks like some of them may even be true," he said, making me revise my previous judgment of his humor level. "Once we got this date scheduled, Brynn has talked nonstop about Eddie and the bookmobile and all the fun books and games and music, and did I mention Eddie?"

The first few kids in the line had received their allotment of Eddie and the accompanying Eddie hair. As they came back around, I pointed out the picture books, and Donna showed them the music and the board games we'd started lending at the end of the summer. The whole thing was going smoother than if I'd planned it for a month.

"Look at that," Andrew murmured, nodding at

the way the kids were exclaiming over the books they were pulling off the shelves. "They're excited about reading."

"The Eddie Effect," I said, smiling.

"Or is it the Bookmobile Effect?" Andrew gestured at the kids who were still waiting in line.

Only they weren't just waiting; they were looking at the contents of the shelves, running their hands over the bindings, and pulling books out to take a look. I could already tell that it would take forever to straighten up the bookmobile, but the time would be well worth it. An investment of sorts.

"The Bookmobile Effect," he said again. "Bringing books and the love of reading wherever the road takes you."

I beamed at him. "Would you mind writing that down in letter form and sending it to my boss? Because I'm still having to justify the expense."

Andrew looked around. "Yeah, this can't be cheap, can it? And after what happened the other Saturday . . ." He caught my expression. "Oh. Sorry. You probably didn't need a reminder of that."

Didn't need and didn't want. I put on a smile and changed the subject, but the gleam had gone out of the day.

That evening, my loving aunt met me at the door and handed me a piece of paper as soon as I released Eddie from the carrier.

"We need a few more things for Thanksgiving," she said.

I scanned the lengthy list, then turned over the paper and read the other side. "What are fennel seeds?"

She gave me a look. "Do you really want to know?"

Of course I didn't. I was perfectly happy to be the grocery store–goer, the table setter, and the cleaner-upper. The last thing I wanted was any part of the actual cooking. The one time I'd tried to partake in the annual ritual, back in my graduate school days, when I couldn't afford the gas to drive home, had been a meal of overcooked Cornish game hens and undercooked potatoes.

I pointed at the list. "All I want to know is where to find fennel seeds."

"In with the spices," she said. "Don't be too long—I'm making fajitas for dinner and the chicken is almost done marinating."

After rezipping my coat, I headed back out, thinking for the zillionth time how lucky I was to have Aunt Frances in my life. Someday I'd want to buy my own house, but until I could gather up a nice down payment, there wasn't any likelihood of that happening.

Standing on the bottom step of the porch, the wood creaking a bit underneath my weight, I read the list one more time. It was long, but none of the items was bulky (except for paper towels) or heavy (except for a can of tomato soup), and, since I'd spent most of the day sitting, I eschewed taking the car and went on foot. Without a doubt, I'd regret the decision before I got halfway back, but I pushed that thought out of my head and started walking.

Just outside the grocery store, however, my fast walk slowed to a slow stroll and then to an amble. Denise Slade was getting out of a car not thirty feet away from me. If I used exquisite timing, I could keep my head down while studying the list and avoid eye contact altogether. After all, the last time I'd seen her, she'd said it was my fault that Roger was dead. Why would I want to open myself up to another round of that? Plus, there was the little matter of Roger's sister's lawsuit. I wasn't sure whether Denise was on board with it, but this was one librarian who really didn't want to find out.

It was tempting to avoid her. So tempting that I pulled the list out of my pocket and unfolded it. But then my mother's voice boomed inside my head: "Minnie, don't let me catch you taking the easy way out."

Why her voiced boomed, I wasn't sure, since my mother was a soft-spoken woman who only raised her voice if there was imminent danger of bloodshed. Well, that or if someone happened to mention a dislike of history.

But, once again, Mom was right. Denise was

grieving, and grief could make you lash out at people. I should forgive her and do what I could to help.

Even if I don't want to?

I asked the question of my mom via mental telepathy, which I was pretty sure didn't work.

Especially then, came the answer.

I sighed and put the list back into my pocket. "Hey, Denise," I said. "How are you?"

She jumped. "Oh. Hi, Minnie."

A long moment of silence went by. Just after it got extremely uncomfortable, I asked, "I heard you were in a car accident. That must have been frightening. I'm so sorry."

She nodded slowly. "Thank you."

I looked at her. Denise normally talked at a rate a notch faster than the rest of the world, but right now she was speaking as if she were translating in her head. That, in addition to her unusual politeness, indicated that something was seriously wrong. Of course, it could have been her way of dealing with Roger's death, but this wasn't carrying the sense of grief.

"Are you sure you're okay?" I asked. "You weren't hurt in that crash, were you?"

"Fine," she said vaguely. "I'm fine. It's just . . ."

My baser self, the part of me that deeply wanted to escape into the store, warred with the part of me that remembered my mother's admonitions to treat others as we would like to be treated. For years I'd thought she'd meant that people should be nicer to me, but I'd eventually caught on.

I took a step closer. "Just what?"

Denise looked at me, anguish on her face, and the words she'd been holding inside came rushing out.

"It's that deputy. Wolf-something. He talked to me, said that someone might have been trying to kill me, that someone had done something to my car to make it crash, that you said Roger had my hat when he was killed, that it might have been me who someone wants dead, that Roger . . . that it was me . . . that I should have been the one, not him . . ."

Her sentence dissolved into a racking sob. I stepped close, put my arms around her, and let her hang on to me as she cried and cried and cried.

When her body stopped shaking, I gave her a hard hug and released her. I searched my pockets, came up with a tissue that probably hadn't been used, and held it out.

She took it and blew her nose. "That deputy detective wanted to know if I had any enemies, if anyone was angry at me. Can you believe it?"

Um. "What did you tell him?"

She found a dry part of the tissue and blew again. "That anyone who has lived a full life has enemies. Take Shannon Hirsch. She's hated me for thirty years, ever since I beat her out for the basketball team's cheerleading squad. You wouldn't believe the stunts she's pulled on me since then."

Denise tried to hand back the tissue, but I shook my head. "Anyone else?"

"I told that deputy I'd think about it." She dabbed at her nose. "Don Weller is another one. My neighbor. For months he's done nothing but try to make my life miserable, ever since that fence of his."

It was a big step from high-school rivalries and neighbor irritations to murder. I knew Don through Rafe—Don taught at the school where Rafe was principal—and couldn't imagine that cheerful man wanting to kill anyone. Then again, do we ever know what truly motivates another person?

Denise swallowed and took in a few breaths. "If I was the one supposed to die, if Roger died because of me . . ."

I waited, wishing I could help, knowing there wasn't anything I could do.

"How am I going to tell the kids?" she asked in a whisper, but I had no answer for her. I gave her another hug, told her to call me if she needed anything, and went in to the bright lights of the grocery store.

Inside, I pulled out a small cart and looked back outside.

Denise was still standing on the sidewalk. Just standing and looking at nothing.

"All right, already," I told my mother, and went out again. "Hey, Denise? Do you have a minute? I could use some help with this grocery list. Aunt Frances made it out for me, and I have no idea where half this stuff is." I proffered the crumpled sheet of paper.

She wiped her eyes and took the list. "Fennel seeds? You don't know where fennel seeds are?" She make a clucking noise. "Goodness, you do need help, don't you? Come on. Did you get a cart? No, not that one, it has a wobbly wheel. This one will do." She pushed a cart toward me. "Are you coming or not?"

I gave her a crooked smile. "You bet," I said.

After I'd dried and put away the last fork from dinner, I hung the dish towel on its wooden rod and went to see what Aunt Frances was doing.

I found her sitting on the end of the couch, her long legs out in front of her, a blanket and a book on her lap. I flopped on the couch across from her and tipped my head to see what she was reading. *The First 20 Minutes*, by Gretchen Reynolds.

It was a book on exercise, a very odd choice of reading material for my aunt. As far as I knew, she'd never exercised in her life. She stayed active with housework and gardening and spent a lot of time on her feet, but I couldn't make my brain visualize her in running shorts.

She turned a page. "I like to know what I'm missing," she said. "And from what I've been reading, I'm not missing much."

Personally, I enjoyed working up a sweat every now and then, but I'd once heard Aunt Frances say that perspiration meant you should stop working so hard. I was pretty sure she was joking, but I also wasn't sure I wanted to find out and remove all doubt.

I kicked off my shoes and tucked my short legs up underneath me. "I'm surprised Eddie isn't on your lap."

"He was," Aunt Frances said, "but I think my choice of reading material disturbed him. He abandoned me a few minutes ago."

There was an odd *thump, thump, thump* noise. Frowning, I turned, trying to pinpoint its origin. "What's that?"

Aunt Frances flipped another page. "It started soon after your cat left me, so your guess has to be better than mine." She looked at me over the top of the book. "Do you have a guess?"

We sat there listening to the nonrhythmic thumping. "Not a clue," I said. "Five bucks says it involves paper products."

My friend Rafe and I regularly made five-dollar bets on everything from the price of a cup of coffee in Australia to the date the last bit of ice on Janay Lake melted. And I suddenly realized it had been a while since I'd seen Rafe. Since he was a principal, this often happened when school started, but it was almost Thanksgiving.

"No bet," Aunt Frances said. "I think he's in the bathroom."

Where there were all sorts of paper products available for shredding purposes. And "shred" was indeed the word; Eddie didn't just yank the toilet paper off the holder; he ripped great paper chunks off it all the way down to the core. If there was a newspaper or a magazine handy, he sank his claws into the middle and dragged them out to the edge. And he didn't just claw at the top tissue that poked out of a box; he reached inside with his slinky paws and pulled out as many small pieces of tissue as he could.

Aunt Frances put her book down as I stood. "Why do you think he shreds that stuff?" she asked. "Is he trying to teach you a lesson?"

I snorted. "If he is, the only thing I'm learning is to be grateful that he hasn't started ripping up books."

But as I walked down the hall, getting ever closer to the thumping noise, I wondered. What, exactly, did Eddie get out of clawing and biting apart paper products? Was he sharpening his claws? Was he acting out some kitty aggression?

"Or," I said, walking into the bathroom, "do you just like making a mess?" The large room was painted in periwinkle blue from the waist up and was white beadboard from the waist down. A

Hoosier cabinet held towels and soaps and various Up North memorabilia that the summer boarders had accumulated over the years, but the room's focal point was the biggest claw-foot bathtub I'd ever seen in my life.

Eddie's head popped up over the edge of the tub.

"What are you doing?" I asked.

"Mrr," he said, and dropped back down.

Thump. Thump. Thump.

I eyed the small stack of magazines on the corner of the Hoosier cabinet's counter. All were intact. "What do you have in there?" I walked closer. "Because if you've taken some of those skipping stones from the jar over here, Aunt Frances is going to have your hide. Those things will chip the porcelain something fierce."

As I neared, I realized that the sound was more like a *roll . . . thump . . . roll . . . thump . . . roll.* "Eddie," I said, looking down, "if you're not the weirdest cat on the planet, I don't want to meet any who are weirder."

My furry friend ignored me and continued to thump a rubber ball against the tub. He'd whack it with his paw, sending it rolling across the tub's floor, watch it thump against the tub wall, then watch it roll back toward him.

The small red, white, and blue ball had been a giveaway to kids during Chilson's annual Fourth of July parade, and, until recently, it had been part of the Hoosier cabinet's memorabilia collection.

How a cat could have moved it from the cabinet to the tub was another thing I probably didn't want to know.

Eddie batted the ball one more time, then looked up at me.

"You know," I said, "if you don't pay attention, that ball's going to—"

The ball thumped Eddie in the foot. He jumped high and fast, his tail fluffing up to three times its normal size.

I shook my head, returned to the living room, and reported to Aunt Frances.

"Hmm." My aunt got a faraway look on her face. "That tub. For years I've thought about enclosing it with a beadboard surround. Lots of room for the bubble bath bottles and soaps. Wouldn't that be nice?"

Eddie jumped up onto the couch, the ball in his mouth. "Mrr," he said, dropping the ball onto my lap.

Aunt Frances looked at him. I looked at him.

"Does he want to play fetch?" she asked.

I picked up the ball and tossed it underhanded across the room. It bounced and eventually rolled to a stop in the doorway to the dining room.

Eddie plopped down, his back to me.

"I'm guessing *no* on the fetch thing," I said.

"Mrr," Eddie said.

"Glad I could help," I told him.

"Mrr."

"Anytime."

"Mrr."

"Don't mention it," I said.

"Mrr."

"Not a problem."

"Mrr."

"That's what—"

"Shhh!" Aunt Frances said. "I'm trying to read over here."

"Sorry," I said meekly.

"Mrr," Eddie said quietly.

"Isn't that what I said?" I asked.

"Mrr."

"Well, sure, but—"

With a sigh, Aunt Frances got up. "When you two are done playing Abbott and Costello, let me know. I'll be in the bathtub."

I grinned at Eddie, and I could have sworn he grinned back.

Chapter 11

I was at my desk the next morning, busy with work schedule readjustments of the "I'll work every Saturday in December if I can have the day after Christmas off" variety, when my phone rang.

"Minnie, you need to come upstairs," Stephen said.

I looked at the ceiling. "Okay. When—"

"Now," he barked, and the phone went silent.

"Huh," I said, replacing the receiver. The last Wednesday morning of the month had been the library's board meeting time since there'd been a library. I got along with all the board members and willingly appeared before them when I requested things, from a new copy machine to the book-mobile, but never once had I been summoned.

I slugged back the last of my coffee as I glanced at yesterday's postcard from Kristen. *Key West: shorts, flip-flops, tank top. Chilson: insulated boots, down coat, wool hat, lined mittens. Duh.* Somehow this reminded me to check for Eddie hair. I picked the most visible ones off my clothes and headed upstairs, trying not to guess why my presence was being requested, and not doing a very good job.

Guess number one: They'd found out about Eddie.

Number two: Mitchell Koyne had offended a board member so badly that life as Mitchell knew it was about to end.

Three: Something had gone horribly wrong with the library's roof and we had to lay off half the staff to afford to fix it. *Would you like to be first, Minnie?*

Four: They'd found out about Eddie.

Five: Someone had hacked into the library's bank accounts and stolen all our money.

Six: Someone had hacked into the library's

lending records and was tweeting about who had read *Fifty Shades of Grey.*

Seven: They'd found out about Eddie.

My face was set as I walked into the wood-paneled conference room. I didn't know if it was the lack of natural light or the darkness of the walls or the furnishings, but I was rarely at my best in a space that was so pretentious that it edged into irony.

Stephen had selected a large dark table, black leather chairs with high backs, and, yes, black leather blotters that sat in front of each chair. At the far end sat the white-haired Otis Rahn, the board's current president. Stephen was at his right hand and Sondra Luth, the board's vice president, sat to Otis's left.

The other five board members were strung down along the sides of the table, with no empty chairs between them, making the end closest to me completely vacant. Which was strange, because Stephen usually sat on the end opposite Otis, and the empty chairs were usually randomly spaced.

As I looked at the formal seating arrangement, I got a very bad feeling. "Good morning," I said.

Instead of the smiles and "Good Morning, Minnie" greetings that I normally got in return, I received a series of solemn nods, going from left to right around the table like a tiny library board version of the wave.

"Please take a seat," Otis said, indicating the chair at the opposite end of the table from him.

I didn't want to sit there. I would much rather have sat next to Linda Kopecky, retired high-school English teacher and avid reader of suspense novels, but I followed instructions and pulled out the chair.

Never before had I noticed what a nasty noise the casters made on the thick carpet. It was a soft, squishy noise as horrible in its own way as fingernails on a chalkboard. I sat, grabbed the table's edge to pull myself forward, since my feet didn't quite touch the floor, and folded my hands on the table, making me the ninth person in the room who was doing that.

I kept a pleasant expression stuck on my face, trying to appear the embodiment of the cooperative assistant director. The others shifted, looked at each other, looked at Otis, looked at Stephen, looked at their hands.

My feeling slid from Kind of Bad to Uh-Oh, This Is Going to Be Really Bad.

Stephen broke the silence. "Minerva, you know that the board is well aware of the incident that took place on the bookmobile the Saturday before last."

My first instinct was to correct him—the incident, as he was putting it so delicately, had not taken place on the bookmobile. It had happened nearby. But I kept quiet and didn't nod. I kept my gaze calm and steady. And, since he hadn't posed a question, I didn't say anything.

There was a short pause. When I continued to keep quiet, he went on. "As I told you earlier, Tammy Shelburt, sister to Roger Slade, is bringing suit against the library for negligence."

"She's hired one of the most aggressive law firms in the region," Bruce Medler said. "They have an extremely high rate of success."

I looked at him. Bruce was one of those guys with hair so short, he might as well have been bald. We regularly tried to top each other with bad puns, but just now I didn't feel like telling him that writing with a broken pencil was pointless. And again, since there was no question, I remained silent.

"We've spoken to the library's attorney," Otis said gravely. "One of his recommendations to strengthen the library's case is to accept your resignation."

My skin suddenly felt a size too small for my body. There had to be something I could say to convince them that the advice of their attorney was absurd, but I couldn't come up with a single thing.

Stephen cleared his throat. "I've told the board that the library will not function properly without an assistant director. The position is essential to operations. The board, however, has not yet taken a vote. This is why I called you upstairs."

To what—speak in my own defense? I looked around the table. If eye contact, or lack of it, was an indication of how they'd vote, my chances were about fifty-fifty. I was starting to get an inkling of what sacrificial lambs might have felt like.

Sondra, the vice president, leaned forward. "Another of the attorney's recommendations to strengthen the library's case is the suspension of bookmobile operations until the matter is settled."

I shot to my feet. "No!" As soon as I stood, I knew I'd made a mistake; strong emotions weren't allowed in the boardroom—the wood paneling was supposed to keep them all out. Plus, I was presumed to be a reasonable and rational adult. Leaping out of my chair didn't exactly paint a picture of a reliable assistant director. But it was too late. I was up and needed to make the best of things.

Laying my palms flat on the table, I took in a deep breath and released it. I'd been taught the technique at my self-defense classes and felt my brain click into gear. Which was good, because in many ways, this was self-defense. I was under attack, the bookmobile was under attack, and I needed to be smarter than I'd ever been.

I studied each of their faces, then said, "It speaks well of this board that there is concern regarding the tragic events that led to Roger Slade's death."

Heads nodded, and I nodded back, feeling like a

bobble-head doll that wasn't quite in tune with its fellows.

"The sheriff's office and I have had multiple conversations," I went on, "and they feel that they're close to making an arrest." Of what I felt had to be the wrong person, but now wasn't the time to get into that.

"A careless hunter," Bruce said solemnly.

"They couldn't tell me." I looked around the table. "But there was a discussion regarding the possibility of murder."

A collective intake of breath stole most of the air from the room. Clearly, no one had once thought that Roger's death could have been anything except an accident. *Interesting.*

"But," I said, "there is no reason to punish the bookmobile for any of this. In the days since Roger died, bookmobile attendance hasn't decreased and no one has called to cancel a stop. Matter of fact, I've had a request for an additional stop."

I stood as straight and tall as I could, which wasn't very, but since I was the only one standing, it worked out. "Garaging the bookmobile would deprive our patrons, the people who might need us the most, of access to everything that we offer."

Spreading my arms wide, I gestured at the entire library, at the entire world. "Our mission statement is to provide materials and services to the entire community, not just the people who have the wherewithal to make it to this building." I let my arms fall to my sides, hanging my head just a little. "Keeping our patrons from harm is, without doubt, the most important thing. But please think about how much harm it could do to deprive them of books."

I sat down, already wishing I'd said something different. Of course, I couldn't remember ever getting to use the word "wherewithal" in a sentence, written or spoken, so that was a tiny bonus.

At the other end of the table, the board members and Stephen had a short, whispered conversation. Otis looked down the length of the dark wood. "Minnie, thank you for your time. We'll let you know when we make a decision."

I walked back downstairs, my feet making Eddie-sized thumps on the steps. There was no way I was going to be able to get any work done until I heard from the board, so I grabbed the new ABOS coffee mug I'd picked up at the last Association of Bookmobile and Outreach Services conference and headed to the break room. If the next day hadn't been Thanksgiving, I would have pawed through my desk drawer for change enough to get some chocolate from the vending machine, but maybe coffee would suffice.

Holly was on her way out of the room, but she took one look at my face and backed up. "Are you okay? No, you're not. I can see that something horrible has happened. Sit down. I'll get you some coffee—don't worry, I didn't let Kelsey make it this morning—and you can tell Aunt Holly all about it. Oh, and take a brownie. Josh's mom dropped them off."

I let Aunt Holly take charge, not even objecting when she cut off a huge slab of brownie and put it on a napkin in front of me. "Eat," she commanded. "Then talk."

Three bites later, I started to feel a little less shell-shocked. Two more and I was almost ready to talk. We adjourned to my office so I could be close to my phone, and I told her what had happened upstairs. Well, except the part where I might be forced to resign.

Holly objected in all the right places. "Are they nuts?" she asked, her face a little pink. "The bookmobile is the best thing that's ever happened to this library! Sure, this new building is awesome and everything, but has it changed anyone's life? People who come here were already coming to the library, maybe a few more, but not like the bookmobile. Did you tell them how many new library-card forms you've completed out there?"

I smiled. "You should have talked to the board instead of me."

She shook her head rapidly. "No way. I freeze up something silly if I have to speak in public."

"The board meetings aren't like that," I said.

"It's just a bunch of people sitting around a table."

"And all of them staring at you when you say something. I'll pass, thanks." She gave a mock shudder. "But, hey, I wanted to tell you that I had to give up on Facebook."

Facebook? Why . . . ? Then I remembered. My concerns that Stephen had learned about Eddie felt long ago and far away.

"No matter who or what group I tracked," she said, "I couldn't find anyone who would have liked the same collection of groups Stephen would. So either he's being smarter about this than I would have guessed, or he's just not on Facebook."

"Well, that's good," I said.

"Maybe, maybe not." She pursed her lips. "The way I figure it, he's got to be out there somewhere. Lurking. Spying on us. That's the way he is, right? So he's there, taking notes. I just have to figure out where he is. Twitter might be more his thing."

"Or," I offered, "he might not be on social media at all."

Holly shook her head. "No, I don't see it. It's too big of a chance for him to gather up information."

She was making him sound like a grand spymaster. Stephen had his quirks, and it wouldn't hurt him to attend a few workshops on playing well with others, but he was an excellent library director, and I was starting to feel a little sneaky for, well, sneaking around about him.

"Thanks for doing this, Holly," I said, "but I don't want to take up so much of your time. If Stephen knows about Eddie, there isn't much I can do about it until he decides to tell me." Of course, if the board was going to fire me or keep the bookmobile from running, Stephen wouldn't have to do anything.

I sighed.

Holly, who was a mother and therefore had that supermom sense for noticing the slightest mood anomalies, gave me an empathetic glance. "Yeah, I know. You're worried about what the board is going to say. When they call, let me know, okay?"

My phone rang. For two full rings, I just stared at it. My insides felt tingly and my head felt two sizes too small. When the third ring started, I snatched up the receiver. "Minnie Hamilton," I said. "How may I help you?"

"The board has made a decision," Stephen said.

My mouth's dryness was immediate and absolute. There was no way I was going to be able to say a word until I got some fluid into it. I scrabbled for my coffee mug and took a long gulp. "What did they say?"

"They chose not to take a vote on requesting your resignation, at least for the time being."

"Okay," I said slowly. "What about the bookmobile?"

He let out a sharp breath. "Your point about the possibility of murder pushed that discussion in a completely new direction. The board now feels that if Roger Slade was, in fact, murdered, the library cannot be seen as negligent. We had a short conference call with the library's attorney, and while he isn't in complete agreement, he did agree that the case against the library would be weaker if murder could be proved."

"So, I can keep the bookmobile on the road?"

Stephen barked out something that might have been a laugh. "Is that all you care about—the bookmobile?"

I wanted to say that I cared about a lot of things—world peace, finding a clean source of energy, and discovering a way to walk in the rain without getting mud splatters on my pants—but I was pretty sure Stephen's question was rhetorical.

"The case will first appear in court the second Wednesday in December," Stephen said. "How they got it on the docket so soon, I don't know, but they did. If you care so much about the bookmobile, you'd better solve this situation before then." He banged the phone down.

Slowly, I returned my own receiver back to its cradle.

"What?" Holly demanded. "What did they say?"

The small tent calendar on my desk was on November. I flipped it over to December and counted the days until the second Wednesday of the month. "Two weeks," I murmured. "I have two weeks."

"For what?"

I looked at her, looked at the calendar, then looked back at her. There was only one real answer to her question. "To figure out who killed Roger Slade."

Thanksgiving came and went with a flurry of cooking (Aunt Frances), a massive amount of dishwashing (me), and a stunning show of eating ability on the part of everyone who came for dinner.

Our ten guests included two former boarders who were now married to each other, an elderly couple that Aunt Frances and her long-dead husband had been friends with, a husband and wife and their two children from one street over, and two strays.

My stray was the widowed Lloyd Goodwin, one of my favorite library patrons, whose children couldn't make the trip north this year, and Aunt Frances had invited a man whose name I never did get right. It was Brett, Brent, or Brant, and since he seemed to answer to any of the three, I gave up figuring it out before dinner was ready.

"Where did your stray come from?" I asked Aunt Frances when I popped into the kitchen to check on turkey timing. "He's hot, for an older guy."

And he was, in a white-haired, sturdy-shouldered sort of way. He was also a bit on the pompous side, but since he'd laughed at my jokes, I was trying to forgive that.

"Hardware store," my aunt said. "He kindly helped me see the difference between wood screws and metal screws."

I laughed. "And that turned into an invitation to Thanksgiving dinner?"

"Minnie," my aunt said severely. "No one should have to eat Thanksgiving dinner alone."

An undeniable fact. I grinned at her. "You're a nice person. Did you know?"

"The salt of the earth. Now get out of my kitchen unless you want to carve the turkey."

I couldn't think of much I wanted to do less, so I skedaddled back to our guests until I was summoned for plating duty. At first, Eddie stayed on the stairs, observing through cautious eyes, but he eventually came down to join the fun and shed on everyone that he could.

The rest of the afternoon and evening zoomed past with good food and fine friendship, and I tumbled into bed glad to have been able to forget the library board's dictate, at least for a day.

The next morning I wasn't scheduled to work until afternoon. Tucker had just come off the night shift and finally had some free time, so he picked me up and took me to the Round Table for breakfast, which I hoped would be a place free of cat allergens.

Sabrina, the diner's waitress extraordinaire, sat us in a booth, gave us menus, and poured coffee. "Her," she said, nodding at me. "She'll want cinnamon French toast with real maple syrup and sausage links. What'll you have?"

Tucker opted for coffee and a look at the menu.

"Gotcha." Sabrina wrote down the order and started to tuck her pencil into her bun of graying brown hair.

"Hey!" I pointed to one particular finger on her left hand. "Is that what I think it is?"

The cool, collected, and seen-everything-at-least-once-and-probably-twice Sabrina blushed. "No one else has noticed," she said.

We both looked to the back of the restaurant, where Bill D'Arcy sat hunched over a computer, as per usual. But there was one difference. His left hand, which was busy with typing away at the financial transactions that made him scads of money, caught the restaurant's light and displayed a shiny wide gold band on his ring finger.

"Had all the paperwork set," she said. "We were at my sister's for dinner yesterday, and the only thing I had to do was make sure the minister showed up at halftime."

I laughed, and Tucker congratulated her.

"Thanks, hon," she said, beaming. "Now, how

long do you think it'll take me to get rid of those awful brown curtains he has?"

Fifteen minutes was my guess, which pleased her, and she headed off with a smile on her face.

Tucker was giving me a quizzical look. "What?" I asked.

"Just now," he said. "That's the first time you laughed since I picked you up. You usually laugh a lot more often. Is something wrong?"

His expression of caring concern made my throat close up tight. I swallowed some coffee to loosen it up, then said, "The library board met yesterday. I was called upstairs half an hour after they started." My throat felt weird again, so I preempted its closing by sipping more coffee. When in doubt, add caffeine.

"What did they want?" Tucker asked. "Is there some problem?"

"The board is worried about a negligence lawsuit." I swallowed again. "Some of them think they might have a better case if they fire their assistant dir—"

A man walked past and a slight breeze blew over my arm and lifted a cat hair off my sleeve. The black-and-white piece of former Eddie wafted up into the air, where it turned lazily about, as if it were searching for the perfect new home.

"Umm . . ." Tucker flattened himself against the back of the booth.

The breeze faded as quickly as it had come, and

the hair dropped like a rock, heading straight for my boyfriend's lap. Sliding fast, Tucker zipped to the booth's far end, and the Eddie hair fell to the floor.

"Safe," I said, smiling. But there was no answering grin on Tucker's face. On the contrary, he was frowning in the direction of the stray hair. "And this," I said, "was supposed to be a cat hair–free zone. It's this fleecy material." I poked at my sleeve. "It's a pet-hair magnet. I promise I'll never wear anything like this around you again."

Tucker nodded. "Probably a good idea."

That was unfortunate, because I'd been joking. Fleece sweatshirts were the primary component of my wintertime casual wardrobe. If I couldn't wear fleece around the allergic Tucker, I'd have to go out and buy new clothes, which wasn't part of my budget.

I wrapped my hands around my coffee mug. "Our relationship was a lot easier in the summer, back when I wasn't wearing clothes that attract so much Eddie hair." I laughed.

Tucker didn't. His attention was still on the threat that had come so near. "Yeah," he said, "it was, wasn't it?" Then he shook his head and sat up. "But you were talking about the library board. Someone was negligent?"

He hadn't been listening to me. Or listening, but not hearing. A sinking sensation manifested itself somewhere in my insides, halfway between my heart and my stomach. It was a feeling I'd had a few times before in my life: the one that came just before heartbreak.

"Minnie?" Tucker asked.

I gave him a quick smile and returned to the saga of the library board. But as I talked, all I was really thinking was one thing.

The end is near.

Chapter 12

Tucker didn't break up with me during breakfast, but when he dropped me off at the boardinghouse, there wasn't any happy hug, either, even though the offensive fleece was covered up by my winter coat.

I dawdled away the rest of the morning by doing some online Christmas shopping, concluding that my engineer father might actually like the three-dimensional map of Janay Lake, and that even though my nieces and nephew might want the newest version of the latest video game *(So real, you get motion sickness!)*, they weren't going to get it from me.

After a lunch of leftovers and a short game of Bounce the Ball in the Bathtub with Eddie, I changed into library clothes and headed out.

The day was partly sunny, partly cloudy, the

kind of weather that had you zipping and unzipping your coat as clouds passed over the sun. I was in unzip mode, my face turned up to the radiating warmth that might not be back until April, as I turned the last corner. My thoughts were wandering from the bookmobile to Tucker to Eddie to the library board and back around to the bookmobile. Since I was so busy thinking, I didn't notice that the library's door was opening until it banged into me.

"Oh, goodness, I'm so sorry!" A woman exclaimed. "I didn't hurt you, did I?" She readjusted the bag of books she was carrying.

"Not your fault. I'm the one who wasn't paying attention." I looked at the woman and burrowed through my brain for her name. *Blond. A little older than me . . . got it.*

"Thanks for not running into me, Allison."

She smiled, said, "Have a nice day," and walked toward the parking lot.

I stood, sort of watching her climb into a silver sedan that looked expensively new, but mostly enjoying the sunshine. But then a cloud moved over the sun and the temperature plummeted, so I went inside.

Where Denise Slade was standing in the entryway, arms folded and frowning. But not at me; at Allison Korthase.

"Are you okay?" I asked.

Denise's frown went deeper. "For a new member

of the city council," she said, "that woman could stand to learn some manners."

I'd been the one who hadn't been paying attention to where I going; it hadn't been Allison's fault at all. But there was no way Denise was going to listen to me so I said, "I didn't realize you knew her."

Denise made a rude noise. "This is Chilson. There's maybe half a degree of separation between everyone in town. Of course I know her."

I murmured something noncommittal and marginally polite, and started moving away. But Denise wasn't ready for me to leave.

"Everybody says she's so nice. Ha." Denise sniffed. "That woman doesn't know the meaning of the word 'nice.' And she hates cats. Says she's allergic, but I think she just hates them, and how can you trust someone who doesn't like cats?"

I didn't see the connection between cats and trust, but decided not to ask for an explanation.

"You know what she's really like?" Denise pointed her chin in the direction of Allison's brake lights. "She's cheap. That fancy car? Her brother-in-law runs a car dealership downstate. He gives her a deal, so she leaves town to buy her cars."

It actually sounded pretty sensible to me, and I didn't even have a brother-in-law.

"And she's always first to our book sales." Denise folded her arms even tighter. "She wants to look at the new arrivals, just to make sure she gets ahead of everyone else."

This was getting deep into the Gossip Zone, a place my mother had warned me about. I smiled and started edging into the building. "Sounds like you should try to recruit Allison to the Friends of the Library."

"Her?" Denise rolled her eyes. "Not in a million years. She always thinks she knows the best way to do things. One of those people who never listens to anyone and thinks she's the center of the universe, if you know what I mean."

I nodded in solemn agreement, but Denise wasn't waiting for my response.

"We're down a member, thanks to Pam Fazio's hissy fit, but we're not desperate enough to ask Allison Korthase to join. Not now, not ever."

Another mental note got jotted down, this one to ask around about the history between Denise and Allison. "I saw Pam the other day," I said. "I hadn't realized she'd quit the Friends."

"Really?" Denise narrowed her eyes. "How could you not have known? I thought everyone would be talking about it."

The unhappy twist of her countenance reminded me of my mother's statement that if I made a face often enough, it would freeze that way. "Well, I—"

"I can't believe you didn't know." She shook her head in exasperation. "So, you never heard what she said?"

"About what?"

Denise put her hands on her hips. "What she said to me! She went into a tailspin about something—I don't even remember now what it was. She stomped to the door and said, 'Don't bother asking me back. I won't be back, not unless you die and someone else gets to be president.' Then she whipped around and left." Denise snorted. "Like I'd ever ask her to come back. Pam was more trouble than she was worth, always arguing about every little decision. I mean, honestly, how could anyone care so much about the hours the used bookstore is open?"

There was a pause, which I realized meant she wanted me to agree with her. Off in the distance, the courthouse's tower clock chimed the hour. *Saved by the bell.* I nodded in its direction. "Sorry, Denise, but I'm scheduled to start work right now. Hope you had a good Thanksgiving."

My parting sentence had been a social sentiment said without thought, and I wanted to kick myself when I saw the darkness fall across her face.

Of course she hadn't had a good Thanksgiving. Her husband was dead and the day must have been an endurance test beyond all measure. I'd heard the family had chosen to have a private funeral the day before Thanksgiving, with a memorial service next summer. And now Christmas was coming, with all its enforced cheer. The prospect must have been horrific to her.

So I stepped back to her side and gave her a fast, hard hug.

"Thanks," she whispered, then coughed and pulled away. "I wanted it to be a nice day." She looked at me and half smiled. "But it was pretty horrible."

I tried to think of something to say, but there was really only one thing. "I'm sorry."

The smile stayed on her face. "You'd better get going. I don't want Stephen marking you tardy."

When I reached the door, when I had it half open, I paused, not wanting to look back, but knowing I should. If I looked back, if she was still standing there, if she still had that half smile stuck on as if it were painted on, I'd have to go back and do what I could to help.

But she was gone.

I'd barely had time to bring my office's computer to life when the phone rang. "Good afternoon. This is Minnie Hamilton. How may I help you?"

"I think you've helped me quite enough already," a male voice growled.

It was a familiar voice, but not familiar enough for me to identify the speaker. I hated when people did that. "Excuse me," I said, "but I didn't catch your name."

He coughed directly into my ear, and I hoped no one else used his phone, as the cough sounded horrible.

"Detective Inwood," the detective said, sounding more like himself. "Am I correct in saying that you sent Mitchell Koyne to my office?"

I sat back, grinning, and crossed my ankles. "Mitchell said he had information about Roger Slade. I thought the investigating detective should have all possible information about a murder victim."

"It's not necessarily murder," he said stiffly. "There's still a strong possibility of accidental death." I snorted, but he ignored me. "Besides," he said, "having a list of Mr. Slade's third-grade classmates isn't intrinsically useful to the case."

"No?" I asked, though I was thinking *Too bad. That's what you get for being so hard on Ash Wolverson, you big bully.*

"No," he said, "and I'm quite sure you knew that."

"All information can be useful," I said in my librarian voice. "It's just a matter of finding the correct application."

"I see what you mean," the detective said, sounding entirely unconvinced. "And do you have any more information?"

From the tone of his voice, it was easy to tell that he didn't want to hear anything I had to say. "Since you asked," I said, "there is one thing." His sigh was sadly audible. The man really needed to work on his people skills.

"Go ahead," he told me. "I'm all agog with anticipation."

I almost laughed, but caught myself just in time. "Detective, if you don't want to listen, all you have to do is say so." I heard a snort, but couldn't decide if it was sarcastic, humorous, or illness derived.

"As you said, Ms. Hamilton, all information can be important. I just hope you don't have as many pages as Mr. Koyne did."

While it was tempting to say "more," just to hear his reaction, I merely told him about Pam Fazio, about her abrupt and angry departure from the Friends, and about her parting shot, which could be considered a threat.

Detective Inwood listened, then said, "Thank you, Ms. Hamilton. We'll continue to pursue the investigation until all avenues are exhausted."

I wasn't sure how an avenue could get tired, but decided against criticizing his metaphor. "There's another thing."

"Sorry, Ms. Hamilton. You mentioned one point of information, not two."

My eyes opened wide. "Oh. Uh . . ."

The detective laughed. "Got you. Now, what were you saying?"

So, the law enforcement officer actually had a sense of humor. Who knew? "The other day, Denise rattled off the names of people she said might be considered enemies. I just wanted to make sure she'd told you, too."

"She did indeed," Inwood said, his voice dry as

every cake I'd ever made. "She gave us the name of a local attorney, a middle-school teacher, a retail-store owner, and the director of a nonprofit organization."

"They don't sound exactly like prime candidates for murder, do they?"

"Ms. Hamilton," he said tiredly, "in my experience, absolutely anyone can commit murder."

As I hung up the phone, his words echoed around inside my head. *Anyone can commit murder.*

By midafternoon, the thick clouds had all blown off and it was suddenly a clear and beautiful day.

The library was nearly deserted on this day after a holiday, Stephen was out of town, and I'd worked so many unpaid library hours the past two weeks that I found it easy enough to turn off any guilt my mother could inflict on me from afar.

I slipped on my coat and stopped by the front desk to tell Kelsey I'd be back in an hour.

"Sounds good," she said vaguely, turning a page of the book she was reading.

A different assistant library director might have smacked down any employee caught reading during working hours, saying that there were always things to do, but I had no problem letting people catch their breath on quiet days, which were few and far between.

I walked through and past downtown to the area

where buildings that had been residences in the days of yore were now renovated into professional buildings. Doctors, dentists, engineers, and there, in a white clapboard house with a widow's walk up top, was the attorney's office I was aiming for.

A small brass plate on the red front door told me I was about to enter the law offices of Powell, Hirsh, and Carter. Inside, the hardwood floor was covered with patterned carpets that I hoped could tolerate the sidewalk salt that people would soon start to track inside.

"May I help you?"

A woman with short dark hair, a sheaf of papers in her hand, and a pair of reading glasses on her head was giving me a polite, questioning look.

"I wasn't sure you'd be open today," I said.

"Technically, we aren't." She laughed, hefting the papers. "But there's work to do and it's always quiet on this day, so I figured I might as well get a head start on next week."

A number of tiny clues were piling up, from her age to her air of ownership, so I went ahead and asked, "Are you Shannon Hirsh?" Although Denise had claimed Shannon to be manipulative and full of hate, the woman seemed nice enough.

"Every day," she said cheerfully. "And you are?"

I introduced myself, and started in with the spiel I'd manufactured on my walk over. "I've been thinking about setting up a will. I don't have any dependents and hardly any assets"—while

Eddie was priceless to me, I was pretty sure the appraisal professionals out there wouldn't put a proper value on him—"but I figure it's worth doing, no matter what."

Shannon nodded, her dark hair bobbing with her. "Always a good idea to have your estate in order."

"I hadn't thought about it much before," I said, "but Roger Slade's death really got me thinking. Such a shame, and such a shock, too."

"He was an extremely nice man." Shannon put the papers down and studied me closely. "Minnie Hamilton. From the library. You're the one who—"

"Yes," I said quickly. "Like I said, it was a shock."

"I imagine." She gave a sad smile. "Or, rather, I don't want to imagine."

"It's not as if I knew him very well," I said, watching her closely, "but I feel . . . somewhat responsible."

"For what?" She raised her eyebrows. "For some moron's stupidity? How can that possibly be your fault?"

"It was because of me that he was there at all," I said. "If it hadn't been for me, if it hadn't been for the bookmobile, he would never have been there in the first place." And no matter what, I couldn't get away from that awful truth. Deep down, no matter what I said to people and no matter what people said to me, I knew I was partially responsible.

Shannon snorted. "Come on back. Let me show you something."

She led me through a rabbit's warren of hallways, conference rooms, and offices to the back of the building, where the windows of her corner office looked out over a backyard that was well tended, even in late November. The office was a typical attorney's office: a few restrained prints of flowers, lots of files, three-ring binders, books, and . . . trophies?

"Take a close look," she said, waving toward the crowded shelf.

Curious, I squinted at the tiny lettering engraved into the brass plate of a trophy so tall, it was scratching the underside of the shelf above. When I saw what the award was for, I stood bolt upright and stared at her. "Are these all . . . ?" I gestured at the rest of the shelf.

She shrugged. "I don't really care about them anymore, but they make you take them. I started winning when I was just out of high school. The bug caught me and I'm still shooting."

And, apparently, still winning. I glanced at the date on the plaque in front of me. Just this summer, Shannon had won first place for a shooting award in Fort Gratiot, Michigan. The trophy to its right proclaimed that last year she'd won third place in a national competition in Colorado.

She tapped a tall trophy. "So, you can see, when I say it's not your fault, I know what I'm talking about. No hunter worthy of the name would ever shoot someone accidentally, not like poor Roger was shot."

I disagreed about the fault thing, but she was entitled to her opinion, even if it was wrong.

"Roger was far too nice a guy for Denise," Shannon said, sitting on the edge of her desk, next to the framed pictures of people I assumed were her husband and children. "No idea what he ever saw in her—she's been a pain in the you-know-what since she was born—but it's a shame what happened." She sighed. "No one deserves that, not even Denise. And certainly not Roger."

"Someone told me," I said, "that you and Denise were big rivals in high school."

She smiled. "A more accurate assessment would be that Denise hated me. If I said it was because I beat her out for first-chair flute in sixth grade, would you believe me?"

"Yes," I said promptly.

Shannon laughed. "So you know Denise. You'd have thought she'd have been satisfied after she made the basketball's cheerleading squad and I didn't, but no, she's kept up this silly rivalry for years. The only reason she went after Roger in the first place was because he took me to prom."

I blinked. No one had told me that.

"All these years later," Shannon was saying,

"and Denise still wants to one-up me any chance she gets. You'd think she'd have let that high-school attitude go by now, but she hasn't grown out of it."

It seemed odd to me, but then, I found lots of things odd. The duck-billed platypus, for one. Blue cheese for another. And then there was the oddity of a black-and-white tabby cat who liked to tell me exactly what he thought.

"Of course," Shannon said, laughing, "the feeling is mutual. I never miss an opportunity to one-up her, either. Not that I get many chances these days, but if I see them, I take them." Her grin faded. "Well, maybe I'd pass if I saw one right now. Poor Roger," she said, sighing, and I wasn't sure whether she was talking about his death or his life of being married to Denise.

I took a stab in the dark. "Do you know of any history between Denise and Allison Korthase?"

Shannon's eyebrows drew together. "My guess would be something about downtown. Allison's on the Chamber of Commerce board and Denise always has suggestions," she said, smiling tightly. "Now." She slipped down into her office chair. "Let's talk about your will."

I sat in one of her upholstered chairs, because it would be a good idea to get my affairs in order. Adults did that kind of thing, and I was trying to be adultlike, at least most of the time.

But it was hard to concentrate on my short list of

assets when I was thinking about so many other things. About rivalries, about marksmanship, and about what my attorney uncle had once told me—that good trial attorneys were also good actors.

The next morning, Eddie, the bookmobile, and I ventured forth under a sky streaked with clouds of red and gray and a slightly creepy shade of dark blue, and pulled up to a tidy ranch house just outside of Chilson. Eddie looked up at me.

"Sorry," I said, "this isn't a stop. We're waiting for today's volunteer."

At least I hoped we were. If she didn't show up, Eddie and I would be forced to turn around, and I'd have to make the dreaded phone calls canceling the day's stops.

I watched the house, wondering if I should go to the door and knock, was tempted to honk the ultraloud horn but knew I shouldn't, when the side door opened and Kelsey came rushing out, her hands and arms filled with packages. I opened the bookmobile's door, and she came up the stairs, breathing hard.

"Thanks. Sorry I'm late, but my mom didn't show up until a couple of minutes ago, and I had to get her settled with the kids."

I showed her where to stow her belongings, which seemed to be primarily food items, and we were under way before Eddie got in more than three complaints.

"This is going to be so much fun," Kelsey said, reaching forward to scratch Eddie's head through his carrier's wire door. "I'm glad you let me ride along."

Let her? I'd almost wept with gratitude when she'd said she wanted to go. I absolutely had to find some real volunteers. Using the library staff on their days off wasn't a good policy in many ways.

"I brought all sorts of stuff," Kelsey was saying. "I wasn't sure what you liked to eat for snacks, so I packed apples and crackers and cheese and grapes and yogurt." Her voice dropped to a whisper. "And don't tell my kids, but I brought potato chips and dip for this afternoon."

There were definite advantages to having the mother of small children as your volunteer. I didn't want to tell Kelsey that normally we didn't bother to eat snacks on the bookmobile—it wouldn't do to appear ungrateful—so I thanked her and started talking about the day's events.

"Our first two stops are home deliveries. After that we have a school stop, a church stop, a stop for lunch, and two township hall stops."

Ten minutes later, we were at Mrs. Salvator's house, which had a nice, short driveway. I told Kelsey she could make the first delivery. "There's just one thing," I cautioned. "It's easy to get chatting, and ten minutes is all we've scheduled for this stop."

"Got it, Chief." Kelsey saluted me, zipped up her coat, and picked up the plastic bag I'd stuffed with books the day before and labeled with the woman's last name. "I'll be back in plenty of time."

As I watched her knock on the door, then go inside, as per Mrs. Salvator's instructions, I eyed Eddie. "Think she'll make it?"

He yawned, flattening his ears and showing sharp white teeth.

"I agree. That's why the stop is really scheduled for twenty minutes."

"Mrr," Eddie said, which I took as cat applause for my outstanding management skills.

Sure enough, Kelsey came trotting out of the house a little more than fifteen minutes after she'd gone in. "Sorry," she gasped. "But she was telling me all about this book she'd just finished, and I didn't want to walk out on her, you know?"

I did. And that was why I'd made the home-delivery stops twice as long as I'd originally planned. It wasn't as efficient, but we were providing something more than books.

The next home stop had a long, narrow, and hilly driveway. I eyed it, considered my bookmobile-backing skills, and decided to walk up. "I'll take this one," I said.

"Does Eddie get snack time?" Kelsey asked.

I pointed to the cabinet I'd recently stocked. "Top shelf. But don't give him too many. He's prone to carsickness if he eats too much."

"This handsome cat?" Kelsey leaned down to look in the carrier. "Carsick?"

"Mrr," Eddie said.

I ignored him and headed out.

Halfway up the gravel drive, the plastic bags had become heavy enough to make my fingers cramp. "More things they didn't talk about in college," I muttered as I tromped up the back steps of Barton Raftery's fieldstone house. Then again, in college they hadn't told me how much fun it would be to run a bookmobile outreach program, so I decided to call it a draw.

I opened the back door and stuck my head inside. "Knock, knock," I called.

"Come on in," came Barton's voice.

"Shoes off?" I asked.

"Only if they're dirty," he said.

I picked up one foot and eyed the sole of my light boot. Not visibly dirt encrusted, but better to be safe than sorry. I kicked them off and padded to the living room.

"Minnie," Barton said from his recliner. "You are a sight for sore eyes."

Barton, in his mid-seventies, with a shock of white hair and a broad build, was a regular at the library. Every week he checked out a stack of books—heavy on the thrillers, with a smattering of literary fiction and religious history—and only hip-replacement surgery had kept him away.

"It's not me you want," I said, emptying the bags

onto the coffee table, "so much as these books."

"Now, now," he said, reaching for a Daniel Silva novel, "a pretty girl makes anything better."

I handed him a copy of the latest release from Stuart Woods. "Brand-new. You're the first one to read it."

"Ahh, you know how to treat a man right. I tell you what, when I'm all healthy, I'll come out with you on the bookmobile. See if my wife gets jealous."

I smiled, but it must not have been very convincing, because Barton said, "Hey, now. What's the matter?"

One glance at my watch told me I didn't have time to tell the whole story of the library board's intentions regarding the bookmobile, even if I wanted to, which I didn't, but Barton was a nice man and deserved a response, so I said, "I'm still a little upset over Roger Slade."

Barton gave me a look. "Couldn't have been easy," he said. "Finding him and all."

"No, it wasn't."

We shared a short silence, while I thought about Roger and Denise and responsibility and blame and motivations and possibilities too wretched to think about.

"Want to hear a story?" Barton asked. "And it's not about that witchy Denise, either."

Of course I wanted to hear a story. Didn't everyone? "Sure."

He nodded at me to sit down, so I perched on the edge of the coffee table. "Let me tell you something about Roger," Barton said. "A demon behind the wheel of a car, that one. Did you know that he totaled three cars one summer?"

My chin dropped. "Roger Slade?"

"A Ford Mustang, a Pontiac LeMans, and a beat up old Firebird." He sighed. "Too bad about that Mustang. It was a beauty."

Roger had been a speed demon? That didn't sit right with anything I knew about him. Maybe he wasn't the nice guy everyone thought he was. Maybe he had hidden depths that he would have gone to great lengths to hide. Maybe, in spite of the hat, Denise wasn't the intended target. Maybe—

"Then again," Barton said, "with some work, that LeMans could have been a show car. Can't believe his dad let him drive it in the first place."

His dad? I squinted at Barton. "When did this happen?"

He furrowed his brow and stared at the ceiling. "Nineteen seventy-eight? Or was it 'seventy-nine? One of those."

I'd been listening to a tale about Roger's youthful indiscretions. "Nice story, Barton," I said, standing, "but I don't see what it has to do with Roger's death."

"Not a thing," he said, frowning. "What made you think it might?"

"I'll be back in three weeks for the books," I said.

And I would be, whether it was by bookmobile or, if the worst happened, in my own little car, because even if I lost the bookmobile and my job, I would still make sure the books were returned to the library.

At the end of the day, I dropped Kelsey at her house with most of the snack packaging empty. "See you on Monday, Eddie," she said, making kissy noises at him. "You, too, Minnie," she said, and grinned, as I ducked away from any kiss she might send my way. "Any snack requests?"

"You don't have to bring any," I said half-heartedly. "Really, you don't."

"Do you like Rice Krispies treats?" she asked.

"Well . . ."

She laughed and waved good-bye. "Have a good weekend."

When she was gone, I dropped the transmission back into drive and off we went.

"What do you think?" I asked Eddie. "Is Kelsey ready to quit working at the library so she can be a bookmobile volunteer?"

Eddie kept quiet.

"No opinion?" I asked. "Really? The world must be ending."

Eddie rolled over, clearly not finding me amusing.

Cats.

But I kept quiet, too, on the way back to the library, and didn't say a word as I finished the bookmobile cleanup and transferred Eddie back to my car. I was thinking dark, dreary, and depressing thoughts about the likelihood of finding Roger's killer, about the end of the bookmobile, about the end of my job, and about the prospects of ever finding another job that I liked as much as this one.

So when I saw Denise Slade leave the library and walk toward the parking lot, I was more than ready to quit with the depressing stuff and find some answers.

"Denise?" I called. "Hang on a minute, will you?"

Her sigh was visible from fifty feet away, but she waited. "What do you want?" she asked when I got close enough to see the whites of her eyes.

"I heard a story today about Roger that I find hard to believe. About the summer he totaled three cars. Is that right?"

"Right after he learned to drive." She rolled her eyes. "My dad almost didn't let me go out with him because of it. The guys at school called him Triple for months. But from then on, he didn't get a single ticket, not even for parking."

"The other day," I said, "when Allison Korthase was walking out, you didn't have a good word to say about her. I just wondered why. She seems nice enough."

Denise sighed. "Not that it's any of your business, but we don't see eye to eye on politics." The sigh turned into a glare. "Why are you being so nosy, anyway? If you don't have enough to do, you should help out with the Friends more. When was the last time you spent any time in the sale room? Or signed up to work any of our fund-raisers? From the amount of time you spend on the Friends, it seems like you want us to disappear."

Recent widow or not, I needed to straighten things out with this woman. "That's not true, and you, of all people, should know it. You're the one who wanted the library staff to step back from the Friends operations, and you're the one who requested that the Friends be independent from the official library functions. How can you possibly blame me for not involving myself?"

"If you really cared about the Friends, you'd find ways to help." She spun on her heel and marched away.

This time, I let her go.

I also added Allison Korthase to the list of suspects. Politics? Please. Whatever the real reason for their enmity, the fact that Denise didn't want to talk about it was itself suspect.

The list of possible killers was starting to grow, but if I added everyone who'd had a fight with

Denise, I'd have to add myself. It was becoming clear that a lot of people had developed, and possibly even nurtured, a long-term hatred of Denise.

The problem wasn't going to be finding suspects; it was going to be narrowing the field down to one.

Chapter 13

On Sunday morning, after I spent Saturday night intermittently texting with Tucker—who was, of course, busy at the hospital—and to Kristen, who was tending an extremely busy bar in warm Key West, Aunt Frances filled me with stuffed French toast, slightly crispy bacon, and apple slices. Then, when I'd finished the dishes, she told me to go outside and play.

I looked at her. "How about Eddie? Are you going to kick him out into the cold, too?" Outside the kitchen window was a stiff north wind and scattered clouds that had the look of snow.

Aunt Frances smiled. "Eddie and I are going to start our Christmas lists, aren't we?"

My cat, who was sitting up tall on the seat of a chair, rearranged his feet a little and wrapped his tail around himself. "Mrr."

"You know," I said, "all his list is going to be is cat treats, cat toys, and fancy cat food."

"Then we'll have plenty of time for watching reruns of *Trock's Troubles*." She patted Eddie on the head, and he leaned into her, purring.

Those two were clearly ready for a day on the couch. Well, Eddie almost always was, but Aunt Frances was rarely off her feet for that long, and she deserved a quiet day, if that was what she wanted.

"I'll have my phone," I said, "if there's anything you want."

Ever so nicely, she shooed me away. "Get out of here, youngster. Do I have to count to three? One . . . two . . ."

Laughing, I went to the front closet for my coat, and pulled my wallet and cell from my backpack, which was hanging on a hook. "Are you sure you don't need anything?" I called to the living room.

"Git!"

"Mrr!"

Outside, the crisp air stung the inside of my nose and sharpened my eyesight. I breathed in the scent of winter and smiled. Aunt Frances, in her infinite wisdom, had known I needed to get outside. How she'd known, I wasn't sure, since I hadn't realized it myself, but that's why she was the best aunt in the world.

As I walked, thinking about this and that, I nodded and exchanged good-mornings with a woman walking her dogs, a middle-aged couple dressed in church clothes, and a skinny young man out running.

Though I thought I was walking with no particular destination in mind, I soon realized that my feet were taking me to the marina. This time of year, the marina was shut down and deserted, except for the ubiquitous seagulls. Which meant if I wanted to talk to anyone, there was only one person possible.

I picked my way carefully up the front steps of the house next to the marina and knocked on Rafe's door. The steps had been sturdy and fully functional the last time I'd been up them, but with Rafe, you never knew. A project that looked fine to 99.99 percent of the people in the known universe could have a teensy-tiny flaw that would make Rafe shake his head and rip the thing apart.

When Rafe finally finished renovating his house, it would be the most beautiful home in Chilson, but the end date kept moving farther and farther away. After three years of work, he'd managed to wrangle an occupancy permit, but it wasn't the kind of occupancy most people would be interested in.

I made a perfunctory knock on the front door, a heavy thing of oak and leaded glass, and went in. "Hey, are you home?"

"Minnie, you are the answer to my prayers."

I looked in the direction of his voice, which had

come down the wide, stripped-down wood stairs. "What were you praying for, exactly?"

"Someone to bring me another tube of caulk. There's a box in the kitchen."

If you could call it a kitchen. How he'd convinced any inspector to sign off on a house whose kitchen possessed only a utility sink, electricity for a refrigerator, and a series of milk crates for storage, I would never know.

I tromped through the bare studs in the living room and dining room and into the mess. "Had to be a man," I said, still thinking about the inspector. I took two caulk tubes from the box and made my way up the stairs.

Rafe was in a back bedroom. Then again, it might have been the master suite's sitting room. With so many walls gone, moved, or stripped to the studs, it was hard to tell. He'd shown me the blueprints dozens of times, but he'd also made so many changes on the fly that I was pretty sure the house bore little resemblance to the original plans.

I waved the tubes around. "I brought two, just in case. Where do you want them?"

"Anywhere," he said, grunting a little with effort, "just so I won't step on the buggers."

The grunts weren't surprising, because he was standing on a short stepladder, just past the DON'T STEP ON OR ABOVE THIS LEVEL step, trying to caulk a window frame and maintain his balance at the same time.

"You know," I said, "if you went downstairs to the kitchen, got the properly sized ladder, and brought it up here, you wouldn't be running the risk of falling and breaking your neck."

"Risk is my middle name," he said, putting on a deep, gravelly voice.

I snorted, because I knew for a fact it was Theodore. "You probably don't carry your cell in case of an accident, do you? I bet it's in that dusty mess you call a bedroom."

He popped the empty caulk tube out of the gun and held out his hand for a fresh one. "Did you stop by just to give me a hard time, or do you have another, even more nefarious purpose?"

I watched as he took a utility knife from his tool belt and sliced off the tube's plastic tip. Sitting down on a stack of lumber, I said, "I brought cookies." The smell of Cookie Tom's wafting through town had compelled me to buy half a dozen coconut chocolate chips.

He grinned, pointing the loaded caulk gun at the ceiling. "That was my second prayer, you know."

I watched him bead out the caulk in a smooth line. "Is there anything you want me to do?"

"Entertain me. My iPod ran out of juice ten minutes ago."

"How about if I ask you some questions?" Except for his college years, Rafe had lived in Chilson all his life, and if he didn't know everything about everyone in town, it meant someone had only recently moved in.

"My wallet's downstairs next to last night's pizza box," he said. "But I know there's at least two fives in there." Rafe and I had a long history of making five-dollar bets, and one of these days I was going to have to start keeping track of who won most often. Rafe assured me that he had, but since he had memory issues with anything that didn't concern his school or major-league baseball, I wasn't about to take his word for it.

"Different kind of questions," I said.

"Fire away."

The caulk gun clicked as he kept an even bead flowing, and I reflected on how many references we used on a daily basis that had to do with firearms and weaponry.

"Don Weller still teaches at your school, right?" Don was a neighbor to Denise. On his list, Mitchell had noted Don as Roger's neighbor and a sixth-grade teacher, and he was a man Denise had named as an enemy.

"Sure," Rafe said. "Good guy, even if he does cheer for the Green Bay Packers."

"Do you know what Denise Slade has against him?"

"Yup."

I waited. Waited some more. I decided against picking up the circular saw and cutting off the legs of the ladder. "Are you going to tell me?" I asked, spacing out the words.

"Do I get a cookie first?"

"No."

He sighed and moved to the other side of the window frame. "It's typical Denise stuff. He'd put up a few extra sections of fence on the property line between his place and the Slades, not thinking much about it, but she called the city zoning administrator and turned him in for a zoning violation."

"You need a zoning permit to put up a fence?"

"In Chilson, yeah, if it's within eight feet of a property line. Anyway, it was Don's bad luck that there's a new zoning administrator all hot to dot the *i*'s and cross the *t*'s, and he got fined a hundred bucks."

A hundred dollars seemed like a lot, but since I didn't know the least thing about zoning, I kept my opinion to myself.

"But what really got him mad," Rafe went on, "was he had to show up in front of the Planning Commission for a permit review on a night the Red Wings were playing in the Stanley Cup playoffs. Against Chicago."

"Now, that is truly horrible," I said dryly.

"Didn't someone say that sarcasm is the lowest form of humor?"

"That's puns."

He grinned over his shoulder. "You know what's

257

really funny? Denise had better never put a foot wrong ever again, because if she does, Don will be on her faster than flies on dog doo-doo. If she'd kept her mouth shut about the fence, maybe told Don he had a violation but that she wasn't going to say anything to the city if he went and begged for mercy, she'd have made a friend for life. As it is, she's got an enemy forever."

I didn't say anything, but thought about Denise all alone in her house. How hard could it be for someone to break in, especially a next-door neighbor?

"It's too bad about Roger, though," Rafe said. "He was a good guy."

To Rafe, most people were good guys, women included. Only somewhere out there, someone wasn't good. Someone had killed Roger, and someone, I was sure, had tried to kill Denise.

The litany of professions recited by Detective Inwood came back to me. A local attorney, a middle-school teacher, a retail-store owner, and the director of a nonprofit organization.

Shannon was the attorney and Don Weller was the teacher. Was Pam Fazio the store owner? And who was the nonprofit director?

"Say, is it cookie time yet?" Rafe took out the caulk tube, now empty, and tossed it into an open cardboard box.

I shook my head, trying to clear the fluff out of

my brain. But, as usual, all that happened was my hair rearranged itself.

"Sure," I said. "Cookies coming right up."

I spent the rest of the morning and all of the afternoon hanging out with Rafe, alternately helping and being annoyed by him, sometimes both at the same time.

"Why is it," I said with exasperation, frowning at the clamp that didn't quite fit around the pieces of wood they needed to fit around, "that you never get annoyed like I do?"

"Because," he said, taking the clamp out of my hand and replacing it with one he'd fetched from another room.

I waited, but he didn't say anything else. "Because? That's it?"

"What, you want me to say it's because you're a girl? I can, you know. It's because you're a—"

"No," I interrupted quickly, "I don't want you to say that."

"Then don't ask questions that you don't want the answers for."

I stood there, clamp in one hand, wood bits in the other, thinking about questions and answers, about things I didn't want to know. About asking the right questions. And about the cost of finding the answers.

"Hey, Minnie. You going to clamp that wood before the glue dries?"

"I think so," I said absently, and tried to focus on what I was doing.

Half an hour later, Rafe kicked me out. "I'm done for the day," he said, stretching. "I'm headed over to a buddy's to watch the Lions lose another football game."

"And drink beer and eat junk food?" I asked.

He slapped his flat stomach. "Dinner of champions," he said. "Want to come?"

I squinched my face. "As much as I want to bang my fingers with a hammer."

After I washed up in the kitchen sink (such as it was) and dried my hands on my pants (since there was no towel and the paper towels were upstairs) I poked my head into the bathroom where Rafe was showering and yelled good-bye.

"See ya," he yelled back. "Hey, thanks for the help."

"No problem. I'll send you a bill."

"Sounds good. You'll get paid as soon as this place gets finished," he said, and so I was laughing as I left his house.

During the hours I'd been inside, snow had started to drift down. The light was mostly gone from the sky, and the glow from the windows of the Round Table was like a beacon.

I stomped my feet free of snow in the entry-way and slid into a booth. In my life with Aunt Frances, I was on my own for Sunday food after breakfast, and the cold slice of pizza Rafe had handed me for lunch wasn't going to tide me over until tomorrow morning.

"Menu?" the middle-aged waitress asked. For once, it wasn't Sabrina.

"No, thanks, Carol. I'll have an olive burger with a side salad." I wanted fries, but chose the vegetable route. My parents would be on their way back from Florida right now, and my mom's imminent entry into the state was making me aware of my eating habits.

I sat back, uncomfortable at my bookless state, and looked about for something to read. A cast-aside newspaper would do, even if I'd already read it.

"Minnie?"

I turned. Ash Wolverson was smiling at me in a tentative sort of way. In the worn jeans and hoodie he was wearing, he didn't look at all like a sheriff's deputy.

"Hey," I said. "What's up?"

He stood at the end of the booth, looking hesitant. "Are you waiting for anyone?"

"Nope. Have a seat."

I watched him slide in, thinking that I'd never before met a man this good-looking who was also so unsure of himself. "How was your Thanksgiving?" I asked.

"Okay," he said. "How about yours? Did you drive or did you cook?"

261

I laughed. "Mostly I did dishes."

There was a short silence that might have grown uncomfortably long had Carol not arrived with a glass of ice water. She eyed Ash. "You leave your dinner much longer, it's going to get cold, and fried fish doesn't microwave up anything decent."

Which was when I realized Ash had already been in the restaurant when I showed up. The place wasn't that big, making it yet another day in which I wasn't going to win a Power of Observation award.

I started to talk at the same time he did. "Go ahead," he said.

"Thanks." I smiled and then peered at him. Was he blushing? Surely not. "I was just wondering if Detective Inwood has forgiven you for missing the hat."

Ash touched the edges of the paper placemat in front of him. "Hard to tell. He's still letting me work with him, so I figure he can't be too mad."

I wasn't so sure about that, but maybe he was right. "I know you can't talk about an active investigation, but can you tell me if there's been any progress?" *Please let there be progress. Please be close to figuring out what happened. And pretty please figure it out before the court hearing.*

"Some," he said. "We're working with a local conservation officer, putting together a case."

Which wasn't really an answer at all, or at least not a useful one. If anyone asked me, Ash was following far too closely in Detective Inwood's footsteps. No one was, but I was ready if the question came up.

Still, if they were working with a CO, a type of officer who had full arrest powers and was responsible for enforcing the hunting and fishing laws, that probably meant they were still thinking a hunter with remarkably poor shooting ability had killed Roger by accident. And if they thought that, I was sure they were wrong. Denise was the one who—

"Can I ask you a question?"

I blinked away from my thoughts. Ash was studying the table. "Sure," I said.

"Would you . . ." He blew out a breath, looked up at me through eyelashes far too long to belong to a grown man, and asked, "Would you go out with me?"

I blinked at him. Blinked again. "Go out with you?"

Now the blush was evident. "Maybe have dinner and a movie? We could go anywhere you'd like. And see any movie you want. What kind of food do you like? I'll eat anything, and I like almost everything. There's a new place in Petoskey people are talking about and it sounds good."

The poor man was starting to babble. I had to stop him, and fast. "Thanks very much," I said. "I

263

appreciate the offer—really I do—but I'm seeing someone right now."

"Oh."

He deflated, and I felt horribly sorry for him. "I've been seeing Tucker Kleinow for a few months. Do you know him?" Ash shook his head slowly. "He's a doctor," I said, "an emergency-room doctor, at the hospital in Charlevoix. He hasn't been up here very long; this will be his first winter Up North." I suddenly realized I was talking too much, so I picked up my water and took a long drink.

"A doctor," Ash said dully. "That figures." He slid out of the booth and stood. "Sorry to bother you."

"You didn't." I smiled at him, but he didn't see it because he was studying his shoes. "Honest. And I'm sorry you didn't know I was seeing someone."

"A doctor," he muttered under his breath, and trudged back to his dinner.

I wanted to call him back, wanted to make him smile and laugh, but I knew he needed time to get over what he would undoubtedly be considering a rejection. How hard it must be, sometimes, to be a man.

Sighing, I thought about the specific hardships of being a man. Then I thought how hard it was to be a woman. Really, it could be a hardship just plain being human.

I shook my head, trying to jolt free the sadness and the worry. Worrying didn't help anything and it didn't make tomorrow any better. Plus, worrying had the definite minus of making the present worse.

Worrying, I realized with a sudden shock, was what I did when I didn't have anyone to talk to or anything to read. In theory, I could read on my cell phone's e-book app, but that gave me a headache.

So I got up and grabbed a real-estate guide from the rack next to the cash register.

After all, anything to read was better than nothing.

I ate my meal while perusing advertisements for lakeshore homes I could never hope to afford, and tried not to notice when Ash left. The poor guy. I wondered again at his odd lack of self-confidence in a social setting, then stuck a fork into my salad and concentrated on criticizing the multimillion-dollar houses that were for sale.

When dinner was eaten and paid for, I zipped my coat and headed home. One step outside, and I came to a sudden stop. The snow that had been coming down gently when I'd arrived at the Round Table must have been falling heavily ever since. A three-inch coating of white lay over everything in sight—buildings, streets, sidewalks, trees. Even in the winter darkness, the town almost glowed with snow-white brightness.

I stuck out my tongue to catch a few flakes and smiled, because this would be the perfect night to take the long way home and check out the holiday decorations.

On one street there were two armies of wire-framed snowmen on a front lawn, set up in a snowball-fight formation. On another street there was a spectacular display that included a pair of five-foot-high nutcrackers and a slightly creepy ten-foot-tall Santa Claus. Another family had put up a tall pole and strung lights down from the top, creating a massive treelike structure that changed color every few minutes.

But I saved the best until last. Two streets away from the boardinghouse, I stopped in front of a two-story Victorian-era home and smiled.

The front yard had been transformed into a winter fantasy scene. There was a waist-high small village, complete with a train station, church, blacksmith's shop, horse-drawn sleighs, and even a pint-sized ice rink. Adults walked, children ran, and a pair of dogs tussled over a gift-wrapped box. A restrained hand had lit the miniature town with tiny lights that illuminated the scene in a golden tone. I was completely entranced, just as I was every year, and I didn't hear the footsteps until they were closing in on me.

I turned and exchanged nods with my aunt's neighbor Otto Bingham.

"Nice," he said, gesturing at the display. "All in

wood, isn't it? Professionally done, it looks like."

The man can speak? It's a Christmas miracle! I smiled. "I'll tell my Aunt Frances."

"Oh?" He tilted his head slightly to one side. "Did she help put it up?"

Laughing, I said, "No, she made it. Plywood, most of it, with some hard maple for the blocky bits, like the church steeple."

His mouth dropped slightly open. "She made this?"

I pointed. "If you squint a little, you can see the date above the front door of that city hall."

"Nineteen eighty-two?"

"Yup." I put my hands in my pockets. "She grew up helping her dad—my grandpa—in his woodshop, and when she married a guy who lived up here, she made sure to have space for a shop herself." It was in the basement, which wasn't an ideal location, but the addition of an exterior stairway had made it a lot better.

I loved to brag about my aunt. Since everyone in the county knew about her talents, I didn't get to do it very often, yet here was someone right in front of me. *Perfect!*

"She made little projects for years," I said, "but when my uncle died, she got into it more seriously. Before long she was teaching wood shop at the high school." Which was where Rafe had first learned his woodworking skills, some-thing about which I reminded him every so often.

"Teaching?"

"Yep." I grinned, enjoying myself. "These days she's teaching woodworking classes at the community college in Petoskey and kind of tutoring some advanced students for the wooden boat–building school up in Cedarville."

"Tutoring?" Otto asked faintly.

"She loves it—says it keeps her young, even though she spends a lot of hours doing it. And now she's getting into wood turning. You should see some of her work—it's just gorgeous. I keep telling her she should sell some pieces at the art shows in the summer, maybe even the art galleries, but she just keeps giving them away."

"A professional craftswoman," Otto muttered. "That figures."

I glanced over at him. For a second, he'd sounded exactly like Ash had an hour earlier. "What do you mean?"

But he just sighed, said good night, and walked away.

"You know what would be great?" my newest bookmobile volunteer asked.

I glanced over at Lina Swinney. I'd met the young woman at the Lakeview Art Gallery a few months ago. We'd gotten along well, so when I'd heard over the Thanksgiving dinner table that she was taking a semester off from college to help her mom recover from a bout with pneumonia, I'd given her a call. She was glad to help out when she could, but it was another temporary solution to the volunteer problem, and I still needed a real answer.

"You've already had lots of ideas," I told her. "My favorite is spinning Eddie's loose hair into yarn and making a blanket of his own hair for him to shed on."

Lina giggled and patted her own long honey-brown hair. "Do you think it would work?"

I had no idea. I liked reading about characters who knitted and weaved and sewed, but I'd never tried to do any of it myself. One of these days. Right after I finished reading *Gravity's Rainbow*.

"What's your new idea?" I asked. "If it has anything to do with finding a revenue source for the bookmobile operations, I'd be your willing servant for a year, minimum."

I could feel her looking at me with a puzzled expression. Lina was bright and full of energy, but she and I did not share a sense of humor. Not that I was joking about the servant thing—not exactly.

We were headed into the next stop, the parking lot of a mom-and-pop grocery store. Three cars waited for us, even though we were a few minutes early.

Lina flung her arms out, gesturing at the book-mobile's interior. "Look at all this! It's a blank canvas waiting to be filled. It's an undeveloped artistic endeavor. Just think what we could do with the ceiling and walls and even the bookshelves. And it's the holidays, so it's the perfect time to decorate this thing to the max."

Making noncommittal noises, I parked the bookmobile. Lina released Eddie, and we started the stop's setup routine. As we did the small amount of necessary business, Lina kept talking.

"Can't you just see it?" She nodded at the shelves. "Wire garland, maybe, or at least crepe paper. We could put snowflakes up. Maybe get kids to make them." Her face was getting a little flushed. "Or snowmen. Christmas stockings. Stars. We could turn this place into a traveling art show."

"Mrr," Eddie said.

I looked at him. He was sitting near Lina, on the foot-high carpet-covered shelf that ran along both sides of the bookmobile. It served both as seating and as a way for people like me to reach the highest shelf.

"What do you think he said?" Lina asked. "I think he'd like decorations."

She was undoubtedly right, and what he'd like to do most would be to rip them to shreds. There was precedent for that kind of behavior.

"It's a fun idea," I said, "but I'm going to have to say no. I don't have time to put that together." My heart panged. Not to mention the fact that the library board might be looking for a buyer for my single-bookmobile fleet in less than two weeks.

"Maybe next year, though, right?" Lina asked.

I made a sideways sort of nod (which, if she'd been reading my mind, she would have read as "Not a chance"), opened the door, and welcomed people aboard. They were all regulars, and they pushed past me on their way to greet Eddie, who was holding court from the passenger-seat headrest.

Phyllis Chambers, recently retired from a state government job in Lansing and relocated Up North, got her Eddie fix and drifted toward me. I was sitting at the back desk, trying to get the chair to adjust to my height.

"Minnie," Phyllis said, "do you have that gluten-free cookbook we were looking through last time, the slow-cooker one? I don't see it now."

"Let me see if it's been checked out." I tapped at the computer and frowned. "That's weird. It says the book's still here. Well, let's take a look." The 641s were on the right side of the aisle, about halfway down, at Minnie eye-height. I knew the book's cover was dark, but it wasn't there.

"Huh." I stood there, hands on hips, staring at the spot where the book should have been.

I spent a lot of time making sure all the bookmobile books were shelved properly. As in a *lot* of time. Of course, someone could have walked off with the book, but theft was so unusual for our library that even Stephen didn't see the need for the shrieking alarm devices that big-city libraries had. It was far more likely that someone had unintentionally taken it home, so with any luck, it would come back in a week or two.

"Here it is!" Phyllis held the book aloft. "It was in with the biographies."

"Next to Julia Child?" I asked.

Phyllis laughed. "Harry Truman."

"Maybe he took up cooking after he left the White House." I beeped the book through the system. "Glad you found it."

"I wasn't really looking," she said. "I just opened my eyes, and it was there. Wrong place, but I was looking at the right time."

She nodded and went to the stairs. She might have said good-bye, but if she did, I didn't hear, because her words were too loud in my ears.

Wrong place, but I was looking at the right time.

It had the ring of profundity, somehow. Was it possible that I was looking in the wrong place for Roger's killer? Looking in the wrong place for the person who wanted to hurt Denise? Looking in the—

There was a sharp pain in my shin. "Ow!"

Eddie head butted me in the leg one more time, then sat and looked up at me. "Mrr."

"Yeah, you're probably right." I ruffled up his fur. "Without a doubt, I am indeed looking for both answers and profound statements in the wrong places. What I should really be doing is asking you."

"Mrr," he said, and whacked me in the shin again.

By the time we returned to Chilson, Lina was ready to give up college, her future career, and her boyfriend, and do nothing but work on the bookmobile.

"This is the coolest thing I've ever done," she said.

I glanced at her, but it's hard to judge facial expressions when you're carrying milk crates full of books into a library's basement. Though she sounded sincere, even Eddie could sound sincere when he really wanted something. "I'm glad you had a good time." I said.

"It just seems so wrong that you can't get the money to pay someone," Lina said. "I mean, it would be part-time—right?—so there wouldn't be benefits or anything. How much could it really cost?"

Too much, according to Stephen. As we entered the room that held the bookmobile's collection, I shied away from thinking about the odds of the bookmobile program ending altogether and said, "The library's budget is tight."

Which it was, but even when I'd dug up a few thousand dollars to cut, Stephen had latched on to the savings as a way to reduce library costs, not as a way to transfer funds to the bookmobile. In the past few weeks, I'd sent off applications to all the grant possibilities I could think of, but I was way past the deadlines for most of them, thanks to the one that had fallen through. Still, it didn't hurt to try.

"I think it's silly," Lina said, thumping her crate of books onto a solid table. "Everybody knows that you can't maintain a solid staff through volunteers. They're just not a reliable source for long-term operations."

Between young Lina and Thessie, my teenage summer volunteer, I would soon learn all I needed to know about everything. Smiling, I put my milk crate next to Lina's. "I'll be sure to mention that to the library board at their next . . ." *Volunteers.* Denise also volunteered for other groups. And hadn't there been a fuss about—

"What did you say?" Lina turned to me, her hands full of the books she was about to shelve.

"I'd glad you had a good time today," I said vaguely, and tried to concentrate on what I was doing, but my brain was fizzing about something else altogether. Because I'd finally remembered why Denise had fingered the director of a non-profit organization as a possible murder suspect.

I opened the door of the Northern Lakes Protection Association and walked in. As I turned around to shut the door, I looked at Eddie, who was maybe twenty feet away in my nicely warmed-up car. "Ten minutes," I mouthed. Since he'd protested so loudly at the unanticipated stop, I'd let him out of his carrier. He was sitting on it and staring at me out the car window, giving me the Look That Should Kill.

"You're lucky it doesn't," I muttered. "Who else would feed you like I do?"

His mouth opened and closed, but I didn't hear what he said. Which was just as well. I closed the door and turned around.

The room had been painted in shades of blue; a light blue near the ceiling morphing into a medium blue at eye height, then feathering into a dark blue at the floor. On the walls were framed maps of area lakes, and the carpet was a squiggly pattern of blue and green. The whole space made me feel as if I were underwater.

A man was sitting behind a large desk and talking on the telephone. He smiled and held up his finger. He was older than me, but not by much. Then again, he had that whipcord-thin build and hair so short it didn't give a good clue to its color, two things that could conceal a man's age for decades.

"Sure," he was saying to the person on the other end of the phone. "It's your birthday, honey. We can go anywhere you want, even if it is in the middle of the week." He listened. "Grey Gables? Sure. I'll make the reservations. Seven o'clock?" He picked up a pen and scratched a note on a desk-blotter calendar for the day after next. "Yes,

I'll put it in my phone, too. Don't worry." He said good-bye, hung up the receiver, and looked at me. "Sorry about the wait. How can I help you?"

I introduced myself, then asked, "Are you Jeremy Hull?"

Thanks to the photos someone had so kindly placed on the NLPA's website, I already knew I was talking to Jeremy, the organization's director and only full-time staff member, but saying so would have felt a little like stalking.

"Sure am," he said, pushing back from his desk. "Have a seat. What can I do for you?"

I sat into what I immediately realized was a seriously uncomfortable chair for someone my size. If I sat all the way back, my feet would swing in the air like a small child's. Since that wasn't the image I wanted to project—not now, and not ever, even when I had been a small child—I perched on the edge of the seat.

"Have you seen the bookmobile?" I asked. Jeremy nodded, smiling a little. Seeing that, I forgave him for the chair. "Ever since we started up this summer," I said, "we've been having problems finding volunteers to go out on the bookmobile. In a perfect world, we'd have money to hire part-time staff, but I just don't see that happening. I know your organization runs mostly on volunteer power, so I hoped you might have some advice."

He laughed. "Sure. Go back to school and get a

degree in computer science. Make a pile of money, then retire early and spend your time volunteering for the bookmobile."

"Gee," I said thoughtfully. "I never once thought of doing that."

"And on your off days, you could spend some time here," he said. "Just to mix it up. Wouldn't want you to get bored." He laughed again, only this time it didn't sound very happy. "Volunteers are the best part of this job. And the worst."

"So you've had problems, too?"

He leaned back, shaking his head. "You wouldn't believe some of the stories."

Now was the time. "I hear Denise Slade used to volunteer with your organization."

"Denise." He said the word in a monotone. "That's not a story; that's a chapter."

"She's the president of our Friends of the Library group," I said. "Should I be worried?"

He sat forward and put his elbows on the desk. "Can I ask you to keep this conversation confidential?"

I'd have to tell Eddie, but I doubted that would count. "Absolutely."

"Denise Slade," he said, spitting out the consonants, "might be the worst thing that ever happened to Northern Lakes."

"Oh," I said.

"It's too bad about her husband—I was even out there that day, checking levels at the Jurco Dam—

but after what she did, I couldn't find it in me to even send a card. My wife says I should forgive and forget, and she's right, but that just hasn't happened yet, and it's not something I'm going to fake."

I studied Jeremy's tight face. "How long ago did this happen?"

"Almost a year ago, but it might as well be yesterday."

"What did she do?"

He made a disgusted sort of noise. "She was my assistant. Worked hard, cared about the projects, talked more people into volunteering, basically made herself indispensable."

"That all sounds okay," I said. "What went wrong?"

"You must know Denise. What would you guess?" he asked.

I thought a moment. "That your board made a decision she didn't agree with, something she thought was just plain wrong. She told them so in a grand and very public manner, and she walked out."

He nodded, his mouth a straight line. "Bingo. Walked out, didn't look back, didn't leave any notes for the next person, didn't finish up any of her projects—nothing. She left me with a huge mess, and the board blamed me. I almost lost my job because of her. It took a lot of scrambling to hold everything together, and I'm still not sure I've regained the board's complete confidence."

It all sounded pretty horrible, and I said so.

"Thanks." He smiled. "So, I guess the answer to your question about volunteers is to avoid using Denise Slade. The woman is a menace."

We chatted for a few more minutes, tossing around collaboration ideas for next summer, and I left after having exceeded my ten-minute promise to Eddie by only five minutes.

"Oh, hush," I said as I encouraged him back into his carrier. "I don't know what you're complaining about. It's not like you can tell time. And even if you could, you're not wearing a watch."

"Mrr!"

"Yeah, back at you."

When he didn't respond, I looked over at him as I buckled my seat belt. "Now what are you doing?"

He was scratching the side of his carrier, going at it with his claws as if he were trying to dig a hole and escape.

"What—did Timmy fall down the well again?"

He ignored me and kept scratching.

"Even if you did escape, where would you go? The backseat?" I started the car. "And even if you got out of the car, there's nothing over there but the parking lot for the Protection Association. Are you going to volunteer to do their valet parking?"

Eddie flopped down with a loud thud.

"Oh, come on," I said. "That was funny."

He turned his head, ignoring me in a very obvious way.

I laughed. "Love you, too, pal."

"What is your cat doing?" Aunt Frances asked.

Before I answered, I swallowed the bite I'd been chewing. My mother would be pleased to know that at least one of her admonitions had stayed with me. "You know that wooden puzzle of the United States? It's in the living room on the shelves with the jigsaw puzzles."

She frowned. "The puzzle that was a gift from my grandparents the Christmas I was six."

I hadn't known that, and said so.

We sat at the kitchen table, listening to the sounds of a cat playing with something he shouldn't.

My aunt's expression was a little pensive, so I dabbed my face with my napkin and got up. In the living room, Eddie was crouched in the corner, batting at two puzzle pieces, one much larger than the other.

"You," I told him, "are a horrible cat." I reached down, picked up the wooden bits, and carried them and the entire puzzle back to the kitchen. I set the puzzle on the table, checked the pieces for damage and Eddie spit, and handed them to Aunt Frances.

"Michigan," she said. "And Maryland. Do you think he was going for the M states?"

"If he was, he missed Mississippi, Minnesota, and Maine."

"Massachusetts." She counted on her fingers. "Seven. There's one more."

"Missouri."

"Mrr."

We looked down at Eddie. "You missed some states," I said. "Better luck next time."

He jumped onto my lap, then up onto the table. Before I could grab him, he swiped at the Maryland puzzle piece and sent it skittering onto the floor.

"If you're trying to destroy them alphabetically," Aunt Frances said, "you should take out Maine first."

"And if you're trying to do it geographically," I said, picking him up and putting him on the floor, "you still got it wrong, especially if you're trying to go west to east."

The two humans in the room started laughing.

Eddie looked from me to Aunt Frances and back to me. Then he put his little kitty nose in the air and stalked off.

Which only made us laugh harder.

"Don't go away mad," I said, wiping the tears from my eyes.

"Just . . . go . . . away," Aunt Frances managed to finish.

Eddie gave Maryland a final swipe, sending it underneath the stove.

"Hey!" I said, my laughter gone. "That wasn't funny."

He stopped, gave us a look that clearly said *I win—again,* and made a dignified exit.

Chapter 14

T he next day was a library day, and I spent the first part of the morning as I usually did, catching up on the jobs that had piled up when I was out on the bookmobile.

All was well until I opened the last of my forty-three e-mails, from a college friend who was working for a moneyed foundation, and read that she'd never heard of any grants for bookmobile operations. *There are purchasing grants, sure, but, Minnie, basically no one gives grants for operations. You know the theory, that if you can't afford operations, you shouldn't have purchased it in the first place. Good luck, though!*

I sent her a quick thank-you and deleted her e-mail. If I deleted it, maybe it wouldn't be true. Sure, that was it.

But I knew it wasn't.

I put my head in my hands. What had I done? How could I have created a program that couldn't be sustained? What had I been thinking?

Tears stung at my eyes. Tears of self-pity.

"Stop that right now." I spoke out loud, and,

instead of my own voice, I heard my mother's. And Mom was right—this was no time to feel sorry for myself. At this point it didn't matter whether my championing of the bookmobile program had been the right thing to do. This was not a time for self-doubt; this was a time for action. And since, as everyone knew, action was fueled by caffeine, what I needed was a refill.

I grabbed my mug and headed for the break room. It was half past ten, a typical coffee-refill time. If I was lucky, I might even find someone to talk to.

Ten feet from the open doorway, I heard Josh and Holly arguing about something. I slowed, trying to get a handle on the topic before I entered the room, then realized they were fighting about the best way to cook a turkey. Since my opinion on that was simple and irrefutable, I was practically whistling when I entered the room.

"You are so wrong," Josh was saying emphatically. "Hey, Minnie. What's the best way to cook a turkey?"

I picked up the coffee carafe. "Have my Aunt Frances do it."

Holly laughed, but Josh gave a snort of disgust. "That's a cheater answer."

I toasted him with my mug. "But accurate." I couldn't care less about the turkey-cooking methodology as long as I didn't have to involve myself with the actual cooking.

Holly filled her own mug and ripped open two sugar packets. As she stirred them in, she asked, "Minnie, do you know if the Friends are going to have their postholiday book sale?"

"Haven't heard." A tickle at the back of my mind told me that I should have known, that I would have known if I hadn't been so busy with the bookmobile. I took a tiny sip of coffee, hoping that would get rid of the tickle. "Why wouldn't there be one?"

Holly took a sip of her coffee, grimaced, and set it down to rip open two more sugars. "It's just that Pam Fazio was supposed to run the sale this year, and now that she's gone, I wonder if anyone else will step up."

I'd forgotten that Pam had been talked into doing the sale. "I'll ask Denise," I said. The annual postholiday book sale was held in mid-January and was the biggest winter event for the Friends. It was also the only winter event, but the sale was well attended and netted a reasonable amount of money. I would have thought they'd do better having a sale before Christmas, and had at one point said so, but the blank look I'd received had as good as said, "But we've always done it this way. Why would we ever change?"

Josh laughed. "I wish I could have been there to see Pam's farewell scene."

"If we'd known in advance," Holly said, "we could have sold tickets."

I sipped my coffee and realized why Holly had added so many sugars: It was a Kelsey-brewed pot. As I opened the refrigerator door and checked the sell-by date on the small jug of milk, I said, "I was out on the bookmobile that day. I missed the whole thing."

"From what I heard," Josh said, "it was spectacular. Pam just stood up, right in the middle of the meeting, right in the middle of whatever Denise was talking about, and walked out."

Holly took up the tale. "Denise asked her where she was going, told her the meeting wasn't over yet, and Pam said that it was for her."

"Yeah," Josh said. "Denise asked, 'What do you mean, it's over?' and Pam said she was quitting. That the only way she'd ever come back to the Friends was over Denise's dead body."

He laughed again, but his laughter trickled off. "Okay, that's not as funny now as it was before . . . well, before." He shifted, obviously remembering Roger's death and the probable attempt on Denise's life, which was now public knowledge, thanks to Facebook.

I wasn't so sure Josh's retelling was accurate. When I'd heard it from Denise, she hadn't used that quote, and when Pam had told me, she certainly hadn't. Then again, would she have? And if Denise hadn't remembered the events accurately, it wouldn't be the first time.

Then again, maybe Josh's version was correct.

What I needed to do was talk to some other Friends and find out. Of course, what I'd probably hear was yet another version. Who could accurately remember a conversation from that long ago? I could barely remember what I had for breakfast that morning.

"Say, Minnie, I wanted to tell you." Josh went to the doorway, looked left and right down the hallway, then came back. "I have another software update to do on Stephen's computer. I'll tell him it'll only take a couple of minutes. He's sure to stay this time, so I have it all figured out what I'll ask him to find out if he knows about Eddie. I'm almost positive he doesn't know, but what do you think about this?"

Josh sketched out his impending conversation, using an improbable squeaky voice for our boss, but I had a hard time paying attention to Josh's theoretical questions to Stephen because I couldn't steer my thoughts away from the darkest part of the just-told tale of Pam's farewell speech.

The only way I'll come back is over your dead body.

Come noon, I held down the main desk while Kelsey and Holly took their lunch breaks. In summertime, I would have scheduled two people, but now that it was December, the tourists were long gone and the snowbirds had flown south.

Foot traffic in the library was much slower, and there was occasionally time to breathe.

I had just tidied up the last of the morning's book returns when I saw Mitchell slouch his way in. "Hey, Mitchell. What's up?"

He gave a one-shouldered shrug. "Nothing."

It sounded more like a pronouncement than a social response. "Is something wrong?" I asked, then winced inwardly.

Why, *why* had I asked him something like that when there was no Holly around to summon me with a manufactured emergency? A perky Mitchell, which was the normal version, was something I could deal with. A despondent, down-in-the-dumps Mitchell was a different entity altogether, and while I did want to help him, I was also working and couldn't dedicate the rest of the afternoon to jollying him.

He heaved out a massive sigh. "Remember you told me to go to the cops with that list I made? After I gave it to them, I expected that they'd, you know, give me something else to do for the case. Some legwork they don't have time for or something."

Why he would have thought that, I had no idea, but the workings of Mitchell's brain were a deep mystery that I didn't in the least want to solve. "But they're not giving you anything?"

"Nothing." He put his hands in his pockets and stared at the floor. "Not a freaking thing. I've called that detective lots of times, asking if there's anything I can do, but he says the investigation is progressing, and that's it." He kicked at the counter's baseboard. "And now when I call, I don't even get the detective—I have to talk to some deputy."

I turned a laugh into a cough.

"So, now what should I do?" Mitchell asked, kicking at the baseboard again.

He could stop the kicking, for one thing. Then a flash of brilliance struck. "I have an idea."

"Yeah?"

"Well," I said, "on TV and in movies, when the police are stuck on a case, they always go back to the beginning. Start looking at things all over again, trying to see everything from a fresh point of view." It was the vaguest of vague ideas, but if Mitchell picked it up, it might keep him busy for a while.

He was nodding vigorously. "That's a great idea. Go back to the beginning. Awesome. Thanks, Minnie!" He walked off, his hands still in his pockets, but with his posture straight and tall. He turned and bumped open the front door with his hip, and I was suddenly reminded of Eddie.

A new thought pinged into my head: *If my cat were human, would he be like Mitchell?*

I pondered the notion and finally decided that even if Eddie took on human form, he couldn't possibly be anything but an Eddie. No way, no how.

A woman approached the desk and put a stack of books on the counter for checkout. "Something funny?" she asked, smiling.

I laughed and said, "Almost everything, really," and got back to work.

The rest of the noon hour zipped past, not so much because I was busy, but because snippets from recent conversations kept echoing around inside my head.

Anyone can commit murder.

Wrong place, but I was looking at the right time.

The only way I'll come back is over your dead body.

Go back to the beginning.

The bits were banging into each other so much that they were starting to create new sentences all on their own. Unfortunately, none of them made sense. It was when I caught myself thinking *Anyone can look at the beginning* that I knew I had to clear my head if the afternoon was going to be at all productive. As soon as Kelsey returned, I abandoned the front desk, wolfed down my lunch of turkey sandwich and warmed-up mashed potatoes, and went out for a walk.

The snow from the other night was still on the ground, and talk was that it was going to stick this time and not be gone until April. I counted the months in my head, three times, and got to five every single time. It seemed like a lot. "But you'll be gone before the end of April," I said to the snow. "Won't you?"

Happily, the snow didn't answer, which I took as an affirmative. Snow through the first week of April was tolerable; snow after that might be reason to move to a warmer climate.

I walked downtown, enjoying the chill air in my lungs, enjoying the sight of high clouds chasing low ones, enjoying the cheery holiday displays in the storefronts, and enjoying the nearly empty sidewalks. I was having such a nice time soaking in the world and thinking about as little as possible that I almost didn't notice when a tall, thinnish man on the other side of the street waved at me. "Afternoon, Minnie," he said.

A blink or two later, I recognized the voice and returned Jeremy Hull's wave. Then I stopped in my tracks as I saw him open the door of a dark blue vehicle that wasn't quite a sedan and wasn't exactly an SUV. A dark blue vehicle that had half a dozen bumper stickers on its back end, one of which read THIRTY-SEVEN MILLION ACRES IS ALL THE MICHIGAN WE WILL EVER HAVE.

I stared as Jeremy started the vehicle and drove away. Stood there staring until my feet got cold, stood there a little longer, then slowly made my way to the sheriff's office.

When I was ushered to the conference room, I sat in my regular seat. For a moment I debated about walking on the wild side and taking a different chair, but I decided a sheriff's office wasn't the best place to start being wild.

I sat and suddenly realized that, once again, I had no book to read. Worse, there was no reading material anywhere in the room. There wasn't anything, actually, except the table and chairs. A more boring room couldn't possibly exist. I considered going to the front window and begging for a copy of *Law Enforcement Monthly*, or whatever their professional magazine was, but sighed and stayed in my seat.

I'd tipped my head back and was staring at the water stains on the ceiling tiles when the door opened. "I'm pretty sure that's an armadillo," I said, pointing up. "What do you think?"

"Sorry, but I never thought about it." Ash Wolverson walked to the opposite side of the table and pulled out a chair.

I scrambled to sit up straight. "I thought Detective Inwood was going to talk to me."

"He had a phone call."

"Oh." I put my hands on my lap. Put them on the table. Didn't like how that felt and put them back on my lap. Wasn't comfortable with that, either, and wished they could disappear for a while.

Ash took out his notebook. "You had something to tell us?"

He kept his head down, but even so I detected

a faint shade of red on his cheeks. It was some comfort to know that he was uncomfortable, too. As the silence started to lengthen, his color deepened, and I saw that he was, in fact, far more uncomfortable than I was. The poor guy.

"I remembered something," I said. "From the day Roger was killed."

Ash gave me a quick glance, then started writing as I told him about seeing the not-a-car, not-an-SUV, that it had sported a number of bumper stickers, and that I'd just seen Jeremy Hull driving in that same vehicle not far from the gas station. Jeremy had said he was at Jurco Dam, but the dam was miles from there.

"You're sure?" Ash asked.

Once again I saw the thirty-seven-million acres sticker, saw it on the bumper, right next to the decal of the Great Lakes. "I'm sure." I didn't like it, didn't like it at all, but I was sure.

He wrote a few notes and thanked me, but he didn't once meet my eyes.

"You still think a hunter accidentally killed Roger?" I asked.

Ash's jaw tightened. "You know I can't talk about an active investigation."

So what else was new? I nodded and left.

My return walk to the library wasn't nearly as full of cheerful feeling as the walk out had been. Instead of a jaunty saunter, with my head up and my spirits light, I was practically scuffing my feet, with my head down.

I didn't want Jeremy Hull to have killed Roger. Didn't want anyone to have killed him, really. What I wanted was for Roger to be hale and hearty. Swallowing down a clump of sorrow, which didn't sit at all well in my stomach, I climbed the steps of Older Than Dirt.

Though the day outside hadn't been sunny, the snow had brightened things up enough that the interior of the antiques store seemed dark in contrast. Which was my excuse for almost stepping on top of Pam Fazio, who was kneeling on the floor, arranging a display of . . .

"Are those what I think they are?" I asked, my eyes slowly adjusted to the inside light.

Pam glanced up. "Hello, Minnie. Lunch boxes, yes, but with a twist." She moved a Wonder Woman lunchbox to the left, edged a Minnie Mouse lunchbox to the right, and positioned a Bionic Woman lunchbox in the center. On nearby shelves were a dozen more vintage lunchboxes, from Barbie to Holly Hobbie to *Charlie's Angels*.

She bounced to her feet and waved at the display, grinning. "What do you think?"

I studied the attractive, colorful display. "Are lunch boxes an *in* thing?"

"No idea," she said. "But do you see? Every lunch box features a female. A girl! You could use one of these as a purse, a jewelry box, a cosmetics case, even a lunch box." Smiling, she reached to reposition Chris Evert. "These are so much fun, I'm not sure I want to sell any of them."

As I stood there, watching her, I knew I really, really didn't want to find any evidence that would implicate her in Roger's death. Then again, I deeply wanted to find out who'd killed him.

Two wishes, and there was a possibility that they were in complete opposition to each other. Which one did I most want to come true?

I sighed. There was only one true answer to that.

"Minnie, Minnie, Minnie." Pam was smiling at me. "You look sad. What's the matter—too many turkey leftovers? I have just the cure." She beckoned me toward a back corner of her store. The entire place was an eclectic mixture of old and new, familiar and strange, shabby and shiny. Items for sale ranged from a large weathered wardrobe to top hats to leather suitcases to pincushions. Something for everyone, including me, because I often browsed the collection of used books.

"Sit." Pam said, pointing at a ladder-back chair. "Now take your boots off—yes, all the way off— and slip into these." She brandished a pair of antique shoes. They were black, had a small heel, skinny waxed laces, and tops that went six inches past my ankle. I loved them instantly.

Pam grinned. "Had a feeling you'd like those. How do they fit?"

I wiggled my toes. "Perfect." I pulled the laces through the eyelets. "Where did you get these?"

"Now, Minnie, you should know better than to ask an antiques dealer that question." When I started to apologize, she waved me off. "Anyone else, I probably wouldn't tell, but you won't say anything. You haven't spread any gossip about me and Denise, and if you haven't done that, you're probably the most trustworthy person in town."

I started to stammer an objection, but Pam cut me off. "I know this because I hear things you wouldn't believe in this store. People think the staff doesn't have ears, I guess, because it can get worse than a hair salon in here when a group comes in."

It was something I'd never thought about, and probably should have.

"Anyway," Pam was saying, "I bought those boots in Kentucky. I was down there on a buying trip a while back, about two weeks before Thanksgiving. I was late coming home because I called my neighbor and she said we were supposed to get eight inches of snow—remember that? So I decided to stay south." She laughed. "Good thing I did. You wouldn't believe the things in this barn that I wouldn't have found if I'd left when I'd planned."

I was so stupid. If I'd had the sense of a soap dish, I would have found out a long time ago that Pam had been out of town the day Roger had died and thus would have saved myself all sorts of anxiety.

"Tell you what." Pam was looking thoughtful. "I'll sell you these boots for ten percent over cost, and you promise to never again try to scam my morning coffee away from me."

"Twenty-five percent," I said firmly. "And not a penny less."

We bargained our way to fifteen percent over cost, and, as I continued my walk back to the library, I realized that my mood had lightened considerably. New boots, even if they're old, can be a wonderful thing.

My temporarily high spirits crashed that night as I lay in bed, trying to sleep but being all too aware of time ticking away. The court date with Tammy Shelburt was only eight days off and I was no closer to a solution now than I'd been the day I'd met with the library board.

Sleep wasn't easy in coming, and what rest I did get was haunted by uncomfortable dreams of forgetting my high-school locker combination and missing a flight to Paris.

I spent the next day, a bookmobile day, drinking a lot of caffeine and doing my best to be a cheerful and professional librarian. I faked my way through all the stops, but when Lina was gone and the bookmobile was tucked in for the night, I wasn't at my alert best.

Eddie, on the other hand, was wide-eyed and awake.

"Mrr," he said.

"Yeah." Yawning, I buckled my car's seat belt. "You said that before. Lots of times." I started the engine and aimed us in the direction of home. "Over and over. You should work on a broader vocabulary."

He didn't say anything. I did, however, hear a scratching noise.

"Eddie, please don't tell me you're using your carrier as a litter box." I was almost begging, which was never a good plan with a cat. They exploited weakness better than anyone. "We're almost home, and—"

"Mrr."

That "Mrr" hadn't sounded the same as the twelve hundred previous versions he'd vocalized in the last three minutes. I glanced over and had a small panic attack. "Eddie! What are you doing out of the carrier?"

He was sitting atop his former abode, looking out the passenger's window, every muscle in his body at ease. Clearly, he thought he belonged there.

I spent a few quick seconds debating between stopping the car, trying to capture a reluctant Eddie, and shoving him back into the carrier, or just driving carefully and slowly the rest of the way home.

Eddie gave me a look.

"Fine," I muttered. "You win. But you can bet I'll double-check that latch tonight." It was probably my fatigue that had caused me to not secure the latch properly, but there was the odd chance it was broken.

"Mrr!" Eddie inched closer to the window. "Mrr!"

"Yes, my hearing is fine, thank you. Matter of fact, have I ever told you that my family has a long history of keen hearing? There's a story about my great-great-"—I considered the dates and added one more—"great-uncle Archibald. Back in the day, he—"

"Mrr!" Eddie's front feet thumped onto the passenger's door. "MRR!"

I ignored him. "So, back in the day, Uncle Archibald was a cook in a lumber camp. One morning there was—"

"MRRROO!"

Eddie's normal conversational tones were something I was used to; Eddie howls were quite another. "Are you okay?" I glanced over but didn't see any signs of impending stomach upset. Thankfully.

My cat ignored me. Still on his hind legs, he scratched at the window, howling and whining.

"What is with you?" I looked past him. "Did you see a chipmunk? A bird?" If he had, it was gone. "Oh, wait. It's the building, isn't it?" I nodded at a structure of steel and glass and stone. "Well, you're not the only one who isn't fond of the new city hall, but personally, I quite like the design. Form follows function, you know."

Eddie sat down with a plop and gave me a disgusted look.

"You're not familiar with Louis Sullivan?" I *tsk*ed at him. "Your education has a huge hole. My fault, no doubt." Thanks to an engineer father who had a lifelong interest in architecture, I'd ended up with more knowledge on the subject than the average bear, and I was more than willing to share with my cat. "Let's go back to the beginning. Have you ever heard of Stonehenge?"

The cat carrier made a noise. Eddie had slipped back inside.

"Fine," I said. "We'll skip Stonehenge. Let's talk about pyramids."

"Mrr."

"Excellent," I said, and started Eddie's first architecture lesson. That would teach him for escaping the carrier.

Maybe.

After I got home, I put on some going-out-to-a-nice-restaurant clothes, stuck Kristen's latest postcard to the refrigerator *(Key West: fifty percent convertibles. Chilson: fifty percent pickups with snowplow blades.)* and was at the front door when Tucker pulled into the driveway. I hurried out so he didn't have to come into the Eddie-hair-infested house, and in less than half an hour we were sliding our knees underneath a white table-cloth at Charlevoix's Grey Gables. When he'd texted me the day before with a round of apologies for not being in touch and a sheepish dinner invitation for that evening, I'd known exactly where I wanted to go.

The waiter took our drink orders, cited the evening's special offerings, and gave us menus. When he left, I glanced around. The restaurant was mostly empty, as was typical for a weeknight this time of year.

"Something wrong?" Tucker asked.

I faced him, smiling brightly. "Not a thing. How was your day?"

He gave me a look, then started telling a story about a recalcitrant caster on one of the exam-room chairs. Just as he was leading up to the point where I was sure someone was going to get dumped on the floor in a very public manner, the hostess ushered a hand-holding couple to a nearby table.

The man quirked a smile at me. "Hey, Minnie. Seems as if I'm seeing you everywhere these days."

I nodded at Jeremy Hull, wondering whether my guilt over telling the police about his car was manifesting itself in any visible way. It was because I remembered his phone conversation that I'd wanted to come here; maybe I'd hear something, see something, learn something that would tell me one way or another if he'd killed Roger and wanted to do the same to Denise. Coincidental location at the time of Roger's death was bad, but it could be just a coincidence.

Jeremy introduced his wife, I introduced Tucker, and we were on the verge of becoming a jolly foursome when their waiter arrived, took their drink orders, and started reciting the specials.

". . . And tonight's creation by the chef," he said, "is a tenderloin of venison glazed with maple syrup and accompanied by a delectably light cherry sauce. Any questions? Then I'll be back with your wine."

I'd been looking in Jeremy's direction when the venison had been described and had seen him flinch. I caught his eye. "Not a fan of venison?"

He shook his head as he busied himself with unrolling his cloth napkin. "I can't stand the idea of eating the stuff. Haven't been able to since I was a kid and my dad took me hunting."

I could tell where this was going, and I wasn't sure it was a suitable topic for the dinner table. Quickly, I said, "I've heard a lot of stories like that and—"

But Jeremy wasn't paying attention to me. "My dad got a deer a couple of hours into the morning. I was maybe twelve or thirteen. I'd never seen anything dead before, not like that."

His wife reached across the table and took his hand. "Honey, let's not talk about it, okay?" She sent me a smile.

He pulled away. "You know what my dad made me do? He made me dress that deer. Stood over me and told me, step by step, how to—"

"Jeremy," his wife said sharply.

He finally looked at her. Looked at Tucker and me. Realized what he'd been about to say and where he'd been about to say it.

"Sorry," he said. "It's just that ever since that day I haven't been able to stand guns or venison or the sight of blood."

As we made murmuring noises of understanding, our waiter stopped by. "Are you two ready to order?" he asked. "Still thinking about the prime rib?"

"Well, actually," I said, "I think I'll have the salmon." Not that beef was venison, but Jeremy's half-told story was a little too close for eating comfort.

"You know," Tucker said, "I think I'd like the salmon, too."

Our long-suffering waiter nodded again. "Instead of the filet mignon you asked about earlier?"

Tucker smiled at me. "Absolutely."

I smiled back at him, thinking for the first time in weeks that maybe this would all work out.

Chapter 15

During my lunch the next day, I hurried out through the start of what was predicted to be three straight days of rain, and drove a box of donation books I'd been collecting up the hill to the middle school.

Rafe and I had regular bargaining sessions regarding exchanges of labor, and last summer I'd agreed to set up recommendations for an after-school reading program if he did the electrical repair of my houseboat. As often seemed to happen, I was still working on his project when he was long done with mine. Whenever I mentioned this fact, he'd give me a white-toothed grin, say he was just more efficient than I was, and that maybe I should take some lessons from him.

"As if," I muttered, trying to free a hand to open the school's door. Efficiency lessons from Rafe would be about like etiquette lessons from Eddie.

The secretary's desk was empty, so I wandered unannounced through the maze of small offices. "Eddie etiquette lessons would all be about what to do with my tail," I muttered, plopping the box on Rafe's desk.

"When did you get a tail?" Rafe, looking almost professional in a buttoned shirt and dress pants, craned his neck, trying to look around to my backside. "Bet wearing pants is a problem. You going to start wearing skirts? Poodle skirts, maybe?" He smirked.

I pointed at the box. "These are donation books that are on the after-school reading list."

"Hey, cool." He stood and sifted through the contents. Rafe had applied for a small grant to fund the project and it had been awarded, but he'd received only half the money requested. "This will help a lot." He picked up a copy of *Arnie, the Doughnut* and started reading.

I cleared my throat. "Thank you ever so much, Minnie. You're the best librarian ever."

"Huh?" Rafe turned a page. "Yeah. Thanks, Min. See you later, okay?"

I rolled my eyes and walked out. Though the hallways were quiet, I could hear a distant din from the cafeteria. Lunchtime in a middle school. I shook my head, not wanting to remember those days too clearly. To distract myself, I looked into the classrooms through the small vertical windows in the doors, but it turns out you can't see very much that way.

A blare of music startled me. I looked around, saw an open classroom door, and poked my head inside.

Don Weller was seated at a desk, peering into a computer monitor and singing along with the lyrics pouring out of his speakers.

". . . Jingle all the way. Oh, what fun it is to ride in a . . ."

He was so busy singing and working on the computer that he didn't notice my wave and didn't hear my hello. I came into the room, saw what was on the monitor, and gasped.

Don spun around. "Hey, Minnie. What's up?"

I knew he was looking at me, but I couldn't look away from his computer screen. "Isn't that Denise Slade's house?"

He laughed. Or it started out that way; halfway in, it turned into more of a snarl that ended as a sneering sort of sigh. "Yeah. She's my next-door neighbor."

I considered what my strategy should be. "Rafe mentioned your fence issue."

"Wasn't an issue until Denise felt the need to turn me in." He whacked at the keyboard. "She could have said something, could have said, 'Gee, Don, did you know you need a fence permit? Just stop by city hall and talk to the zoning administrator.'" He was snarling again. "'Doesn't cost much. Paperwork's simple. Just make sure you get one, because the penalty is a little fierce.'"

He thumped on his computer's mouse, changing the screen away from the image of Denise's house, whacked at the keyboard, thumped some more. "But, no, she didn't do any of that. What did she do? She waited until I finished putting the dang thing up, then made the call. Freaking tattletale," he muttered, whacking away.

"What are you doing?" I asked.

"Hang on . . ." He made a few more thumps and whacks, then shoved his chair back for me to see. "Wait for it."

The screen went black. As I watched, "We Need a Little Christmas" started playing and lines of large white text scrolled up into view. *Denise Slade, 1038 Ridgeline View, Tuesday, November 25.* The text scrolled up and away; then Denise's house slowly appeared. The night photo showed a house brightly lit with tiny lights. Red, green, yellow, and blue, the lights outlined every window, every eave, every corner, and every post on the wide porch. It was attractive, in a showy sort of way, but I was glad I didn't live next door to it.

"That's a lot of lights," I murmured.

Don snorted. "You ain't kidding. But the thing is, she's violating the rules."

"There are rules about Christmas lights?"

"Our subdivision has a homeowners' association," he said. "No one is supposed to have holiday lights up before Thanksgiving—no way, no how. That there?" He stabbed at the screen. "It's a flagrant violation of the rules, and after the fence thing, I swore that if she ever stepped out of line for anything—and I mean *anything*—I'd be on her so fast, her head would spin."

His head must spin at a very slow rate, because Thanksgiving had been a week ago and his head looked as if it were in the same position it had always been.

I studied the screen and saw that it wasn't a still image—it was a video, and the lights were starting to blink. "Oh, my," I breathed.

"Yeah." He stared at it with a fierce expression. "Right next door. She turns it off at midnight, just like the rules say, but I go to bed at eleven and have to try to sleep with that stuff pulsing away. Doesn't matter how many curtains we hang up; the lights still get through. By New Year's, I'm going to be seriously sleep deprived."

I wished him good luck and walked out, thinking about rules and laws, about expectations and holidays, about families and friends.

And about neighbors.

Boxless and errand-free, I drove down the hill and back into town. I'd hoped to eat lunch at the Round Table and get the scoop from Sabrina on her new husband Bill's treatments for his macular degeneration, but there wasn't time after my conversation with Don.

I snagged a parking spot directly across the street from Shomin's Deli and five minutes later, I walked out the front door with my new favorite sandwich: green olive and Swiss cheese on sourdough. I also walked out into precipitation. A fairly heavy version. It wasn't exactly rain, but it wasn't snow, either. I stepped back into the shelter of the store's entryway and, one-handed, since my other hand held my lunch, I tried to wrestle my hood out of my coat's zippered collar.

"Stupid curly hair," I muttered, wrestling away. Most people's hair could survive a little wet with no ill effects. Mine would spring into an unshapable mass at the slightest drop.

As I grunted with my hood-raising efforts, an ancient and battered SUV pulled up to the curb. Allison Korthase got out, jogged through the falling slush, and went into the eye doctor's office next door.

I looked at the SUV, mud covered from bumper to bumper, then at the eye doctor's. Hadn't Allison been driving a sedan the last time I'd seen her? I mentally shrugged, and, hood in place, left the shelter of the entryway and started back across the street.

"Minnie?"

I jumped. Allison was standing on the curb, a small white plastic bag in her hand. She looked a little different, and it took me a second to realize the difference was that she was wearing glasses. "Oh," I said, ever the brilliant conversationalist. "Hi, Allison."

She nodded. "Thought that was you. Your height and that hair are dead giveaways."

Which meant that my hair was escaping the

hood and would be a mess the rest of the day. Nice. I nodded at the SUV, catching a glimpse of contents that could have passed for the product line of a nice-sized used-sports-equipment store. Hockey sticks, snowshoes, a bow, a gun case, at least two sets of skis, and what might have been a lacrosse stick crowded up against the window, giving the impression that more layers lay underneath. "I didn't recognize the vehicle."

She gave a small grimace. "My husband's. Mine's in the shop for some recall thing, so I'm stuck driving his for the day. So embarrassing. I asked him to at least get it washed, but you can see how far that got me."

I smiled and tried to pull my hood up even farther. "Did you have a nice Thanksgiving?" Which I should have asked when I'd seen her at the library the other day, but better late than never.

Allison jiggled her bag. "Would have been nicer if my new contact-lens prescription had come in on time. I spent the day having my glasses steam up every time I opened the oven door."

Yet another reason to be grateful for twenty-twenty vision. Which I hadn't had since I was ten, but since the idea of corrective eye surgery gave me the willies, I didn't see that changing anytime soon. Happily, my contacts and I got along just fine.

"How about your Thanksgiving?" Allison asked.

I was about to answer when the slush suddenly

turned to straight rain and began falling in big fat drops. We both said quick good-byes, and I scampered across the street to my car. A few minutes later, I was at my desk, biting into my sandwich and reading the e-mails that had multiplied during the hour I'd been gone.

Josh sidled into my office. "Hey, Minnie, you got a minute?"

As I was nodding, Holly came in after him. I looked from one friend to the other. "What's up?" I asked.

"Stephen," they said simultaneously.

"What's he done this time?" I asked. "Recommended *Helter Skelter* to a nine-year-old?"

They ignored me. "He knows about Eddie," Holly said, at the same time Josh said, "I'm positive he doesn't know about Eddie."

I put my sandwich down. "Hmm. One of you has to be wrong. I wonder who it is?" They pointed at each other. "Right," I said. "Josh, you were here first. What's your proof?"

"It's like I was saying: I was in his office the other day, checking up on his computer. I pretended to pick a cat hair off my sleeve, see, and said, "Looks like a cat hair. Wonder how that got on me? And he didn't say a word. Didn't blink, didn't move, didn't do anything." He grinned. "See? If he'd known about Eddie, he would have said or done something."

"Oh, please." Holly rolled her eyes. "This is

Stephen we're talking about. He has the best poker face ever."

"Yeah?" Josh folded his arms across his chest. "What's your proof that he knows?"

"Pinterest," she said. "He has an account."

"He does?" From what I knew, Pinterest was all about pictures. Pin a picture to your account's board. Make comments. Make comments on other people's pictures. It sounded fun, but I was wary of the time-suck factor.

"Yeah, it's an open network, so it wasn't hard to find him. He's pinned a lot of photos of antique cars."

I ran over the top of the sports-loving Josh's surprise about Stephen having any interests outside of books. "So, how does Eddie come into this?"

"Stephen pinned a picture of this old car that had a cat sitting on its hood, and made a comment that the owner didn't deserve to own it if he was going to treat it like that."

"What kind of car?" Josh asked.

Holly and I looked at him.

"What? I'm just saying it's important. If it was an antique Aston Martin, or, something like a Duesenberg, I'd have to agree with him."

"You are such a guy," Holly said.

He shrugged. "Goes without saying."

I thanked them for their conclusions, but I wasn't sure either one had definitive proof. A few

311

weeks ago, I would have been concerned. This week, however, the Secret of Eddie was way down my worry list. Not that I had a list, but if I did, that's where it would have been.

When I sighed, my friends exchanged glances.

"All right." Holly dragged over the spare chair and sat herself down. "Tell Aunt Holly what's wrong. And don't leave anything out, because I'll be able to tell if you do."

I opened my mouth to say I was fine, that everything was fine. But before the first denial was out of my mouth, I knew I couldn't do it.

"Tammy Shelburt's negligence suit against the library starts next week," I said, "and if the sheriff's office doesn't arrest Roger's killer before then, the library board will probably take the bookmobile off the road. The library attorney said it will help the library's case."

Holly gasped. "Seriously? I mean, I know you told me they might, but I figured they'd have come to their senses by now."

"No one has told me anything different."

"Geez." Josh shoved his hands in his pockets. "What are you going to do?"

I looked at my computer monitor, which had gone into screen-saver mode and was now showing a slide show of bookmobile photos. "The only thing that will save the bookmobile is figuring out who killed Roger Slade. So that's what I'm going to do."

Holly half laughed. "If anyone else told me something like that, I'd laugh in their face. But you know what? I believe that you'll do it. Right, Josh?"

He nodded. They both smiled at me, and I smiled back, because if they could believe it, then I could, too.

By the time I left the library, the light had completely gone from the day. It was a school night for Aunt Frances, so I was on my own for dinner. She'd left the porch light on for me, and when I opened the front door, I called out, "Eddie? Hey, Eddie?"

No feline came bounding over to greet me. I put my coat in the closet and wandered through the house on a cat hunt. "Eddie? Where are you, pal?" No Eddie on the couch, no Eddie on the dining-table buffet, no Eddie in the kitchen or in the downstairs bathtub.

I went upstairs. No Eddie on or under my pillow, no Eddie on any shoes in my closet. No Eddie in my aunt's room, and no Eddie in the upstairs bathrooms. I stood at the top of the stairs and called again. "Eddie?" There was no need to get worried—of course there wasn't—but there was a chance he could have scooted outside when the door was open and no one had noticed. He could have been outside all day. He could be lost, cold and shivering and—

Something thumped me in the back of my knee. "Ahh!" I jumped and yelled at the same time.

"Mrr."

I put my hands on my hips and looked down at my cat. "Funny, mister. Very funny. I was calling and calling you. Where have you been?"

He sat down and started cleaning his back paw.

"Okay, I can see you don't want to talk about it. But you could at least give me a hint."

He glanced at me, then switched to cleaning the other back paw.

I sat on the edge of the bed, feeling the need to talk to someone. About the bookmobile, about the library board, about Roger and Jeremy and Pam and Don and all the things I'd learned in the last two and a half weeks. And about how none of it was adding up to a motive for murder.

"Mrr."

"Thanks," I said, "and I'm sure you're right, but your advice would be more helpful if I could understand cat speech."

Eddie had nothing else to say, so I reached into my backpack for my cell phone. "Now or never," I muttered, and tapped in the name. "Hey, Denise," I said when she answered. "Do you have a couple of minutes?"

"Not really." Her voice was hard to hear over what sounded like a large crowd. "I'm down in Traverse City, eating at Red Ginger with some friends."

My mouth watered. Red Ginger was an Asian restaurant with a hefty list of sushi offerings. I didn't get there often, because of the distance and the prices, but it was still one of my favorite places to eat in Traverse. "This won't take long," I said.

Even over the background noise, I could hear her sigh. "Fine. Hang on." She made excuses to whomever she was with. "There. I'm headed downstairs, but our food is coming soon, so I can't talk long. What do you want?"

Condensed conversation was ideal. I skipped what I'd planned as an introduction and, talking fast, went straight to the heart of it. "Remember when I saw you right before Thanksgiving, outside the grocery store, and you mentioned some people who might be your enemies?"

"Yeah. What of it?"

Sometimes it was really hard to be nice to people. At least certain people. "Can you think of anyone else?"

"You mean, is there anyone else running around who might want to kill me?" She laughed. "The police are about to arrest the guy who killed Roger—they've told me so. And that slice in my radiator hose probably came from some mechanic who cut it accidentally. Really, Minnie, is your life so boring that you have to manufacture drama?"

Boring might be nice for a change. "Can you think of anyone else?"

"Minnie, you're being—"

"Can you," I cut in forcefully, "think of anyone else?"

"I already gave the police all the names I could think of," she said. "I'm sure they've followed up on everyone."

Or not, because they were sure they knew who the guy was.

"Just think a minute," I told her. "Assume there's someone else. Assume someone does want to kill you. Assume you're still in danger."

"That's a lot of assuming," she said, chuckling. "You know what assuming does, don't you? It makes an—"

"What about Allison Korthase?"

She huffed in a breath, but didn't say anything for a moment. Then . . . "What about her?"

"Would Allison want to kill you?"

"Well, she might if she knew. But she doesn't."

"Denise," I said warningly.

"Oh, keep your shirt on. All I meant was, there's no way Allison could know it was me."

"Know what was you?"

She sighed. "When Allison was running for city council, she came to a Friends meeting. She talked about literacy and the importance of libraries, and how if she was elected she'd support the library any and every way she could."

"That was a problem?" I asked.

"It wasn't that she showed up," Denise said. "It was what she said."

"I don't understand."

"Her speech," Denise said impatiently. "Part of it sounded weird. Different from the rest of what she was saying. Right off the bat, I thought she'd copied it from someone, so I started writing it down. When I got home, I typed it into the Internet and I was right." She chuckled. "Allison had pulled from one of Roosevelt's Fireside Chats. She didn't think anyone would notice, but I did, so I sent her an anonymous note."

The insides of my palms were tingling. "Then what?" I asked.

"Nothing." Denise puffed a breath of air into the phone. "In the note I told her that people knew what she'd done and she needed to clear her conscience if she was ever going to amount to anything. I said she needed to write a letter to the editor and admit she'd stolen that speech. She didn't, of course, because there's no way that woman would apologize for anything, but I did my duty. Still. There's absolutely no way she could have known it was me who wrote the note."

It all made an icky sort of sense. Denise was seeing her anonymous request as a way of righting a wrong, but Allison would have seen the completion of that request as grounds for public vilification.

I remembered the high-quality signs she'd posted far outside the city limits. Remembered the biographies of female heads of state she'd checked out of the library. Remembered her comment about Washington, DC.

This was a woman with lots of ambition. A woman who wouldn't let anything get in her way.

I was pretty sure my mother wouldn't approve of anonymous notes that were almost poison-pen letters, but I was glad Denise hadn't signed her name. It meant Allison didn't have any reason to do anything to Denise. "Her plans go far beyond Chilson," I murmured.

"What's that?" Denise asked. "Never mind. I have to go. I'm missing dinner." She hung up, Stephen style, and I was left with a silent phone in my hand.

Eddie bumped his head against my shin. I looked down. "I don't suppose you have an opinion on what really happened the afternoon Roger died. You were there, after all. Do you remember anything?"

He stopped cleaning and sat very, very, still, looking at me intently.

"Go ahead," I encouraged. "You can tell me."

"Mrr." He shifted forward a little and said it again, a little louder. "Mrr!"

"Yeah, that's what I figured." I sighed and patted him on the head. "I'll be back in a couple of hours, okay?"

"Mrr."

I gave him one more pat and started down the stairs. "Of course I'll drive carefully."

"Mrr!"

"Yes, I promise to be home before midnight."

"MRR!"

I grabbed my coat, pulled my wallet and keys out of my backpack, and opened the front door. "Yes, I promise not to do what the cool kids do just so I can try to be cool, too." And I slipped out the door and shut it before he could finish one more "Mrr."

Half an hour later, I was checking the time on my cell phone and walking into Charlevoix's hospital. Five minutes ago, assuming there were no emergencies that needed tending to, Tucker would have gone on his dinner break.

He didn't know I was coming, but we'd had such a nice time last night at Grey Gables that I figured he wouldn't mind a surprise visit. If he wasn't there, then no harm, no foul. I'd go home and call Kristen.

I trotted down the stairs, one hand on the cool metal railing, thinking about our good-night kiss. It had started out as polite, had gone into the tender mode, then had suddenly taken a hard turn into passionate. Where this was going I wasn't sure, but I was liking where we were right now. A lot.

The cafeteria wasn't crowded, and I spotted Tucker almost immediately. He was sitting with his back to me, a tray of food in front of him.

He was leaning forward, obviously talking to someone, but there was a half wall blocking my view of his dining partner.

I slowed, not wanting to interrupt what might be a private medical conversation. Maybe this wasn't a good idea. Some people didn't like surprises, and maybe Tucker was one of them.

A woman's laugh rang out, and Tucker laughed, too.

My slow walk became an even slower shuffle.

Fingers reached out toward Tucker. Female-shaped fingers. He took the woman's hand and squeezed it.

I stopped dead. My mouth opened to say something, anything, but although my face muscles moved, no words came out. For an eternal moment I stood there, locked in place, sure that there was no world outside of my bubble of shock.

Then a nearby clatter of silverware broke me free. I could breathe again, and I could move.

So I did. Out the door; up the stairs; and into a cold, rainy night.

An hour later, I was sitting in the living room with Eddie at my side, watching a DVD of *Raiders of the Lost Ark*, when my phone bleeped.

"Incoming text," I murmured to Eddie. "Think it's important enough to interrupt the movie?"

Eddie yawned and rolled over. Since I had no

idea if that was a negative or positive response, I leaned forward to pick the phone up off the coffee table. It was time for Aunt Frances to leave the college—it was possible she was having car trouble. Or maybe it was Kristen, responding to my earlier message. Or my mom, although we usually talked on Sunday nights. Or any number of library employees, calling in sick for the next day.

"Or not," I said out loud. It was Tucker. I thumbed open the message.

Sorry, can't make the movie tomorrow night. Call you later.

I tossed the phone, sending it skittering across the table. My toss had been a little too hard, and it fell off the other side, dropping onto the carpet with a small *thud*.

"It's over," I said quietly.

Eddie stood and climbed into my lap. I gave him a few pats and felt his purr start to rumble. But even the strength of an Eddie purr wasn't going to do the trick—not tonight, not now.

I kissed the top of his head. "I'm headed out for a walk, okay? I'll be back in a little while."

The night's chill air bit into me as I went down the porch steps. I zipped my coat to the top, where it brushed the bottom of my chin in a slightly uncomfortable way. Staying warm was always a trade-off in winter, since it so often involved being uncomfortable, whether through too many layers of clothes, just the time involved to put on proper boots, or the squishing of your hair with a warm hat.

I stopped halfway down the front walk and looked up. While rain clouds still covered most of the sky, there were spots where stars were spangling through, twinkling down from so many unimaginable miles away. Many people found perspective while looking at the stars; I usually found myself wishing I'd brought out a luminous star chart. I was okay with identifying the simplest constellations, the dippers and Orion, but I wouldn't have been able to find Cassiopeia on a double bet with Rafe.

The stars twinkled, the Milky Way glowed, and since it was too early to expect to see any northern lights and my toes were getting cold, I headed for the sidewalk. A jaunt of a few blocks would help set my mind straight. If Tucker had found someone else, well, I'd learn how to move on. I'd done it before; I could do it again.

With my mind made up to be cheerful, I headed out, head high. If Tucker didn't want me, then I didn't want him, either. It was his loss. It was—

The light slam of a door turned me around. Otto Bingham was standing on his front porch, looking across to the boardinghouse.

"Hi," I said.

Otto jumped at the sound of my voice.

"Nice night," I went on, "if you're a polar bear."

He nodded in my general direction, then turned back around and put his hand on the door handle.

With an internal flash of light and heat, I'd suddenly had enough. Enough of Tucker, enough of Stephen, the library board, and definitely enough of this man, who had spoken to me only once in all the times I'd been friendly to him, and even then it had been a short and strange conversation.

"Mr. Bingham," I said firmly, using my librarian voice as I marched up to him. "Why do you walk away from me almost every time I talk to you? If I've done something to offend or anger you, please tell me so I can make amends. It seems as if you're avoiding me, and I hate being on bad terms with my neighbors."

Otto Bingham stood quietly, his hand still on the oval doorknob. "I'm . . . I'm not avoiding you. It's just . . ." He stopped talking and shook his head.

"Just what?" I practically shouted. "It's my hair? You can't stand curly hair—is that it? Or maybe you don't like short people? Which is a silly prejudice, but that's pretty much an oxymoron. Or, wait, you hate librarians. You were scolded by one as a small child and still haven't recovered. Or it is that you have an innate hatred of cat hair, and, since I have a cat, you have to hate me, too?"

Suddenly, I realized that I was waving my arms and shouting at the top of my lungs. Mom would not have approved, and actually, I didn't approve of myself, either.

I dropped my arms and took a deep breath before starting my apology about having a bad day, about being tired, about having no excuse for that kind of behavior. But before I got out the first "I'm sorry," I heard an unexpected sound. Otto Bingham was laughing.

"It's the curly hair," he said. "No doubt about it."

I peered up at him. "You're joking, right?"

"Of course I am." He pushed open the door to his house and stood back, inviting me in. "If you have a few minutes, I have a story to tell you."

Who could resist a story? I sent a quick text to my aunt *(At Otto's—be home soon)* and followed him inside.

Chapter 16

In short order, Otto settled me into a small room that was closer to being a parlor than any room I'd ever set foot in. A pint-sized fireplace sent out a cozy glow over the two wingback chairs that faced it. Occasional tables, small bookcases, and scenic paintings decorated the space in a way that was elegant without being uptight, and I was still admiring it all when Otto came back into the room with two glasses of wine.

He'd shed his coat and was wearing crisp jeans and a smooth buttoned shirt. "I hope you like this," he said, and cited the year and varietal.

When he started to talk about the vintner, I put up my hand. "Sorry, but I wouldn't know a smooth finish from sandpaper. My best friend, Kristen, owns a restaurant here in town, and she's picked all my wines for me since the day she caught me drinking white zinfandel." Which I still liked, every once in a while, but I would unhesitatingly say I never touched the stuff if she ever asked.

Otto gave me a pained look but said, "You have a cat, so I hope you don't mind a little cat hair. Though I try to keep this room free of the stuff, it's a difficult task."

I laughed and picked an errant Eddie hair from my pant leg. "Here," I said, handing it over to him. "We'll call it a draw."

We exchanged cat names and cat antics for a bit, and when that conversation started to lag, he said with a sigh, "But I lured you in with the promise of a story."

"You did," I agreed. "I recommend starting at the beginning."

"Always a good idea." Otto sipped his wine. "And I suppose the beginning of this particular story starts last summer with Leo."

I sat up straight and almost spilled my glass. Which would have been a shame, because the wine was extremely good. Maybe Kristen's lessons were finally rubbing off. "Leo Kinsler?"

"The very one. Leo and I have been friends since high school."

Leo had also been one of my aunt's boarders last summer. He'd driven off into the metaphorical sunset with another of her boarders and, every so often, we'd get e-mails or Facebook posts from the pair.

"Late last spring," Otto was saying, "Leo told me he was coming up here for the summer, to stay in a boardinghouse, of all places. Now, don't look at me like that. My images of a boardinghouse were based on my great-uncle's Depression-era stories. I tried to convince Leo to stay home where he belonged, where we could golf all summer like always, but he was intent on coming north."

I blinked. "Leo golfs?"

"He's a seven handicap."

"Is that good?"

Otto looked at me over the rim of his wineglass. "I take it you're not a golfer."

While I was excellent at miniature golf, I suspected that wasn't what he was talking about. "So, Leo came up here in June, against your advice?"

"Stubborn bugger," Otto said, nodding. "But he loved it up here. Every time we talked or e-mailed, he'd paint this picture of a northern Michigan Shangri-la. He talked about Chilson, about how it sits on the edge of Janay Lake and next to Lake Michigan, about how the people are open and welcoming. He described the countryside, with its hills and lakes and winding roads. He told me about the boardinghouse, about the maps thumbtacked to the knotty pine walls, about the bell someone always rings before meals. He talked about the other boarders." Otto studied his glass. "He talked about you, about Eddie, about the bookmobile. And . . . and he talked about Frances."

With a blinding flash of the obvious, I saw all. Leo had spun Otto a fantasy so vivid that he'd fallen in love with my aunt without ever meeting her. *Good job, Leo,* I thought sourly.

"I drove up in early September," Otto said, "and Chilson was everything Leo said it was."

"Really?" I found that hard to believe. I loved my adopted town dearly, but it was in no way a fairy-tale place. Real people—with real problems and real personalities—lived in it, and real life was often messy.

Otto smiled. "I gave up wearing rose-colored glasses decades ago, Minnie. Too many of my clients were elected officials. I knew Leo's description glossed over some bumps. But overall, I've found that he was right. The second week I was here, this house went up for sale. I told Leo, and he said it was fate."

I made a rude noise in the back of my throat, and

Otto laughed. "That's more or less what I told Leo, but I bought the house anyway. I've been enjoying myself immensely, settling in and getting to know people around town."

"But not my aunt Frances."

He slid down in his chair a little, diminishing himself. "No," he said quietly. "Not her. I'd been working up the courage to knock on her door and I was almost there, but then the other night you told me about her woodworking skills, about her teaching. What does a woman that interesting and accomplished need with a man like me? What can I offer her? I'm a retired accountant. It's hard to get more boring than that." His shoulders sagged, and his wineglass came dangerously close to tipping over.

I eyed him. He seemed sincere, but I barely knew the man. What guarantee did I have that he wasn't some crazed stalker who would make my aunt's life miserable?

"Here." Otto pulled a cell phone from his shirt pocket. "Let me call Leo. You can ask him anything you like about me." He quirked up a smile. "Well, anything except what we did to Mr. Lane's physics room after school that day."

He pushed a few buttons and handed me the phone. "Otto!" Leo said. "It's warm and sunny in southern Texas. How's northern Michigan?"

"Cold and rainy," I said, smiling. "And it turns out that Eddie isn't fond of snow."

There was a pause. "Minnie." Leo laughed. "You have got to be kidding me. Otto actually introduced himself?"

Sort of. "To me. Should I introduce him to Aunt Frances?"

"Ah." Leo chuckled. "He hasn't worked up to that, has he? Otto is a great guy, and I can say that because I've known him for more than fifty years. He's the best CPA I've ever met, but he's as horrible with women as he is good with numbers. He managed to get married once, but she died years ago and they didn't have any children. He's been alone ever since."

I stood, walked to the fireplace, and kept my voice low. "If my aunt was your sister, would you introduce them?"

Leo snorted. "I did introduce him to my sister, years ago, but she went and married a guy who owns a masonry business. Minnie, all Otto needs is a break. He gets stage fright something horrible when he meets women. I bet you've seen him a dozen times, coming out of his house but then going back in."

Clearly, Leo knew Otto very well.

"All he needs is a break," Leo repeated. "Do me a favor and introduce them. If things don't work out, it wasn't meant to be. But if they do, well, we'll have two less lonely people in the world."

I wanted to object, to say that my aunt wasn't lonely—how could she be with me in the winter and a houseful of boarders in the summer? But I knew better. Every so often, I saw her sadness, saw how solitude scraped at her.

After thanking Leo, I handed the phone back to Otto and asked, "Do you know Denise Slade?"

His blank look instantly convinced me that he didn't. If he had known her, he would have shown some sort of reaction. Not that a newcomer to Chilson was likely to have killed Roger in an attempt on Denise's life, but you never knew—*anyone can commit murder*—and I had to protect Aunt Frances. As much as she would let me, anyway.

"Come over Monday night," I said. "After dinner. I'll make the introductions. Now stop looking so scared." I put my hands on my hips and gave him a mild version of the Librarian Look until he smiled. "That's better. I'm a very good introducer, and the two of you will be friends in no time."

Otto got up to fetch my coat. "Maybe this can wait," he said tentatively.

"Monday night," I said.

On my way back across the street, I started laughing out loud. I was about to matchmake the matchmaker. If there weren't the specter of the bookmobile's demise hanging over my head, and the very real possibility that someone out there was still trying to kill Denise, I would have thought that life was very good.

• • •

The next morning, the rain was falling down so heavily that I drove to the library. I arrived early and scampered through a number of tasks that would look at me sorrowfully and shake their heads in despair if I didn't get them done. But as soon as I finished the last have-to job, I shut my office door and went back to my desk with one thing on my mind.

Save the bookmobile.

Which meant figuring out who killed Roger. Which, I was sure, meant figuring out who wanted to kill Denise.

There was the tiniest twinge of Mom-induced guilt that hovered in a back corner of my brain, but I told it to go away. Yes, I was at work and could have been expected to be, well, working, but keeping the bookmobile on the road was my job, too.

I grabbed my purse and, for the first time ever, left the building without telling anyone.

Forty-five minutes later, I was standing at the edge of the Jurco River, looking at the Jurco Dam. I was also shivering, because I wasn't dressed properly. Jeremy had said he'd been here the day Roger was killed, and I'd seen his car about ten miles away from the gas station. If he was here at the time he'd said he'd been, there wasn't enough time for him to get in place to shoot Roger, not with the condition of the gravel road I'd just traveled.

331

I glanced back at my poor little sedan, which was now coated with thick spatterings of mud, courtesy of the rutted road.

So now my only problem was: How could I confirm or deny the time Jeremy had been here? If he hated Denise enough, he might have overcome his aversion to blood and guns.

I stood at the end of the small dam, watching the water rush through, down, and away. *Checking water levels,* he'd said. Water levels above the dam? Below the dam? Both? There were so many things I didn't know; dam knowledge was just one more.

"Hang on," I said out loud.

There, fastened to the end of the dam, about three feet off the ground, was a metal object that looked like a really boring mailbox. I stepped sideways down the shallow slope toward it. The gray metal box was about eighteen inches tall and a foot wide.

I slipped on the slushy ground and slid sideways against the box, grunting as my hip hit a sharp corner. Score one for being short. If I'd been taller, the box would have smacked me in the thigh instead of my softest part.

"Please don't be locked," I said on a breath, feeling around for a catch on the box. "Please . . ."

My fingers found a fastener. With a quiet *click,* it released, and I swung open the door. Inside was a clipboard with a pen attached. On the clipboard was a stack of papers warped from dampness. On the papers were a series of numbers and dates and times and abbreviations.

I pulled the whole thing out and started studying. "Hello."

I jumped and almost dropped the clipboard to the wet ground. Up above me was a woman about my own age, dressed in a warm-looking dark knit hat, heavy boots, dark green pants, and dark green winter jacket, to which a gold shield was pinned. "Hi," I said. "I was just, um, looking at the data."

The conservation officer nodded. "Jeremy Hull's work, mostly, but I take the readings when I'm over here. So does the other CO for the county, Officer Wartella. I'm Officer Jenica Thomas."

Wartella had been the CO I'd talked to what seemed like months ago. "Really?" I asked. "Taking readings is part of your job?"

She nodded but didn't say anything.

"This is my first time out here. Can you explain this?" I pointed to the sheet. "The dates and times I get, but some of these others don't make a lot of sense."

"No problem." She scrambled down to me, sure-footed on the wet, muddy surface. "Date and time, as you said. Those are the initials of the person recording the data." She pointed. "Next is an abbreviation for the weather condition. Sunny, raining, and so on. Then temperature, then the elevation above and below the dam, which is plus or minus from a mark on the dam wall."

Now that it was explained, it all made sense. "How accurate are these?" I asked. "I mean, what if someone writes down a wrong number or something?"

Officer Thomas pulled in a breath. "Incorrect elevations should show up as an anomaly."

"What if it was the wrong time?" I persisted. "What if it was, say, the time-change weekend and someone wrote down the old time instead of the right one?"

The CO considered my question seriously. "It's possible," she finally said, "but unlikely. The people trained to take these elevations are competent and conscientious folks who take this effort seriously. None of us is likely to compromise the data by making an error."

"Why a clipboard?" I asked. "Why isn't it entered into a computer?"

"It is," Officer Thomas said. "We have an extensive data set for this monitoring project. We just like to have the paper copy in case it needs to be used in a court of law." She waited a beat. "Do you have any other questions?"

"No. All set." I tucked the clipboard into its home and shut the door. Jeremy couldn't be the killer. I knew it for sure now.

A few minutes after I snuck back into my office, there was a knock on the door. Holly poked her head inside. "Minnie, it's break time. I made cupcakes yesterday for Wilson's classroom, and there are a few extras."

"Sounds good," I said vaguely, not taking my eyes off the monitor or my fingers off the keyboard. "I'll be there in a little bit."

Holly said something, I made an ambiguous noise, and she retreated, shutting the door softly behind her.

There was another knock on the door.

"I'll be there in a second," I said, still typing.

"Don't go yet." Mitchell slipped into my office and shut the door behind him. "Slipped" being a subjective word, of course, because it was hard for anyone that tall to be unobtrusive. "I got something to show you."

"What are you doing here?" I squinched my eyes shut and opened them again. "Sorry, I didn't mean it like that. It's just that you're never at the library before noon." I leaned back, rotating my shoulders and flexing my fingers, all of which I suddenly realized were very, very stiff.

"True that." Mitchell nodded seriously. "Why ruin a good morning by getting out in it, is what I say."

I frowned and, for the first time in hours, looked at the clock on my computer. *Half past one? How can that be?*

"What're you doing, anyway?" Mitchell came around my side of the desk. "Working? Hey!" He pointed to the monitor before I could bring up another file to cover what I was doing. "You're working on who killed Roger, too." He put his hands flat on the edge of my desk and started reading. "Huh. You got a lot of the same stuff I did, only with more extra stuff. Like lots of details." He read the narrative I'd been constructing all morning, the story of everything I'd learned about Roger and Denise.

He grunted and stood more or less straight. "How come you're doing this?"

For a brief moment, I considered confiding in Mitchell. Telling him about the library board's ultimatum, about my flashes of empathy for Denise, about my guilt and my responsibility for Roger's death, about the possible end of the bookmobile.

My sanity restored itself a nanosecond later. The absolute last thing I needed was Mitchell's bumbling, though well-intentioned, assistance.

"Just trying to help," I said. Which wasn't much of an explanation, but with any luck, he'd accept it.

"Yeah, I can see that." He nodded. "That's like what I'm doing here," he said, pulling a pile of yellow legal pad sheets from where he'd stuffed them inside his coat. "Can you guess what this is? Just read; see if you can figure it out."

It was another multipage listing of names, and this one was even longer than the list he'd prepared of all the people Roger had ever known. Much longer.

I scanned the handwritten sheets. Most of the names I didn't recognize, but every few lines I'd pick out one that I did. Pam Fazio. Kelsey Lyons. Josh Hadden. Don Weller. Holly Terpening. Jeremy Hull. Donna Beene. Allison Korthase. Bruce Medler. Sondra Luth. Otis Rahn. Shannon Hirsch. Stephen Rangel. Minnie Hamilton.

I squinted up at Mitchell. "What's my name doing here?"

"Yeah." He grinned. "What kind of list do you think it is?"

As far as I could tell, it was a list of all the people who lived in Chilson. "I have no idea."

Mitchell picked a pen out of my old ABOS coffee mug and, as he wrote a title on the top page, said the words out loud. "Anyone Who Has Ever Said Anything Bad about Denise Slade."

I started to object, but stopped and felt ashamed of myself. Yes, every so often, I ignored my mother's oft-repeated maxim about not saying anything if I didn't have anything nice to say. I'd probably said uncomplimentary things about Denise, and if I'd said them within Mitchell's hearing, I should be doubly ashamed.

"Yeah." With a finger riddled with hangnails, Mitchell tapped at my name. "Once I heard you say that Denise sees everything in black and white. It didn't sound like a compliment, you know? So I had to put you down."

Thinking about it, I had to agree.

Starting at the top of the list, Mitchell began telling me exactly why each of the names were included. Ten minutes later, he flipped to page two. "And Bruce Medler? That library-board guy? Well, this one day, I heard him—"

"Wow, I'm sorry, Mitchell," I said, getting to my feet, "but would you look at the time? Why don't you type all that up? Then e-mail it to me."

"Yeah?" Mitchell gathered up his papers. "That's a good idea, Minnie. Real good. Must be why you get the big bucks, right?"

"Right." I ushered him out, shut the door behind him, and went back to my desk.

She sees everything in black and white.

I sat down and got to work.

Chapter 17

During my typical walk from the library to Chilson's downtown, I made sure to admire the sunlight on the steeple of the Methodist church, the stonework on the former corner gas station–turned–real estate office, the window display in Upton's Clothing, and the smells from Tom's Bakery.

But instead of doing all that, this time I walked

toward the deli, with my head down against the unending rain, thinking hard. Which was why I didn't see the small child until I almost ran into him.

"Whoa!" I jumped back before I knocked the poor thing to the sidewalk. "Sorry about that."

His mother, or at least the woman I assumed was his mother, turned around and called. "Brody, what are you doing? I told you to hang on to my coat." Her arms were full of shopping bags, a diaper bag, and an infant. "Hurry up, now."

But the boy, who might have been five, didn't move. He pointed at the sky. "Look, Mommy! It's a bald eagle!"

"That's nice. Now hurry up. We have a lot to do." Mommy, busy and harried, didn't look up, but I did. There was, in fact, a large bird floating about up in the sky, wings spread wide, head turning left and right, looking for whatever it was large birds look for. In this case, probably a late lunch.

"It's a bald eagle," Brody said, and it was instantly clear to me that the kid wasn't going to move until Mom admitted that the bird was an eagle.

"Of course it is," Mom said, sending me a busy smile. "This nice lady thinks so, too, I bet."

I squinted up at the bird. In summer, sitting on the front of my houseboat, I'd see eagles every once in a while, but in spite of the bookmobile's bird book, I was no expert and I didn't want to name the bird incorrectly. Librarians aren't big on that kind of behavior.

"I'm not sure," I said. "Maybe, but I can't quite see if it has a white head or not." Even if it didn't, if I remembered correctly from a long-ago science class, it could still be a bald eagle, a young one, since their heads didn't get fully white until they were about five years old.

"Eagle." Brody stomped his foot. "It's a bald eagle."

"Actually, it is."

The three of us turned. Shannon Hirsch stood a few feet away, squinting a little as she watched the bird. "Big one, too, so it's probably a female."

"I told you." Brody stomped his feet again, making small splashes on the wet sidewalk. "It's a bald eagle."

"You can tell?" Mom asked. "For sure?"

"Without any doubt." Shannon grinned at me. "The trophies in my office? Having bizarrely sharp vision made winning all those a lot easier."

Mom thanked her and escorted Brody to their next task.

I looked at Shannon. "Have you won anything lately?"

"Not hardly," she said. "My competition guns are at the gunsmith for maintenance. I usually do my own cleaning, but I've been too busy."

"How long have your guns been out?"

"A month. About the longest month of my life."

"Who do you use?" I asked casually. "Someone local?"

"There's a guy down in Grayling I trust, but he's been slammed with work because of hunting season. I should have known better, right?" She smiled ruefully. "Well, back to the trenches."

We made our mutual good-byes and walked off in different directions.

Inside the deli, I found myself in line—if you could call the two people in front of me a line, and once you'd lived Up North for a full year, you did—behind Pam Fazio.

"Hey there," she said. "Didn't you say you have a couple of nieces?"

I nodded. "Katrina is fifteen, and Sally is eleven." I also had a nephew, Ben, who'd been born in the middle. "If you have any ideas for Christmas presents, I'm open to any and all suggestions."

"Got a shipment yesterday," she said, "and the container—"

There had been conversation going on around us at the occupied tables, but the instant Pam had said the word "container," everyone stopped talking.

"Yes," she said, laughing and spreading her arms wide in invitation. "Yesterday was container day. I'll have everything unpacked by early next week."

"Where was this one from?" someone asked.

"Ireland," Pam said, putting on an Irish accent. "With lace and glass and sideboards from foggy green coasts. With boots and books and bottles and crates full of things unseen."

"Books?" I asked. Pam made regular trips overseas, buying hither and yon and packing everything into a massive container that got stowed on a ship and eventually arrived in northern lower Michigan.

"Of all sorts. And," she said, winking broadly, "some lovely hand mirrors that might be just the thing for young nieces."

It sounded perfect. "How about a present for a thirteen-year-old nephew?"

"Now, Minnie," she said, dropping the accent. "There's only so much even I can do for you."

I laughed and was really, really glad that this nice woman wasn't a killer.

The afternoon flew past as quickly as the morning had. Just as I was thinking that it was time to pack up and go home, my phone rang. The line was full of pops and static, and I wasn't sure there was anyone on the other end, but I said hello and gave my name anyway.

"Minnie . . . you?"

I stood, as if that might help the reception. It didn't, of course, but at least I'd tried. "Cade? What's up?"

"Nothing . . . just closed . . . auction . . . price was . . . thousand dollars."

He sounded excited, but that had to be the line's poor quality, because there was no way he should be pleased about selling a painting for a thousand dollars. I'd looked up his work and had been shocked to find out that some of his larger paintings had sold for six figures. In front of the decimal. Not that a thousand dollars wasn't a nice donation to the library, but I'd held out hopes for more. "Thanks for letting me know," I said. "I'm happy the family even considered the library."

"Not . . . library . . . thousand . . ."

"Cade? Are you there?"

Nothing. The line wasn't just quiet—it was dead.

I returned the receiver to its cradle. So much for the library board being thrilled with my fundraising efforts. They'd see the thousand-dollar check, pat me on the head (in so many words), and ask what I was going to do for them next month.

"Stop that," I said out loud. As in, stop feeling sorry for myself. Stop acting as if there was nothing I could do to find Roger's killer. Stop acting as if there was no way to save the bookmobile. Stop acting as if I was scared of the library board and the pending lawsuit. Stop acting as if I was a helpless pawn in the game of life with no options and no way out.

What I needed to do was remember how much

I'd accomplished and move on from there. I was smart, on good days, and resourceful almost always. I would figure this out. Whether I'd figure it out by next Wednesday was another question, of course, but I wasn't going to worry about that now. Right now I was going to go home and eat whatever Aunt Frances was making for dinner.

I pulled on my coat, grabbed my backpack, and was about to shut down the computer for the weekend when my e-mail program dinged with an incoming message.

Read or don't read; that was the question.

"Don't read," I said, and powered down. Whatever it was could wait until Monday.

Over a meal of fettuccini with various types of squash in some sort of olive oil–based sauce, I told Aunt Frances about my day, about how I'd fact-checked as many of my theories as I could, and about the conclusions I'd reached.

"First, I typed up reasons why Roger could have been the intended victim all along."

"Mrr," Eddie said. He was sitting in his new favorite spot: the seat of a rocking chair that had been moved into the corner of the kitchen from the screened back porch. You would have thought rocking chairs would be anathema to a creature with a long tail, but Eddie seemed to like it. "Mrr," he said again.

"Yeah." I nodded agreement. "It wasn't a very

long list." My own list had been inspired by Mitchell's lists of names, and maybe someday I'd tell him that. Probably not, but maybe.

My conclusion, arrived at after hours of typing, researching, and thinking, was that Roger was exactly who he appeared to be. A happy man, content with his place in life and comfortable in his own skin. Maybe he had made enemies at some point, but if he had, I hadn't found any, and that's a hard thing to hide when you've lived in the same small town your entire life.

I speared a piece of squash. "So, I went with the working assumption that Denise was the intended target."

My aunt gave an unladylike snort. "Good luck. That one has done nothing but make enemies since she was a child." She contemplated her fork. "I suppose I should feel sorry for her. Maybe she was born that way, maybe she can't help having a personality like a hacksaw, but there are some people who make empathy hard."

"Mrr," Eddie said.

Aunt Frances and I looked at him. He looked back, blinked, then started licking his front paw.

"Anyway," I said, turning my attention back to the topic at hand, "Denise has alienated half the town."

"Is that all?" my aunt murmured.

"But alienation," I went on, "does not necessarily an enemy make."

Aunt Frances got a questioning look on her face. "So what makes an enemy an enemy?"

"Exactly!" I beamed. "That was the next phase of my research."

"You researched enemy making?" She smirked. "What did you do, Google it? Bet that turned up some interesting links."

"Mrr!" Eddie glared in her direction.

Aunt Frances laughed. "I don't think he likes it when I make fun of you."

"We have a bond."

"Sorry, Eddie," my aunt said.

Outwardly mollified, Eddie curled himself into a cat-sized ball, thereby withdrawing himself from our conversation.

"One conclusion of my research," I said, "is that the result of irritating someone is most often a distancing effect."

I could see a puzzled expression on my aunt's face, so I knew I wasn't making complete sense. It was all straight in my head, though. "Pam Fazio, for instance. Denise annoyed her to the point that she walked out on the Friends."

"And said that she'd only return over Denise's dead body," Aunt Frances added.

I squirmed a little. "Yes, but that's just something people say. And anyway, Pam was out of the state that day on a buying trip." A fact I'd confirmed with one of her neighbors.

Aunt Frances nodded. "Okay, we can eliminate

Pam. But what about the others you've talked about? That new council member, Allison. Plus Jeremy Hull, Don Weller, and Shannon Hirsch."

"Jeremy." I lined my mental ducks up in a row. "He holds a nasty grudge against Denise for leaving his organization in a tight spot and for almost getting him fired. Plus I saw his car out there the day Roger was killed. But I confirmed that he was checking the water levels at the Jurco Dam and the timing doesn't work. The data sheets have an entry for time of day, and Jeremy's job hangs on being accurate, so it doesn't make sense that he did it."

I'd done some checking up on Jeremy and had quickly found out that although his reputation for management wasn't outstanding, he was reported to be a top-notch environmental scientist. And he was smart; if he'd wanted to kill Denise, he would have figured out a way that didn't include falsifying data.

"What about Don Weller?" Aunt Frances asked. "Seems to me anyone who lived next door to Denise would end up wanting to kill her."

I grinned. "You should have seen that video he made. Don wants revenge, all right, but he didn't hate her enough to kill her." And I had no doubt that someday he would get his revenge. Not for a year or two—he was a decent man and would wait until the shock of losing Roger had diminished—

but someday he would gleefully turn her in for some minor infraction.

"Then who's left?" My aunt thought back. "Allison Korthase. And Shannon Hirsch."

Shannon's sharp eyesight and honed shooting skills made it unlikely that she would have mistaken Roger for Denise, but what if I was wrong and Roger had been the target all along? Or maybe Shannon intended to kill both Slades, righting an old high-school wrong that had festered for years. I shivered at the thought.

"This afternoon," I said, "I ran into Shannon, and she said her guns are at the gunsmith for maintenance. She said he was in Grayling, so I made a few calls and tracked him down. He's had her guns for almost five weeks."

For more than a month, Shannon's guns had been out of her hands. Roger had died three weeks ago. Ergo, Shannon had not killed him. Okay, she could have borrowed a gun or purchased a new one, but I didn't see it. Not for someone who'd just said the month without her guns had been the longest of her life. And that meant . . .

My aunt twirled a last bit of fettuccine onto her fork. "Have you talked to the police about this? You do realize that they're trained investigators and are paid to do this kind of work."

I picked at the remains of my dinner. One thing I hadn't told Aunt Frances was that Ash Wolverson had asked me out on a date. The uncomfortable awkwardness between us would pass soon enough, but right now it was still, well, uncomfortable. And since Detective Inwood pushed the legwork of the investigation to Ash . . .

"I'll call the detective on Monday," I said. "Besides, I really don't know anything, not for sure. All I have are guesses and theories."

"But the killer doesn't know that," my aunt pointed out. "She or he is still out there. Denise could still be in danger."

"That was two weeks ago," I said. "Nothing has happened to her since then. I bet the killer got cold feet, realized that getting away with one murder was a minor miracle, and won't try again."

My aunt looked at the rocking chair. "What do you think?"

Eddie opened his eyes and made a silent "Mrr."

Aunt Frances frowned. "Are you sure he doesn't understand us?"

"Pretty sure," I said, but my mind was still circling with the thought that had been haunting me for days.

Anyone can commit murder.

Chapter 18

Early the next morning, soon after I'd finished dressing and just as I was toweling off my hair, my cell rang. Since I was busy watching raindrops pelt against the window, I decided it was time to get some help from my roommate.

"Hey, Eddie, would you get that, please?"

My cat, who was lying in the exact middle of my bed, which was the same place he'd spent the entire night, no matter how many times I'd tried to gently shove him to one side, didn't even lift his head.

"Some help you are," I said, picking up the phone. "And after all I do for . . . uh-oh." The incoming call was from Donna, my volunteer for the day.

"Minnie?" a voice croaked. "It's Donna." There was a pause, and I heard a distant, racking cough. "I'm so sorry," she said when she came back, "but I woke up sick. I really don't think I should come out on the bookmobile today."

"Absolutely not," I told her. "The last thing you need to do is go out in this weather. Read some of Jan Karon's Mitford books, and I'll see you when you're better." I ended the call and immediately started another one. "Kelsey? It's Minnie."

Two short sentences of explanation later,

Kelsey said, "Let me think. My mom's in Chicago for her annual Christmas shopping trip, and my husband's working today. I'll call around and see if I can find a sitter for the kids."

Which she might or might not be able to find, and, even if she did, there was no way the sitter would be in place in half an hour, which was our appointed departure time.

"Thanks anyway, Kelsey," I said. "I'm sure I can find someone else."

But who? I scrolled through the numbers in my phone and called Holly.

"Oh, wow, Minnie. I'm sorry, but I promised the kids I'd take them to the indoor water park at Boyne today. They've been excited about this all week."

I told her not to worry about it, and called Josh.

"You want me to do what?" He laughed. "Let me guess: I'm not going to get paid, either."

"I'll pay you myself," I said, "if that's what it takes."

He must have heard the near desperation in my voice. "Hey, I was just joking. I'd help if I could, especially if Eddie's coming along, but remember? My buddies and I are going to the Michigan State game this afternoon and the Lions game tomorrow."

The voices and the road noise in the background suddenly made sense. In my half panic, I'd forgotten about the weekend he'd been talking about since August. "Sorry," I said. "I forgot. Have a good time, okay?"

I stared at my phone. *Now what?* I'd exhausted all the library staff I felt able to call at this hour on a Saturday morning, Lina was out of town, and there was no way I was going to call Stephen and beg for his help. I'd go back to school, get a PhD in biochemistry, and clone myself before I did that.

I looked at my phone list again. "Hah," I said. "Got it." I stabbed at the DIAL button and was surprised when it was picked up half a ring later.

"Morning, sunshine," Rafe said cheerfully.

I squinted in the direction of the marina. "You sound wide awake."

"Of course I am. Why wouldn't I be?"

"Because you're never awake before ten on Saturdays during the school year."

"Au contraire," he said. "I am always awake by seven thirty on the mornings that my kitchen appliances are to be delivered."

My last hope circled the drain and dropped down. "Oh. That's nice."

"Liar," he said. "What's the matter?"

I debated lying some more, but knew he'd call me on it. One of these days, I really had to work on increasing my obfuscation skills. "I just needed some help this morning."

"Sorry about that. I would if I could."

"Yeah, I know. Thanks anyway."

I stared at the phone. Sighed. Sighed again, this time so heavily that Eddie went to the trouble of picking up his head to look at me. I dialed one more time.

"Denise? It's Minnie. I have a big favor to ask . . ."

Nine hours and eight stops later, I was regretting that I hadn't given up and simply canceled the day's bookmobile trip. I was also starting to regret the dark clothes I'd chosen to wear, as they were a perfect magnet for Eddie hair, but I'd been regretting Denise's presence far longer. I was reaching the end of my patience and I hoped that I could keep my temper in check, at least while there were bookmobile patrons on board.

For eight hours and fifty-five minutes, Denise had been on her smart phone whenever she'd found coverage, texting, creating Facebook posts and tweets—and reading them out loud to me as she typed—about how brave she was to go out on the bookmobile so soon after her husband was killed on it, how important she was to the book-mobile's outreach, and generally patting herself on the back so hard I was surprised she didn't have a repetitive-stress injury.

But, in general, the stops went smoothly enough while Eddie, from his seat on the console, surveyed his small kingdom with a judicious eye and made the occasional comment.

At the last stop, a busy mother of three small children, who was checking out a pile of picture books, turned to him. "Eddie, what do you think? Is it time for my oldest to start chapter books?"

He studied her for a moment, then said, "Mrr."

"Thought so," she said, and added another book to the stack. "Thanks."

I shook my head. My cat was a better librarian than I was. Of all the things Stephen didn't need to know, this had to be in the top two.

A few minutes later, I shooed everyone out. Thanks to the heavy rain, we'd arrived at this last stop of the day a little late and, thanks to my disinclination to cut a stop short, it was now past the time we should have closed up shop and headed home.

"Thanks for coming out in this weather," I said to the last exiting person. "See you soon." By the time I slid into the driver's seat, Denise had already encouraged Eddie into his strapped-down carrier and was fussing with her phone.

I started the engine and turned on the headlights. It had been one of those days of rain and low, heavy cloud cover, one of those dark gray days that made you want to stay inside with a book and a never-ending bowl of popcorn. It had never truly gotten light outside, and what little there had been was fading fast.

After peering left and right into the gloom, I pulled out of the parking lot and accelerated slowly.

"Can you believe that Shannon Hirsch?" Denise said, thumbing at her phone and making a gagging noise. "She puts the weirdest stuff on Facebook. Want to hear her latest?"

Short of slapping duct tape over Denise's mouth or shoving plugs into my ears, there wasn't any way I'd be able not to. I did briefly wonder why two sworn enemies would be Facebook friends, but there were lots of things I wondered about. The future of space exploration, for one. Why Eddie drank out of the far side of his water bowl, for another.

"She's talking about the books she's given away and wishes she hadn't. Can you believe that?"

I murmured something vague.

"I know, right?" Denise nodded as if I'd agreed with her. "Who cares if she gave away her grand-mother's copy of *Little Women* by accident? I mean, am I asking for sympathy because my husband put my boxed set of *A Song of Ice and Fire* in the sale? Can you believe he didn't know it's the same thing as *A Game of Thrones*? I mean . . . What's the matter?"

She asked this because I was braking hard. When we came to a stop, I turned on the four-way flashers, put the bookmobile into park, and turned to her.

"You gave away a boxed set of George Martin's books?"

"Weren't you listening? I didn't give them away—Roger did."

"To the book sale upstairs?" I asked. "The Friends' sale?"

"You'd rather I take them to the Petoskey library? What's wrong with you?"

"When we were on the bookmobile before," I persisted, "you said you sometimes write in books. Did you write anything in those?"

"Oh, for crying out loud," she huffed. "Is that what this is about—you're worried that the Friends are selling defaced books? Well, gosh, Miss Librarian, I'm so sorry, but, yes, I did write in those books. Anyone who wanted to keep track of all those names would do the same thing. I didn't know I was going to be graded on—"

"That note you sent to Allison Korthase." Denise glared at my interruption, but right now I didn't care about politeness. "That anonymous note. Did you write that by hand or did you print it out on the computer?"

"By hand," she said sulkily. "So what?"

"The Wednesday before Roger died," I said, remembering. Mitchell had handed me the key to the mystery without even knowing it. "Allison Korthase bought that boxed set. Did it have your name in it?"

Denise frowned, not understanding, but then

her face went flat and white. "Yes. It did. Allison knows what my handwriting looks like," she whispered. "She's known for a month."

The police needed to know, and they needed to know as soon as possible. "Do you have reception?" I pointed at Denise's phone.

She glanced at the screen. "Not much."

I turned off the flashers, checked for traffic, and pulled back onto the road. Spotty cell reception was one of the few annoying things about living Up North. I'd have to wait until we got back to Chilson to call the sheriff's office.

The rain suddenly started pounding down full force times two. I flicked the windshield wipers to high and slowed to a safe speed. Denise wasn't talking about the elephant on the bus, so I did. "I think Allison killed Roger. And I think she sliced your radiator hose."

Denise stared through the wet windshield. "Roger was killed by a hunter. Allison didn't kill him instead of me. It's not my fault, and you're being horrible to say so. You're wrong—just plain wrong."

I glanced at Eddie. He was sleeping. So much for him coming to my defense. That bond I'd mentioned to Aunt Frances hadn't exactly stood the test of time. It hadn't even lasted twenty-four hours.

"Allison is smart," I said. "And she's ambitious."

"Now, that I can agree with." Denise nodded.

"You should have heard her, that day at the Friends, going on and on about how she was going to change things. So I asked her, right in front of everyone, 'You're going to do all that here in Chilson?' She went a little pink and rambled on about how anyone can be a catalyst, but I bet she runs for a state office in a few years."

And a congressional seat after that, I thought. *But only if there's nothing in her background to stain her. Only if she never writes that letter to the editor admitting that she plagiarized.*

The rain slackened and I increased our speed the slightest bit. The sooner we got back, the sooner I could tell Detective Inwood about Allison.

Plus, the sooner I could get Denise's voice out of my ears, the better. She had started talking louder to be heard over the rain, and even though the rain was slowing, her piercing voice was still penetrating my skin and going straight into my bones.

I shook my head, trying to get rid of the image, but it stuck, just like the last leaves of autumn were sticking to the road's asphalt.

Denise rattled on about Allison's shortcomings. "That husband of hers, he comes from money, but, then, so does she." She managed to make it sound like a bad thing. "Her grandfather made a bundle down in Grand Rapids, I think it was, doing something with furniture."

She made a gagging noise. "What could be so

new about furniture that it makes someone enough money to live out at the point? There's something seriously wrong with this world when people like that can—Minnie! What are you doing?"

What I was doing was pumping the brakes hard and fast, and there wasn't anything else I could do to avoid what was surely going to happen.

In front of us, directly in front of us, far too close in front of us, was a huge washout. All the snowmelt and all the rain of the past few days had come down the hills and pounded into the side of the road. The runoff had found a weak spot, and the water had won. The gaping ravine felt acres wide and miles across, and if I didn't stop the bookmobile in time . . .

"C'mon," I told the bookmobile. "Stop, already. You can do it."

Denise shrieked. "Minnie! Turn! You have to turn!"

But I couldn't. That would be the absolute worst thing I could do. My truck-driver training had taught me that if I swerved while braking this hard, the bookmobile's high center of gravity would tip us over, flopping us onto the side, or, worse, rolling us over completely. Books would fly off the shelves, each one a dangerous projectile, and we'd tumble over and over. Above all, what I couldn't do was turn.

"Turn!" Denise shouted.

The tires slipped on the wet asphalt, slipped on

the wet leaves, and we kept moving inexorably toward the pit.

"Minnie!" Denise was sobbing. "We're going to die and it's all your fault!"

Seriously? If I'd had even a fraction of a second to spare, I would have shot her one of Eddie's Looks That Could Kill, but I didn't have that much time. I had to steer us straight and I had to pump the brakes and I had to use all my will and strength and might to stop us. I had to stop us. I had to.

Denise's shriek went up an octave and she covered her eyes.

Eddie started howling.

I kept braking. I kept steering.

Braking.

Steering.

Braking . . .

I was almost crying from the tension, my lower lip sharp with pain from biting, my chest tight from holding my breath, my hands so tight on the wheel that they'd never come off.

Slower and slower we went, but we were still coming closer to the edge of the gaping maw. How many feet? Too many.

Then the pavement was gone from view and we were still moving forward.

Denise's shriek escalated to the upper range of an operatic soprano.

Eddie's howls came close to matching hers.

I breathed a silent prayer.

The bookmobile's front tires bumped forward over the edge of the washout . . . and then we stopped.

I turned off the engine immediately. The only things I could hear was rain spackling the windshield and the *tick-tick-tick* of the cooling motor.

"We're . . . not dead?" Denise uncovered her eyes.

"Not even close." But I wasn't sure how stable we were. The washout looked wide, but the light was so poor that I couldn't judge the depth. Ten feet? Twenty? I didn't know and couldn't guess. And if so much of the road had already washed away, how much more might go with it? "We need to get out, okay? Slow and easy."

"I'm out of here." Denise flung off her seat belt and scrambled for the rear door.

"Easy, pal," I told Eddie. He was cowering in the back corner of his carrier. "Sorry about the noise. I'll make sure it never happens again, okay?"

He hunched back ever farther, clearly not believing me.

"Yeah, can't say I blame you." I released his carrier and lifted him free. "You were even closer to her than I was, and your ears are a lot more sensitive than mine."

"Mrr."

"You are such an Eddie," I said, lugging him the length of the bookmobile and down the steps. "You really couldn't be anything else, could you?"

"Now what are you talking about?" Denise demanded. "Are you talking to that cat again? That's so weird. I like cats and all, but you—"

Eddie said, "Mrr!" at the same time I heard an odd metallic *thunk!* kind of noise, and before my brain could register what the noise was, the report of a rifle reverberated back and forth across the hills.

Someone had shot at us. At the bookmobile. At my cat.

Denise screamed and ran around to the other side of the bookmobile. Even in the murky dark, I could see her arms waving in the air as she scuttled to safety. Eddie's carrier was firmly in my hand and I walked hurriedly to where Denise was crouching behind a tire. I thought fast and hard, trying to push down the red-hot fury that was rising in me.

Someone had shot at Eddie, dammit, and whoever it had been was going to pay and pay hard.

I took a deep breath and tried to assess our situation in a calm and rational manner. This was difficult, because I was so angry that I wanted to charge up that hill, shouting angrily at the top of my lungs, but I knew that would be stupid in the extreme.

Calm. I needed to stay calm and figure out how safe we were behind the bookmobile. But I had no idea. All I knew for certain was someone up the hill was shooting at us. Then again, maybe the shooter was already gone, but from here there was no way to know.

"Wh-what are we going to do?" Denise asked.

Her teeth were chattering, but I was pretty sure it wasn't from cold. I felt a surge of sympathy for her. Three weeks ago today, her husband had been killed, and here she was, afraid for her own life, her children one parent away from being orphans. Sure, the children were adults, but they still needed their mom.

I looked at her. "Do you have your phone?"

"My what? Oh. My phone." There was a rustling as she searched her pockets. "No, I must have left it . . ." She gasped out a giggle. "It's in my hand. How stupid—here I am looking for it and it's in my hand."

Now was not the time to give Denise a hug and tell her it was okay to be stupid once in a while. "Do you have any reception?" I asked. "Call nine-one-one. Tell them we're disabled and that a shot—"

Ping!

We ducked, because we couldn't help it, and as the rifle's report echoed, Eddie thudded up against the back of his carrier, hissing.

"That shots have been fired."

"I know how to call nine-one-one," Denise

snapped, thumbing the phone, which lit her face with a faint blue glow. "And the reception's crappy. I can't believe you got us stuck out here in the middle of nowhere. Of all the places to run into a washout, you—Oh, hi," she said into the phone. "What's my emergency? Well, I have a couple of them going on."

Ping!

This time, the bullet slammed into the ground at the back of the bookmobile.

Denise shrieked, and I felt sorry for the person at the other end of the phone.

I laid a hand on Eddie's carrier and knew what I had to do. "Here you go, bud." I unlatched the door and swung it open wide. "Can't have you trapped in there." In the short time we'd been outside, my eyes had started adjusting to the dim light. Objects were beginning to have defined edges, and Eddie's carrier was one of them, making it a clear target for anyone inclined to turn it into one.

"Half an hour?" Denise asked loudly, even as I tried to shush her. "What do you mean it'll take someone half an hour to get here?"

Outstanding. Denise's voice carried like no other. If the shooter was listening to us—and there was every reason to assume so—the shooter now knew we were sitting ducks for thirty minutes. Even if someone showed up in half that time, there was still plenty of time to . . . to . . .

I soft-footed it to the rear bumper. Unless the shooter had a night scope, there was no way my small and dark shape could be seen. And if the shooter were good, Denise would have been picked off the second she'd fled the bookmobile.

My breaths were short and quick as I stood there, convincing myself of my safety. I studied the hillside, looking for signs of life, looking for anything, really, and there, not a hundred feet away, was a slight widening in the treetops. A narrow trail. Perfect.

As noiselessly as I could, with my hair pulled forward to cover my pale face, I slipped out from behind the bookmobile.

Behind me, Denise was still talking to the 911 dispatcher. For the first time, I was glad her voice was so loud. Her talking would focus the shooter's attention. I could quietly make my way along the trail and carefully sneak up to see who was doing the shooting. All I needed was an identification. All I needed was to see if it was Allison or Shannon or someone I'd never considered.

Because maybe I didn't know who was shooting at us. Maybe I'd never met this person. Maybe I'd never once checked out his books or answered his questions about how to set up an e-mail account. Maybe this wouldn't be as bad as I'd thought.

Slightly cheered, I walked slowly across the road and started up the hill. Eyes detected movement like nothing else, so I made no sudden moves and tried not to think about how stupid I was being. On a scale of one to ten, this was probably way on the high end. Eddie would have an opinion on that, but he'd skittered under the bookmobile when I'd opened the carrier door, and I hoped he'd stay there until this was all over, one way or another.

The leaves under my feet were saturated with water, and I was suddenly grateful for all the rain we'd had. Wet leaves were quiet; dry leaves were noisy. Then again, if we hadn't had so much rain, the road would never have washed out and we wouldn't be in this mess, so I stopped the efforts of appreciation.

Every few steps I took, I stopped and listened. Denise was still talking, rain was still dripping down, and, unless spontaneous combustion was a dark and soundless reality, whoever had shot at my cat was still on this hillside.

I pressed on, moving ever closer to the shooter, treading quietly up the path, feeling my silent way in the gloom through trees and brush and rocks.

She had to be up here somewhere. Had to be—

Bang!

The rifle fired, and I saw a flash of light. From the end of the gun's barrel, I realized. By shooting, the shooter had revealed her—or maybe his—location: off to my left and slightly down the hill.

Excellent.

I edged closer. But not too close. All I wanted was a positive identification. I wasn't hero material. All I wanted was to see who this person was.

I was practically tiptoeing through the forest, which was silly, but I couldn't stop myself. With my gaze fastened on the spot where I'd seen the flash, I took slow steps closer and closer. I heard the rustle of fabric—the shooter was moving!

Not breathing, I froze solid until there was another rustle and some metallic noises that I couldn't identify. Something gun oriented, no doubt, and I suddenly wished my self-defense classes from last summer had included working with rifles in the dark.

Then my brain clicked.

Reloading the magazine. The shooter was filling up the rifle's magazine with new bullets. Which was bad, but there was a good side. Her—or his—attention would be on the work at hand, not on what might be approaching from the rear.

I edged forward, oh, so quietly, breathing slowly and evenly, my skin tingling with tension. Every cubic inch of me was wide awake and alert.

Closer . . .

Just a little closer . . .

There was a plastic-sounding *click,* and a tiny circle of light appeared. The beam from a tiny flashlight danced around, illuminating the ground, a small pile of bullets, the magazine, the rifle, and a hand gloved in black.

Show me your face, I thought fiercely. *Show your face!*

The flashlight dropped to the ground and the shooter muttered a low curse. Another black glove reached to pick up the flashlight, and, as it picked it up, the beam skidded across the shooter's face.

I gasped, loudly enough to be heard.

The shooter picked up the rifle and pointed it in my direction. "Who's there? Come out right now, or I'll shoot!"

There was nowhere to run. Nowhere to go. No possible place to hide, and there was a gun pointing straight at me. How could I have been so stupid?

Possibilities flashed through my mind. It was dark. If I ran, there was a good chance the bullets would completely miss me. And there was a good chance there weren't any bullets in the rifle anyway, with that magazine on the ground. Maybe there was one in the chamber, or maybe there were two magazines. I didn't know enough about guns to know what was most likely, but I did know I wasn't going to stand here and get ordered around by the person who killed Roger Slade.

"It's Minnie, isn't it?" Allison Korthase said.

I heard a sound behind me, from down low. Not a swish, exactly, but not a rustle, either. Something in between, or maybe a combination. A swistle? Could there be such a thing? And if not, why? More to the point, why was I having such inane thoughts when a gun was pointed at me?

"I know it's you," Allison said, her voice growing louder. "Where are you?"

Right. Like I was going to tell her. Do that, and I might as well mark my location with a flare while screaming "Shoot me!"

Allison's small flashlight beamed into life. "I know you're there, Minnie. It can only be you. I can still hear Denise down there, yapping away to nine-one-one. I'm so cold," Allison whined in a Denise-like voice. "I'm so scared. I'm so worried about being killed." Allison dropped the mimickry. "Like anyone cares."

The flashlight danced closer to my feet. I edged backward. If I could get a little farther away, I'd make a run for it, bullets or no. In my opinion, which wasn't exactly expert but was all I had, Allison was ready to kill again, and I needed to get clear of her murderous intentions.

"Come on," she said impatiently. "I know you're just a librarian, but there's no reason for you to be such a scaredy-cat."

Just *a librarian?* I opened my mouth to argue the point, but before I could say a word, my retreating heel found a rock and I fell to the ground hard, arms windmilling, the air rushing out of me in a painful "Oof!"

"There you are." Allison chuckled, and her voice turned snide and sarcastic. "What were you trying to do, run backward? How stupid are you?

You'd have thought that someone with a job like yours would be at least a little smart, but here you are, in the woods alone, up against someone like me, who is smart and has a gun. Stupid." She practically spat the word. "Stupid!"

I'd been pushing myself back, trying to get out of her reach, moving away from where I'd fallen, doing my best not to be stupid, when the swistle noise ran past me and toward Allison, a low, rumbling growl moving along with it.

"Eddie!" I shouted, scrambling to my feet. "No! Get back!"

Allison screamed. "Get it off! Get it off!" The rifle clattered to the ground.

In the last vestiges of the day's dim light, I could see her waving her arms, flailing at Eddie, who was growling, hissing, and climbing up her back, all at the same time.

I ran forward and scooped up the rifle, momentarily unsure whether to hang on to it or to fling it into the woods, where neither one of us would be able to find it until daylight.

"It's a bobcat," she yelled. "It's a mountain lion. It's going to kill me! Minnie, get it off!"

She was in a full-blown panic. Allison, I suddenly realized, was afraid of cats. She wasn't allergic, as she'd claimed to Denise. She was scared.

I turned and placed the rifle behind a tree.

"Minnie!" Her shrieks were becoming tinged with desperation. "You have to do something!"

Oh, I'd do something all right.

"You're a good boy," I told Eddie. He was on the back of Allison's neck, clutching onto the collar of her coat for all he was worth and howling into her ear. "If you can hang on a little bit longer, we'll be good."

"MRRR!!" he said, which I took for agreement.

I lifted up my coat, unbuckled my belt, pulled it off, and pushed the belt's length through the buckle, creating a loop. I stepped forward and bumped into Allison, making her scream just a little louder.

Grabbing one of her arms, I looped the belt around her wrist and pulled it tight. She struggled, but I held hard and reached around for her other arm. "Now would be a good time," I panted to Eddie, "for you to help out just a little more."

He scrambled up off Allison's back and onto her shoulder, where he gripped hard and yowled like the hounds of hell. Even I was a little startled by the volume of noise coming out of my thirteen-pound cat.

Allison sank to her knees, whimpering.

I took hold of her free arm, pulled it behind her back, and wrapped my belt tight around both wrists, looping and tying it firm.

"Get him off," she whispered, tears in her words. "Please, just get him off."

And after a minute, I did.

Chapter 19

Minnie?" Denise's shout came from far below. "Are you all right up there?"

Me and Eddie both, thanks. "We're fine," I called. "You can tell the dispatcher that I have the shooter disarmed and—" And what? Saying Allison was in custody wasn't accurate. "Disarmed and incapacitated. Send the police up here, okay?"

"Incapacitated" still wasn't quite right, but I'd come up with the right word eventually. Probably at three in the morning, as Eddie was deciding that the top of my head was the best place for him to sleep.

At this particular moment, however, the cat in question was nestled in my arms and purring like a champ. I patted my furry little friend on the head.

"Mrr," he said sleepily.

"Get that cat away from me," Allison said. "This is all her fault, you know."

I frowned. "Eddie is a boy."

"Don't be stupid," she snapped.

Eddie gave a low growl and, in the dark, I felt Allison shrink away.

"Sorry," she muttered. "What I mean is, it's all Denise's fault."

"Really?" Though he'd seemed light enough a

few minutes ago, Eddie was gaining weight rapidly. I felt around with my feet, found a good-sized rock, and sat down. I'd stand up with a wet rear end, but it would be nice to rest for a little. I rearranged Eddie on my lap. "What did Denise do?"

"It's all so stupid," Allison said.

She had a thing for that word. "What is?"

"I wasn't trying to pass off someone else's speech as my own," she explained in the patient voice that grated on me like nothing else—far worse than fingernails on a chalkboard. "I just forgot to make an attribution that day I talked to the Friends of the Library. A simple mistake, that's all. I can't believe that Denise was trying to ruin my career over it!"

Eddie shifted, lost a little of his balance, and dug his claws into my thighs. *Ow.* "She told me all she wanted was a letter to the editor correcting the mistake."

"It would have ruined me! They would have said I was a liar, a cheat! Every time anyone Googled me, it would come up, again and again. I'd never be able to escape it. All because of one stupid speech."

"And you have plans," I said. "For the future."

"Exactly." Allison sounded satisfied. Why, I couldn't imagine, but the tone was unmistakable. "A term on the city council, a couple of terms as a county commissioner, and eight years from now

I'll run for the state legislature. One term there and I'll be forty-nine, the perfect age for me to run for a national office."

Assuming she won all those elections, of course, but I decided not to mention that small detail. "That's quite a plan."

"Yes," she said. "Don't you think it's time for a female president?"

I blinked in the dark. "Of the country?"

"Why not go straight for the presidency from a state seat? Why taint yourself with the inner machinations of Washington? Why not go straight to the top? Take you. Why don't you angle to get Stephen's job? Or work at the State Library? Even better, the Library of Congress? Think of the things you could do. Why are you limiting yourself?"

I could think of a lot of reasons, but the primary ones were that I liked my current job, that I loved where I lived, and that Eddie wouldn't like living in a city. He was a small-town cat, just like I was a small-town girl. Why would I want to fit myself into a square hole when I was a round peg?

"Ah," Allison said, even though I hadn't said a word, "you're just like everyone else in this town. Stuck in a rut. Happy with the status quo. Living with blinders on." She made a rude noise. "Not me. I'm going places. I'm not going to let someone like Denise ruin my life. I'll get out of this— just wait and see."

Though a good defense attorney could do wonders, I wasn't sure how being on trial for murder, even if she was found innocent, could help her political career. Then again, who knew? It was a weird, weird world and stranger things had—

A swooshing noise startled me and I felt instant intense pain. I fell back, rolled to the ground, and curled into a fetal position, cradling my forehead. Allison had jumped to her feet and whacked me in the head with her own noggin.

"Mrr!"

"Get out of my way, you . . . you cat! Get away from me!"

More swooshing noises. Allison was trying to kick Eddie, and here I was, lying like a lump. I tried to scramble to my feet, but dizziness sent me back to the ground. Eddie was hissing and growling and yowling.

"Leave him alone!" I got to my hands and knees and crawled to the nearest tree. "Don't you dare hurt my cat!" I grabbed the rifle I'd propped up and stood. Swaying, I staggered forward toward the scuffling and swung the rifle around by its barrel. "Leave him alone!"

The heavy stock of the gun thumped against something softish. Allison yelled, and I whacked again. She fell to the ground and stayed there.

In the distance I heard slamming doors, male shouts, and Denise's voice directing them up the hill. Never had I been so happy to hear that penetrating sound.

Feet thudded in our direction. The glare of bright flashlights skittered over the trees and reached our group of two humans and one feline. "Got them!" someone called.

Allison tried to get up again, but I flipped the rifle around and pointed the business end at her. "You killed Roger," I said. "You tried to kill Denise, and just now did your best to kill my cat." Which was boiling my blood something fierce.

"What if I did?" she spat. "Shooting Roger was a mistake, but they'll understand. I have answers. I have ideas, excellent ideas. I have plans!"

The feet and the lights reached us.

Willingly, I surrendered the gun, and as soon as I detached Eddie from Allison's leg, I let them lead me away.

Denise was already gone by the time I reached the road, taken away in one of the three patrol cars that had arrived one after the other.

As I watched, Allison was brought down, her hands in front of her, wrists together. She didn't look at me as a deputy put her into the back of the second patrol car and didn't speak until the deputy started to close the door.

"I'll get out of this," she said to the air over my head. "Just you wait and see."

The deputy shut the door, went around to the

driver's side, and started the engine. He made a three-point turn and accelerated, the car's taillights winking out of view as it went around the curve.

"Minnie, are you okay?"

I turned. Ash Wolverson, a flashlight in hand, stood nearby.

"Fine," I told him. "Really. The rain stopped a few minutes ago."

"The rain did, yes. But precipitation didn't. You're covered in snow," he said. "Let's get in my car."

"Eddie, too?" My cat, who had had enough of my cuddling, was slinking around my legs, pausing every so often to whack my shin with the top of his head.

"From what I hear, he's the hero of the hour." Ash scooped Eddie up into his arms and scratched him behind the ears, just the way he liked it. "He can walk all over the dash if he wants."

So the three of us climbed inside into the warmth, but I still shivered.

"You've got to be wet, through," Ash said. "I should get you home."

I shook my head. "My phone's in the book-mobile. Can you call the garage? I need to get a tow truck out here."

Ash nodded and started pushing buttons on his radio.

Which was good, because there was no way I

was leaving the bookmobile until it was safe and sound. Or at least on solid ground. The knowledge that it might have suffered serious damage was depressing. If the bookmobile was out of commission for an extended period of time, it would take more than Eddie's purrs to make me feel better.

"Mrr," he said from the dashboard.

Well, maybe they'd make me feel a little better.

"You're all right," I told my furry friend, "for an Eddie."

"He's a pretty cool cat." Ash gave him a long pet. "His fur is silky. Not like any cat I've ever had."

Wonderful. Eddie already thought he was one of a kind. Now he had the stamp of approval from the sheriff's department. Outstanding. I half smiled. What we really needed was an Eddie stamp of approval. A sketch of his face with a paw print for a signature. We could stamp his food dish. And the back of the couch. And the rocking—

"You'll need to make a statement," Ash said.

Reluctantly, I steered my thoughts back to the unfortunate and unhappy present.

"She admitted to killing Roger," I said. "Right before you got there. She said it was a mistake." I swallowed, hating that Roger had died. And now Denise would learn with certainty that it was her threats that had unhinged Allison to the point of murder, that Allison had indeed killed Roger, thinking he was Denise.

I sighed, wondering how long it would take Denise to learn to live with that knowledge, with that guilt, and I hoped she'd be okay. Poor Roger had been in the wrong place, just like that book on the bookmobile.

"Mrr." Eddie jumped onto my lap and flopped down. His thick purrs started to fill my empty spaces, and I leaned down to kiss the top of his head. He really was a pretty good cat. Even without the qualifier of being an Eddie.

"You're shivering," Ash said.

"I'll be okay," I said through chattering teeth.

He gave me a long look and smiled. "Yeah. I bet you will be." And then he reached forward and turned up the heat.

On Sunday, after sleeping late and waking with Eddie curled into the crook of my elbow, I poked at the breakfast Aunt Frances cooked for me and then walked through the snow to the sheriff's office to give my statement.

I'd been exhausted the night before when I returned home, and even more exhausted after I'd texted Tucker and called Stephen. But a good night's sleep, and, after my visit to the sheriff's office, a nap and a phone call with Kristen ("Your cat has excellent taste in women") revived me to the point of smiles, if not laughter. Aunt Frances,

Eddie, and I spent the evening eating pizza from Fat Boys and binge watching episodes of *M*A*S*H*, and my sleep that night was clear of dreams.

The library was quiet and dark when I arrived early on Monday morning, and first thing, even before starting up my computer, I called the garage for the bad news.

"Ah, it's not so bad," Darren said. "Nothing structural—just a little body work. And it won't take much to patch up those bullet holes." He paused. "You're all right, right?"

His concern made my eyes sting a bit. "I'm fine," I said. And I would be. Denise was safe, Eddie was safe, and the bookmobile would live to ride again. Somewhere, anyway.

I thanked Darren and looked at the number on my e-mail's in-box with disfavor. How, exactly, could I have received seventy-three e-mails since leaving the library on Friday? Once again, I patted myself on the back for making a firm vow to never check library e-mail when I wasn't working. I could have, sure, but why? There wasn't much that happened at a library that needed instant attention.

Then again, seventy-three e-mails . . .

I pushed back my chair and stood. This required coffee. Maybe even Kelsey coffee. With a mug or two under my belt, I'd be ready to tackle anything.

But before the coffee was done brewing, the

entire library staff was in the break room, all wanting to know what happened on Saturday, all with twisted stories of what they'd heard had happened.

"Denise got shot, is what the guys at the Round Table were saying," Josh said.

"The poor bookmobile!" Kelsey was almost crying. "I heard it was totaled!"

"What about Eddie?" Donna asked, her face creased with concern. "No one's said anything about him. Is he okay?"

Holly looked me up and down. "Someone told me you were in the hospital, in the ICU, but that was probably wrong."

I grinned at her. "Probably," I said and, for no reason other than the fact that I was surrounded by friends who cared about me, my dark mood lifted and the metaphorical sun came out.

Then came the voice of doom: "Minerva."

My compatriots froze solid. "Good morning, Stephen," I said cheerfully. In the past two days I'd almost destroyed the bookmobile, faced down a stone-cold killer, and edged away from an uncomfortable situation with Ash Wolverson into what might be friendship. There was nothing Stephen could do that would topple me.

"Upstairs," he said tersely. "Now."

As soon as the door shut behind him, my good friends started chattering about the pending possibilities.

"Is he going to fire you?" Kelsey asked.

"If he does," Josh said, "can I have your office?"

"Don't be an idiot," Holly scolded him. "Stephen would never fire Minnie. She's too important."

Unfortunately, I was old enough to know that everyone was expendable. "Only the library board can fire me," I said. But I hoped now that everything was out in the open, they wouldn't. After all, with Allison in jail, Tammy's lawsuit couldn't be valid. Then again, what did I know about the law? Reading Scott Turow's books wasn't exactly the equivalent of a law degree.

"Oh . . ." Donna said. We all turned to look at her. The sound she'd made had been almost one of pain.

"What's the matter?" I asked.

She wouldn't meet my gaze. "Yesterday morning," she said, picking invisible lint off her sweater, "I drove past the library on the way to church. There were a bunch of cars in the parking lot, and I couldn't figure it out until I saw Otis Rahn come into church a little late."

The room spun in a fast, whirling circle, and I put my hand on the wall to steady myself.

"The board met on a Sunday morning?" Kelsey whispered.

As one unit, they all turned to look at me, but I didn't look at them. Didn't want to see their pity, or hear their worry or anything at all except normal library complaints about recalcitrant software and mistakenly shelved books. "I'd better get going," I murmured, and headed upstairs in Stephen's wake.

When I entered his office, Stephen was standing at one of the windows, looking out across the snow-whitened rooftops of downtown Chilson.

"Ah, Minerva," he said without turning around. "Please sit down."

No way was I going to sit while he was still on his feet. If I was going to get fired, I'd take it standing tall. All sixty inches of me, which always sounded taller than five feet.

"I have a number of things to discuss." Stephen tilted his head. "Four, to be exact. Number one." He held out the index finger of one hand. "Due to our phone conversation on Saturday, I called an emergency meeting of the library board. We met yesterday morning, and, as you might be able to imagine, we had a number of issues on the agenda."

"Yes," I said quietly. "I can imagine."

"With such a decided resolution to the dangers threatening the bookmobile, the board reached a quick consensus regarding the vehicle's future." He paused and turned slightly. Not enough to make eye contact with me, but that was nothing new. "The bookmobile itself has a future, correct?" he asked. "With regard to its physical condition?"

I told him what Darren had said, and he went back to staring out the window.

"The board has no issues," he said, "with the continuance of the bookmobile program. Ms. Shelburt has dropped her lawsuit against the library."

"That's great." Happiness and relief rushed through me. "But I still need to find funding for it."

Stephen shook his head, and my propped-up spirits started falling again. He sighed. "Minerva, don't you read your e-mail?"

My chin went up. "Of course I do. It's the first thing I do every workday, and the last thing I do before I leave at night."

"But you don't check your e-mail on your days off."

He made it a statement, and my chin went up even farther. "No," I said firmly. "I do not. I'm salaried. I work at least sixty hours a week, and when I leave this building, I'm done working until I come back to the building. I resent the implication that I'm not working hard enough, and if that's what you—"

Stephen turned to face me and I stopped midstream, because he was . . . well, he was smiling. "Minnie, you amuse me."

"I . . . do?"

"If you'd read your e-mail, you would have learned that the auction of Russell McCade's artwork, the proceeds of which are coming to the library, fetched an astronomical price. One of the highest prices ever for one of his works."

"Highest?"

Stephen nodded and was still smiling when he told me the number. Which was when I did sit down. Cade's broken phone call and his excitement suddenly made sense. When he'd talked about a "thousand dollars" that was just the tail end of the six-figure amount that was going to the library.

Only . . . what else had he said? I looked at my boss, not wanting to know but having to ask. "Is there a problem with the donation? Cade called Friday, but the connection was bad, and I could have sworn he said something about 'not the library.'"

Stephen went back to the window. "Apparently Mr. McCade has used his powers of persuasion to convince the family to donate the proceeds not to the library, but to"—he paused—"the bookmobile. That's the second item I wanted to discuss."

Though I was already sitting down, I wanted to sit down again.

"The library world," Stephen went on, "is buzzing with the news. I'm surprised you haven't received phone calls about this."

Not yet, but I had received seventy-three e-mails.

"The Chilson District Library," he said to the window, "is becoming a library of note, and I have to say that you, Minnie, are primarily responsible." He gestured toward his desk. "I've received a letter of support for the bookmobile from an Andrew Burrows, a kindergarten teacher at Moulson Elementary, I believe. It is signed by sixty-two people."

I opened my mouth, but nothing came out.

"The library board and I have received numerous such comments. Each of the letters, phone calls, and e-mails we've received speak of you and the bookmobile in great and glowing terms."

Stephen was passing on compliments? Who was this man, and what had he done with my boss?

"This leads me to the third item." He folded his arms and rubbed his chin. "You may not be aware, and as a matter of fact, I quite hope you're not, but I've been grooming you to be the next library director."

I squeaked, but Stephen kept rolling.

"Not for five years and ten months, of course, which is when I anticipate that my retirement savings will reach my target amount, but it's never too early to start training your successor, not if you want your institution to be properly run after you're gone."

Properly? I almost snorted.

"The reason," he said, "that I've been so hard on you the past year was to test you, to see if you have the right stuff. The library board will, of course, make the final decision, but at this point I can say with certainty that the job is yours."

He'd been testing me? The nights I'd worked late, the hair I'd pulled out, the off-hours research I'd done, all in the name of meeting one of Stephen's challenges—all that had been a *test?*

My chin went up again, but slowly it came down. Maybe testing me had been a good way to determine my suitability. There were worse ways. Probably.

"I can see that you're surprised," Stephen said, which was when I realized he'd been watching my facial expressions in the window's reflection. "There's no need for you to make a decision at this juncture, but after all you've done for this library, I thought it reasonable to inform you of my plans."

"Thank you," I murmured. "This is a lot to think about."

"I understand." Stephen pulled out his chair. "If you have any questions, feel free to ask."

As if. I thanked him again and started to stand.

"Oh, and Minnie. The fourth thing?"

"Yes?"

He smiled faintly. "Your cat. I know all about him."

"My cat?" I froze, half-up and half-down.

"Eddie, I believe his name is." Stephen straightened his computer monitor. "I've known he was on the bookmobile from the first week." He chuckled. "Did you really think I didn't know what was going on?"

"Oh. I . . . uh . . ."

"Minerva." Stephen sighed. "If you're ever going to sit behind this desk, you really need to learn to speak more coherently. Please work on that."

"Yes, sir." I stood and, on extremely wobbly legs, I made my way back downstairs, where my friends were waiting for me.

Chapter 20

So, the bookmobile is financially safe and sound?" Aunt Frances asked.

I beamed at her. "Thanks to Cade's painting. It's not enough to create an endowment, but it'll keep us on the road for a long time." My heart sang with happiness at the idea.

"And Stephen has known about Eddie all along?" Aunt Frances asked.

Or that's what I assumed she asked, because she was talking while her mouth was full of popcorn. *Bad aunt.*

For the twenty-first time in the last three minutes, I pushed Eddie's head away from the popcorn bowl. "That's what he said."

I still found it hard to believe. If he'd known the whole time, why hadn't he just said so? I'd spent a lot of energy trying to keep Eddie's bookmobile presence a secret. If I'd known that

Stephen had known, I'd have put that time to better use. Maybe I would have finally finished reading James Joyce's *Ulysses*. Probably not, but maybe.

"So Eddie and the bookmobile will ride again." Aunt Frances reached out, pushed Eddie's head away, and took another handful of popcorn. "I couldn't have managed it better myself." She gave me a wink.

I smiled, but it faded as I studied the fire, its orange peaks dancing. Most of what had happened had been luck, both good and bad. Good that funding for the bookmobile had dropped from the sky, but horribly bad for poor Roger.

"Mrr." Eddie bumped my elbow on his way across my lap.

"Hey!" I pulled his head out of the popcorn bowl. Time twenty-two. "That's not for Eddies."

He gave me a disgusted look and slithered up onto the back of the couch.

"Allison Korthase." Aunt Frances shook her head. "She had so much potential."

She'd had it all, as far as I could tell. Intelligence, beauty, money—yet that hadn't been enough for her. She'd wanted more, much more, and had murdered to get it.

Eddie bumped me on the back of the head. Absently, I reached up to pet him, wishing that I'd been smart enough to figure out before Roger had been killed that Allison had had the capacity for murder. How, I didn't know, but if, for instance, I'd known that—

"Hey!" I saw Eddie's white-tipped paw snaking down to the popcorn bowl. I batted it away. "This is not cat food. Your bowl is in the kitchen."

He turned around and sat on the back of the couch with his hind end against my head.

Aunt Frances laughed. "You should see his face."

"Oh, I have a good idea of what it looks like." If Eddie had the power to disintegrate me on sight, I would have been a small heap of powder months ago. "You know what else Stephen said?"

My aunt did the one-eyebrow thing. "About the bookmobile or about Eddie?"

"Neither," I said, then reconsidered. "Or maybe both."

Aunt Frances looked at my cat. "It's a pity she can't be more clear."

"Mrr," he said.

"Do you want to hear or not?" I asked.

"Yes, please."

"Mrr."

So I told them about Stephen's not-so-imminent retirement and about his plans for my future.

"You don't sound overly excited," Aunt Frances said.

I plunged my hand into the popcorn. Becoming a library director had been my career goal for years. In college, I'd often fallen asleep while dreaming about the library I'd one day direct. Even since moving to Chilson, I'd thought about the changes I might make as director. But in the past year, I hadn't thought about it much. Hardly at all, as a matter of fact.

"I'm not sure," I said slowly, "that I want to be library director, if it means giving up the bookmobile."

Eddie's tail thumped against the back of my head.

"You are so weird," I told him.

"Well." My aunt used the napkin on her lap to wipe her fingers clean of butter. "You don't have to make the decision today."

"Not even this month."

"So no need to worry, right?"

"None."

"Then I say it's a perfect time to pop another bowl of popcorn. Just because it's Monday night doesn't mean we shouldn't celebrate." She stood. "Eddie, you staying or coming with?"

A furry tail whacked my ear.

She squinted. "Was there an answer in there somewhere?"

"Only if you want one."

She snorted. "You two are a match made in heaven. No, don't get up. This way, I get to use as much salt as I want."

Eddie slid down to my lap. "How nice to see you," I said. "It's been so long."

He rotated one and a half times and settled on my left leg. "Why can't you spread yourself more evenly?" I asked. "You know your weight is going to cut off all circulation to my leg in ten minutes. Do you want me to have to lop off my toes?"

Eddie looked partway up to me and opened his mouth in a soundless "Mrr."

"Okay, you're right. I might have been exaggerating a teensy bit."

He settled onto my lap a little deeper and started purring. Yet another argument won by the cat.

Aunt Frances laughed and picked up the empty bowl. "Back in a minute."

I gave Eddie long strokes along his back and thought about what Detective Inwood had told me that afternoon when he'd called.

"She's made a full confession," he'd said, satisfaction oozing out of every word. "A couple of nights in jail, and she was ready to tell everything."

Allison had told him that she'd used snowshoes to get to the spot where she'd shot Roger, and she'd admitted to tampering with Denise's car. "Her intention," the detective said dryly, "was to cut the brake lines, but she knows nothing about cars. She just popped the hood and stabbed at the biggest hose, figuring it was so big because it was important, and what could be more important than brakes?"

I'd frowned. "Why didn't she get on the ground and cut the lines from down there?"

"Because," he said, "Ms. Korthase had just left a meeting. She said she was dressed in dry-clean-only pants and didn't want to get them dirty."

The detective then told me that Allison had been following Denise's tweets and Facebook posts all Saturday. She'd cross-referenced those with the bookmobile schedule I'd posted on the library's Web site and had calculated when we'd be at the road washout.

"The road commission had put up a Road Closed barrier," Detective Inwood said, "but she dragged it out of the way just before you came along."

"I'm glad no one else drove down that road while the barrier was gone." I winced at the idea. "Someone could really have been hurt."

"Yes," the detective said, his dry tone back in full force. "Someone could have." There was a slight pause. "It was becoming clear that the evidence we'd been gathering against the hunter wasn't going to be sufficient for prosecution. In all honesty, we were at a loss for new suspects."

While he wasn't exactly oozing with gratitude, this was probably as close to a thank-you as I was going to get. "You're welcome," I said.

The detective had cleared his throat. "Deputy Wolverson spoke highly of you. He said it was due to your efforts that Ms. Korthase didn't wound or kill Ms. Slade. He said you kept calm in an emergency situation and, if not for you, things could have turned out much worse."

What could have been worse was I could have charged up that hill and been shot, something I wasn't about to tell my mother. Ever. This was definitely a case in which what she didn't know wouldn't hurt her, and Aunt Frances, who had known my mother long before I came along, had already made a pinkie swear not to share that particular bit of information.

Heavy, male-sounding footsteps came across the front porch and were followed by the double stomp of boots shedding snow and a knock on the door.

"I'll get it," Aunt Frances called, hurrying to the entryway. "Minnie, don't you dare get up and disturb that cat." She opened the door. "Tucker! I didn't realize you were stopping by tonight. Come on in."

"Thanks," he said, smiling at her and hanging his coat in the closet.

Aunt Frances made her way back through the living room. "Next bowl of popcorn, coming up fast."

Since I hadn't known Tucker was stopping by, either, I wondered what was up. "Eddie's right here," I said, once again seeing that female hand reach across the cafeteria table. "And so is all his hair and dander."

Tucker sat next to me. And started petting Eddie. With his bare hand. "It'll be fine," he said. "I dosed up before I left the hospital."

"Oh. Well, if you're sure."

"You're mad, aren't you?"

I shrugged.

"Listen, I'm really sorry about the other night, but I was having a conference call with some med-school friends of mine, talking about a fellowship opening they thought I should know about."

"And a fellowship is what, exactly?" I'd heard of them but wasn't clear on the details.

"It's more training," he said. "Specialized medical training that you can get after your residency."

I frowned. "This is something you want to do? I thought . . ." I'd thought he was happy doing what he was doing. I'd thought he was content.

"It's a great opportunity," he said.

"You'd do this in Charlevoix?"

"Well, no. This is a fellowship for sports medicine." He paused. "At the University of Michigan."

"But that hospital is in . . ." I tailed off.

"Ann Arbor," he said. "I could stay with my parents; it'd be a long commute, but it'd be a lot cheaper for me."

"That makes sense," I said slowly. "How long would this last?"

"Two years."

The words were short, but the implication was long. Two years long.

"But it won't be like it's two years," Tucker said. "First off, I may not even get it. Most likely I won't—there will be a lot of competition. And it's not that far from Ann Arbor to here, not even a four-hour drive, so we'll be able to see each other lots of weekends. And this is a research fellowship. I'll have regular hours, not like now."

It sounded okay. Not great, but okay. Still . . .

"Why haven't you said anything?" I asked. "You never even told me you were applying."

"I wanted to surprise you. I thought you'd be excited about this. It's a real opportunity."

It was an opportunity for him, not for me. "I'm not sure I like surprises anymore."

Aunt Frances came in as I was saying so and plopped the popcorn on the low table.

"Please forgive my niece, Tucker. She's had a number of shocks today and they're obviously going to her head."

Tucker stopped petting Eddie. "Shocks? What's the matter?"

But I wasn't going to be distracted so easily. "The other day I stopped by the hospital. It was dinnertime, and I found you in the cafeteria, with . . . with . . ." I couldn't make myself say the word.

"With Rita." Tucker nodded. "Sure. She's a nurse

in the ER, one of those people who like to hug everybody in sight. Her husband is a big movie fan, and I was giving her some trivia for her to stump him with."

Husband. The world brightened into a beautiful place. Silly old me for not being up-front and asking Tucker about her in the first place.

I smiled at him and he smiled at me. My heart started beating a little faster, and I felt myself leaning forward. Behind us, Aunt Frances cleared her throat. "Goodness," she said, yawning, "it's almost my bedtime. Maybe I'll head upstairs to—"

Knock, knock.

Aunt Frances looked at me. "Are you expecting anyone else?"

"Not that I can . . . Oh!" I heaved Eddie onto Tucker's startled lap and jumped to my feet. Ignoring the questions my aunt was flinging at me, I hurried to the door and opened it to the white night.

"I'm so glad you came over," I said. "And you brought flowers—how nice!" I took the bouquet and ushered the new arrival to the living room. "Aunt Frances, this is Otto Bingham, our across-the-street neighbor. Otto, this is my aunt, Frances Pixley."

Otto smiled at my aunt. "It's nice to finally meet you, Ms. Pixley."

Aunt Frances looked at him, put her hand to

her hair, and turned the lightest shade of pink. "Frances, please."

"Only if you'll call me Otto."

"You know," my aunt said, "I've always liked that name." Her face got a little pinker and she started to babble. "Well, what I actually like are palindromes, and especially names that are palindromes. The last one I met was an Izzi. I knew an Anna once, and a Hannah, but I can't think of any other male palindromes. Too bad, isn't it?"

I'd never heard her babble like this, not ever. I knew it was because she was nervous, and she wasn't used to being nervous, but would Otto know that? I clutched the flowers and hoped.

Otto threw back his head and laughed, a deep, rich sound that put me in mind of summer vacation, clear skies, and new books from my favorite authors. Which was when I knew that everything would be all right in the end.

I smiled at my aunt, at Otto, at Tucker, and finally at Eddie. "What do you think of palindromes?" I asked.

Eddie jumped off the couch, padded over to me, and rubbed his chin against my leg.

"Mrr," he said.

Center Point Large Print
600 Brooks Road / PO Box 1
Thorndike, ME 04986-0001 USA

(207) 568-3717

US & Canada:
1 800 929-9108
www.centerpointlargeprint.com